SEVENTEE JEROME

Richard Thornley's books include *Zig-Zag*, *Attempts to Join Society* and *Coyote*. He lives in Worcestershire.

ALSO BY RICHARD THORNLEY

Zig-Zag
Attempts to Join Society
The Dark Clarinet
Coyote

Richard Thornley

SEVENTEEN SEVENTEEN JEROME

Published by Vintage 1999

2 4 6 8 10 9 7 5 3 1

With thanks to Maurice Phillips

First published in Great Britain in 1998
by Jonathan Cape

Vintage
Random House, 20 Vauxhall Bridge Road,
London SW1V 2SA

Random House Australia (Pty) Limited
20 Alfred Street, Milsons Point, Sydney
New South Wales 2061, Australia

Random House New Zealand Limited
18 Poland Road, Glenfield, Auckland 10,
New Zealand

Random House South Africa (Pty) Limited
Endulini, 5A Jubilee Road, Parktown 2193,
South Africa

Random House UK Limited Reg. No. 954009

A CIP catalogue record for this book
is available from the British Library

ISBN 0 09 977301 5

Papers used by Random House UK Ltd are natural, recyclable products made from wood grown in sustainable forests. The manufacturing processes conform to the environmental regulations of the country of origin

Printed and bound in Great Britain by
Mackays of Chatham PLC, Chatham, Kent

PART ONE

Paul

ONE

Friday: 9a.m. to 11.40a.m.

Paul asked Laurie in the morning – he was late for work – he called to her, "Sweetie, that old wallet hasn't shown up, has it?"

She said, "No."

As he went out to the garage, she called, "Your golf shoes are down by the freezer."

He thought, Golf? Since when did I get the time to play golf?

Later in the morning, around eleven-thirty, Paul asked his receptionist to chase up his new driver's license. (When Sheri Sumner had called to cancel her check-up.) Then he sat behind his desk and wondered to himself as to why his wife had linked his wallet to his golf shoes.

His wife was pregnant. Did she want him to take up golf again?

The pregnancy was something he knew. But knew nothing about, what bizarre associations were likely to be made by his wife when carrying their first child. He wasn't thinking about playing golf, nor intending to. And they had no plans to take a golfing trip, not with Laurie being pregnant.

"Doctor Mathiessen, the DMV say that you can drive on the temporary license until they replace the old one."

"Fine by me. I'll take lunch early, Alice."

Alice asked him if she should bill Mrs Sumner; he said not.

Friday: Noon to 4p.m.

Lunch with Bill Matson. Californian-Mexican cuisine.

Friday's exactitude. The overhead fans are cutting lazy, silent circles, stirring asides from other tables. Bill knows more about food than Paul does, and grins. Bill is full of the pleasure at what he has just swallowed and what is to come. His bite firms down on what remains of his smile.

The two men have subjects: for which they have an index, like friends do. They flit haphazardly across this index, between mouthfuls. Their conversation might be described as global, with just the stock topics pinpointed; no boundaries, few features; and so there are convenient expanses which only their appetites can occupy. Once the food is loaded, their lips are sealed. They swathe their mouths in thick paper napkins, leaving grease where their lips touch down.

"Wonderful. This is wonderful food. You think so?"

Paul agrees. This is a new place. They would eat here once more, and then there would be another new place. So they circle. And today's delicacies from the index – medical lawsuits, remodelled houses, new movies, bankruptcies, games snatched from Channels Two through Forty-Six, earthquake insurance, drivers' licenses, white-water rafting in the Rockies – the fans stir and dissolve.

Bill doesn't know what could have happened to Paul's driver's license. Paul hadn't been mugged, so maybe the driver's license got left at a supermarket check-out. Paul doesn't think so. All groceries go on a credit card, and the store doesn't ask him for his ID. Anyhow, that's history, that's out of the way.

Habitually Bill's eyes rove, but today his eyes fall back upon Paul more often than is usual. Their conversation travels on, from point to more mutually acceptable point. Paul and Bill disembark punctually, each in turn, purposefully, criss-crossing the index – the food is wonderful – but the ground on which they alight is not as sustaining as it might be. The topics do not hold. The points of contact are not so much shaky as they are dry, unexpectedly barren. How so? Why? Not because of Paul's thinking about his driver's license, surely? Both men are disconcerted. The food loses its appeal. Their hunger, such as it was, has been dissipated.

Their waitress happens upon them, intuitively.

"Is everything all right here?" She is sure that it is. They reassure her.

"Yes, it's great. Everything's fine."

And they, in turn, are reassured. The food has been wonderful.

Paul knows what is bothering Bill. Bill is bothered about bringing his wife to dinner on Saturday evening.

They pass to a more immediate future.

Paul has three appointments this Friday afternoon. Bill has a consultation and a standard alignment procedure. On some kid's uppers. The consultation will be a pain in the butt. Nobody wants to know that they need dental surgery. You just have to lay it on the line and soothe down the protests. Bill envies Paul! Everybody knows about skin cancer treatment and takes it pretty much as one of life's precautionary measures. Hell, out in the valley they are probably baptising kids with Melanoma as a first name. But try advising people that they need dental surgery and it is like pitching Munibonds.

"Yes, but people are terrified of cancer," Paul reminds him. "They aren't terrified of Munibonds. What I have to deal with is other people's fear."

"That's why you'll never be out of clients."

"I guess so."

He passes on to what is really troubling Bill. He says, "Well, we won't talk bonds over dinner. I guess that tomorrow night we could talk vacations. Family vacations." He smiles.

"Vacations with babies, or without?" Bill grins. He knows a sore point when he sees one.

"With."

On the sidewalk a young guy is smoking a cigarette. Paul stiffens with resentment.

"Hey . . . " Bill chides. "It's great having children. The pain in the ass is now, when everyone talks about it. When the baby isn't there it's like verbal bonding with an abstract. It's like getting stuck talking about art the whole time."

"Okay, so tomorrow night we don't want to talk about babies."

"Yeah, but we will." Bill grins again. "And rightly so."

"Sure."

"But no art."

"Right. Maybe movies. You can't go wrong with movies. Or remodelling the house; Laurie likes to talk colors. Or winter vacations. And anything anyone dreams about. Helen dreams, doesn't she?" he suggests.

"Oh yes, she dreams," Bill says.

"So it's dreams. Talk dreams."

"Can you ever remember them? Who wants to remember them? It's all I can do to invent them any more."

Paul says, "I think we're only there at dinner to listen, you know?"

"That's fine by me. Is this tab yours or mine?"

"Yours. I got it last Friday."

Pass on the rest of the future.

Paul drinks another coffee. Bill signs for lunch. How cheap food is. Plain fact. Paul looks around the restaurant and cannot understand how anyone can make a living out of food. Bill is a good man. In all kinds of ways. Orthodontist plus. He would talk dreams, even European movies. Some Friday lunches they have talked dreams. They could do Saturdays over dinner with wives.

It wouldn't be difficult. There would be some baby talk, but it wouldn't be difficult.

They stand outside in dull sunlight. Bill says, "So what are we having tomorrow? What kind of wine do you want me to pick up?"

"Nothing too fancy. As long as it's expensive."

They smile, and each man puts on his sunglasses.

"Great. Seven?"

"Any time you like."

With a small rim of regret, he leaves Bill.

Driving back in the car he wonders if Saturday night will be difficult. Why should it be difficult? Whose fault would that be?

But then life is blurred with frustration. Him parking the car. Him getting out of the car, not being able to fix on the change he wanted in his life or in Laurie. Difficult.

There isn't any distraction. There isn't any fault.

Four trees. Sunlight. Paul looks around, unseeing.

A strong memory of love sweeps through him, a memory much stronger than nostalgia – love itself, from outside or inside, there is no telling which. He carries the love into his practice. Past the tank of fish. To his office. Where he brushes his teeth and sprays his breath fresh.

He scans the records of the three afternoon patients.

He keeps his first patient waiting in the examination room.

Love settles heavily. Paul feels the whispered rumors of a headache and takes an aspirin, which will also thin his blood. He goes smiling into the examination room.

The second patient of the afternoon doesn't show. There is no phone call, no reason.

He forgets about the headache. Instead, from his office, Paul looks at the heat outside the window. There is no depth to the heat. It hangs, or clings on, like the air in an oven which has been switched off. He feels too clean and too honest. Perhaps he cares too much. He comes back to thinking about Laurie. Love is transparent, clear, like an old intention. Love is Laurie. He is sure.

He wonders, Who holds the responsibility for love? That is the scary part, the unknown. Had they really decided that they couldn't live without each other? They had. They had really decided this.

He can't understand where the decision has come from. Has he ever made any decision, ever, about anything? He has the decision. There is the decision. Made. But the making? What was there in the making? No, there wasn't any making. There was the worry: and then there is the ending of worry, the ending of anxiety, in loving Laurie. He can make decisions about other people – he does so every working day – but he can never make decisions about himself.

Laurie can. Laurie can make decisions about herself. Why should it scare him? That it was decided that they couldn't live without each other. That he doesn't want to live in any other way. That it should be an end to anxiety, and is so, love is.

Love is.

He opens the door and looks through into the front office. Alice is checking through accounts, one after another, killing time. His partner Abe Deane, an older man, has already left for the weekend, lunching at twenty-five thousand feet somewhere. There is no-one in the waiting room. The fish are active, crossing the tank.

"Two in one day," he says, "two cancellations. That's bad."

"You want I should bill them," Alice sympathises.

"Bill the second one, she didn't call."

"She did, just now. And they both have made appointments for the end of next week."

"Okay. That's good."

"Do you want me to bill her for today?"

"No. Thank you, Alice."

It could mean that neither of the women thought that they had any problem. End-of-the-week patients were either very alarmed, or else didn't think they had a problem. If he froze off a melanoma then their skin would be sensitive and scarred, not in great shape for a weekend's poolside entertaining or tennis. In LA, saving lives had to coincide with saving looks.

"Okay."

There are two reasons why he can't let Alice go early. The

practice doesn't look good without a receptionist. More important, he can't risk being left alone with a patient, nor with his nurse. Some doctors achieved sexual malpractice, others had malpractice suits thrust upon them. So, if he stayed until the end of the day, he would participate in an almost British ceremonial of assembly with his nurse and Alice and the lab staff outside the outer door, while it was locked and before they fanned out to their separate cars. This frigid protocol was ridiculous – he felt like decent Jack Lemmon cringing from a rainstorm – but it was the way things were. Abe Deane had no time for it, but then Abe Deane was twice Paul's age and his future lay with the nurse he had married forty years ago. Great working relationships might seem to be reserved for that generation. At Paul's age, even divorce lawyers got divorced.

"You got nothing to do?" Alice notes.

"Sure. No. Maybe."

"You got your babe coming in."

"Yes." In four months. He wasn't counting, and in a year and four months the baby would be one year old. Then two, three. He could get up to three, couldn't see any further, couldn't imagine any further.

"Dog-catcher got you, Doctor. Here she comes now. That's her play car. Classy lady. It don't do not to look busy, now does it?" Alice rebukes him, sweeps away his little thinking; this is not his baby. The arrival is Diana Caviatti, his last patient.

"Alice, I'm not sugar-daddying Mrs Caviatti."

"She got one of her own, I'd say."

Alice doesn't smirk. She has been behind the desk since forever and can get away with murder. He smiles. She expects him to smile.

"Have Julie go with her to the examination room. Five minutes."

"Yes, Doctor."

He takes a delivery of prescription pads from the top of the reception desk and goes to his office, where he locks them in the safe.

He had been taken into the practice nearly three years ago. He had been married to Laurie for five, sleeping with Laurie for seven. Living in Los Angeles for just over three years.

It was natural. From Connecticut Laurie's father had known about real estate. Paul's father ran a lumber company out of Denver.

Laurie had loved Colorado, had majored in law and got taken into a firm which specialised in environmental lawsuits. Paul had not always wanted to study medicine, but had always refused to go into the lumber business; so medicine. He had met Laurie, and each was confident that they had found an ally. It felt like that. They got the best times out of life. They came across a lot of different people, and they wanted to get married because they knew they were different. They loved, evidently, in Colorado.

They had stayed there for two years after their marriage, and marriage hadn't made any difference. New furniture made a difference, but they ignored it, and accepted it. Then Laurie's job wasn't going anywhere. So she didn't care; but she did, she didn't get along with the group of other lawyers. She thought that they were crazy and too single-minded and riding high off confrontations which they set out to cause.

Paul didn't say anything, but he had thought that he saw some of his father's influence pressuring her. They hadn't settled back east, near her relatives; and he knew that Laurie needed family, and so wanted to get along with his family. Marriage, commitment, brought that out in her. For their part, his parents had been delighted to accept her, and they enjoyed her. This irritated him. He felt that they needed to get away.

He had started applying for jobs, strangely enough more on the east coast than on the west. It was the flip side of the coin: he wanted to get to know her family, he wanted her family to play more of a leading part in their lives, in her life. Sometimes he would skip through real estate magazines, and talk to Laurie about movements in population. Maybe the desire to move west was over, maybe people would move back and re-structure the east. She had listened, but didn't react. When they flew to Connecticut one Thanksgiving, he talked with Laurie's father.

Laurie had one sister, no brothers. He felt relaxed with her father, he was appreciated. It was Laurie's turn to kid him about the use of charm, his turn to proclaim a liking for family.

Nothing had come of it, but they both knew restlessness. Then Paul had got offered an interview in Los Angeles, with Abe Deane. He immediately liked Abe Deane, and the interview went well, he got offered the job.

So it was crazy. It was practical, but crazy. Looking down from the Rockies, Los Angeles was the last place on earth they would consider living. It was crazy. But, okay, practically the experience would do no harm. Colorado would always be Colorado, and they could come back. It was crazy, but, one Saturday night, they had both sat down and had gotten high, and had wondered why on earth they shouldn't be crazy. Why not?

Laurie had started angling for west coast contacts – environmental lawyers were a close-knit outfit – and Paul had accepted Abe Deane's offer for him to start work at the end of the summer.

Then they had told both families, and both families thought that it would be a good thing to do, this proving of a direction. It was a project; and everyone had gotten in on it.

Hence the house, 1717 Jerome, which was way out of Paul and Laurie's bracket. Real estate and lumber had pulled together for the new nest. Mentions of loaning were nodded at, indifferently. Paul felt uneasy.

"Why worry?" said Laurie. "We don't want to live in a horrible part of LA. This is just our families showing that they care. Nobody's going to lose on the deal. Your father will pay it off against the company, and my father won't even make a blip in his stocks. If it would make you feel better then we could pay them rent. Just feel good about it. Don't throw it back in their faces."

He had never felt good about it. 1717? Why couldn't they have just gotten a 34?

But no. 34 just didn't hold a candle to the contrived splendor of Seventeen Seventeen.

Paul had house-sat for a friend of Abe's while it was being built. He commuted to Laurie at weekends. He didn't work Fridays at all, he went to stare at Seventeen Seventeen, feeling like an idiot around the specialised craftsmen. In California, these guys all had titles.

Laurie came twice to look at the house. She had been over the plans with her father and didn't care for the construction phase. She disliked construction, there was something surgical about it, she didn't want to know what stretched where, what stitched together how; even if Paul managed to learn about it, she didn't care to know and she didn't want to look. There was to be another house alongside – Paul surmised that Laurie's father was financing the development of what had been a double lot – and Laurie worried far more about this other house, its positioning, its windows, its height, its overlook. One Friday, Paul was amazed to see a whole brand new outside wall being torn down and thrown into a dumpster, subject he figured to Laurie's environmental concern.

When they had moved into the house, he had had no sense of it being a home. It had an office; his office, Laurie said. He couldn't think what to do with his office.

Abe had offered him some advice. "From here on in you have to pretend that you run the house. You never will run the house, but you have to pretend. Like we do at our offices. Alice runs the offices and the nurses run the practice. You just have to pretend otherwise. Make a lot of noise. And when you're used to it, don't let on that you're used to it." Abe had nodded appreciatively.

"You've done all right." He had grinned. "Nobody in this town is going to hold that against you, partner."

Paul had made arrangements to pay off the house. He wanted their independence. Month by month he arranged to have money deducted from his salary. He didn't want the house, but he didn't want anyone else to own it. No-one said anything. No-one seemed to notice.

TWO

Friday: 4p.m to 5p.m.

Last patient, Friday.

Mrs Diana A. Caviatti. Two or three times a year. Whenever she was in Los Angeles. She had a house here, or her mother did. Her husband had houses elsewhere, heading east and on into Europe. Northern Europe, Paul thought. There was northern Europe, and then she talked more about France. She might say, I have a doctor for my skin in California.

She was an A-l client. The first time she came, he couldn't believe he had her. Even Abe lifted an eyebrow, which was his way of rubbing his hands. She had come on a recommendation from an older woman, not her mother, but who knew her mother. Not even. Who worked for her mother. However it was, Mrs Diana Caviatti came to him. (One or two pre-cancerous possibilities. Nothing.) And Abe, and he, had lifted eyebrows and had speculated into assumption over cocktails that there would be more, more Mrs Caviattis, more of her circle, more of her friends, her lunchees, her honorary board co-members. Her social caste. (These women, said Abe, move like mercury. The metal, not the god.)

Diana Caviatti had continued to visit him, but presumably the goddess didn't communicate, or else was one of a kind.

The last appointment on a Friday afternoon: he had once placed her there out of irritation. She hadn't proved convenient by way of increasing his client base, so let her know inconvenience: what wealthy socialite opts for disfigurement on a Friday evening? Diana Caviatti was indifference itself. She could not have cared less. Two, maybe three times a year; hers was the last appointment on a Friday afternoon. In the jock-slot, where the better looking women were booked in, at their convenience, at his suggestion.

This was no big deal, not for him. Abe did the same thing, with his wife in and out of the examination room. Paul had noticed, and now noticed it in himself. Bill laughed and said how it used to be a line or two of cocaine, Friday afternoons, that was the last appointment. Just something to give a little lift to the weekend. Everyone had gotten a little older and so now it was sackable women who provided the high and gave you a little dream to take home to reality. That was all right. Hell, these women knew what they were doing.

Well, Bill knew what he was doing, after hours. Maybe his wife Helen did, for all Paul knew. Paul was never unfaithful to Laurie, not in his consideration.

Diana Caviatti was sitting in the chair. Julie, his nurse, held a ballpoint pen. The pen came between Julie and Mrs Caviatti and that was the extent of their interest in each other, a polite and efficient extraction of personal information. And that was all he wanted of Julie. It was his responsibility to care, to charm.

"Diana," he said, suddenly shy, "so how are things going with you? You'd better fill me in a little on your movements. Just give me some idea here of what you might have been exposed to. Remind me – you're resident where?"

"We're in The Hague. And sometimes on the coast, outside Antibes. But the children go to school in The Hague so that is where we spend most of our time, and my husband has a lot of his business there now."

He stood, intent on preserving the personal eye contact, carefully enhancing formalities. Uncomfortably he realised that he had forgotten her. He hadn't forgotten who she was; but he had forgotten her freshness, he had misplaced that. It wasn't a youthful freshness, nor was it the reconstituted freshness which was so often brashly cultivated as coquetry on the west coast. She was more graceful, less concerned; the attractive, oval face was both pensive and warmly, ironically, amused.

"You don't miss California?"

"Yes, sometimes. Then I come to visit with my mother."

"Is she all right? How's she?"

"She's getting older, but she's well. She had something taken off her arm last year, which has healed. There's a small scar but you wouldn't notice it unless she showed you."

"Good." He remembered this conversation from her last appointment. He remembered the way in which she half held out her arm, the slimness of her wrist, a smooth, olive skin. There was an atmosphere of completeness about her. As far as could be from Los Angeles. As far as could be from the small examination room.

He remembered her mother's cancer being on Diana Caviatti's file, and Julie would have written it down again on the form, to remind him. He would have asked this next question at their last meeting. "And the children don't have any problems?"

"No."

"Do they use sunscreen in Europe?"

"They're starting to. It's not a rule, but most people are aware of it even if they don't use it regularly. They're not so fixated on the problem as everyone here is, you know?"

She smiled pleasantly.

He said, "That's fine. It's great to find people who are both intelligent and relaxed." Which didn't sound as insignificant as he had meant, whether focused on her or on himself. "My wife is having a baby, you know," he hurried, and nodded, and felt a reliable pride, which brought back his smile.

"Oh but that will be marvellous! Please give her my congratulations."

"I will. She's in great shape."

"This is your first, isn't it?"

"Yes, it will be. The first."

"That's quite a roller-coaster of a time."

"I guess it is, yes."

At this point Julie smiled and excused herself and left the room.

"Now," he said, "maybe I should ask you whether you sit outside in the sun, but we'll say that sometimes you sit outside in the sun and sometimes you don't. Have you noticed anything, Diana? On your face, or on your arms?"

"There is some rough skin." She touched her temple, and then her forehead.

"Right. Then we'll take a look at that. If you would just sit back please. Make yourself comfortable, I won't be a moment."

He left her. He wanted to re-establish the normal state of affairs between himself and Diana Caviatti, nothing about their personal lives, nothing about babies. He didn't want emotions brought to the surface. There was enough of that. He didn't want it. In the waiting room, Alice and Julie were standing and watching the tiny television, from which came a low volume of newsmen.

"Julie – would you take Mrs Caviatti a coffee or a juice or something? What's on?" Alice sometimes watched TV during the lunch break, he had no objection. Abe and he might sit in front of a golf game after hours, but not during, and not with women patients in the building.

Julie came away without any complaint, and went to the examination room. Alice changed channels and said, "They arrested some man."

"What man?"

Alice nodded at the screen. "That man. The manifesto man, who killed those people." She kept half an eye on Paul, wanting him to channel through her towards what was on the screen. He didn't want to show any reaction. He felt his hands start to sweat. "You aren't interested in that stuff anymore?" Alice asked.

"No. And it's not what you were watching either." He hoped that an anger would seem appropriate. No intensity. "And it isn't what any patient might want to catch. That's why we have the fish for people to watch. People like fish." He raised an eyebrow, hoping to make her smile and to remove the sting from his reprimand. "We all like fish, remember?"

"We like fish, yes we do," Alice grumbled, "they no trouble."

He saw her unease, and was almost glad of it. "What's wrong," he asked, "is there something else, you were watching?"

"There's trouble, sure enough."

"Where?"

"South Central, where else."

"What kind of trouble?"

"I don't know. Just trouble. Young people. It may be just one of those gang things." Alice switched off the set. "I don't know why I turned it on. Just asking for trouble."

He saw that she was worried.

"Alice, we won't be long now. I'd let you get home, but you know how it is."

"Sure I do. This is my work, same as yours."

"We're nearly done."

Julie came out of the examination room and went to the refrigerator. She took a glass of orange juice and a napkin, and returned, shutting the examination room door behind her.

He composed himself, and opened the door.

"I'm sorry about that, Diana. There was something I wanted to check on your file."

"Anything serious?" she asked. "It can't – "

"No, no. It's nothing at all. I was back-checking what creams I gave you last time. Right, I'll just – " he turned on the faucet and the sound of the water into the sink cut through the weight of the air " - wash up here." Across his mind came the memory of another sink, another bathroom; and the fear, arrested. He squeezed soap out of the bottle, clasped his hands together firmly and rubbed with interlocked fingers, rinsed and reached for the clean towel. "Okay."

This time he didn't look at her eyes, except for a brisk affirmation. This was work. He was aware that she was watching him. She sat straight in the chair, a white shirt, a cream linen jacket, a wide dark green skirt and flats. Light on lipstick.

"Shall I tie back my hair?"

"No. Not for now. I'm going to switch on the light, so you might want to close your eyes, okay?" Grey-brown, almost musk, eyes; calm. She kept her hands crossed in her lap.

He stood at her right shoulder and switched on the light. Beneath her eyelids her eyes adjusted to darkness, the skin rippled quickly beside the mascaraed lashes. The texture of a full foreskin. He scanned across her forehead and hairline with the spectroscope. In three places the skin was harder and rough and had pushed out, no bigger than a pimple, but there was no darker growth at the circumference. He touched each blemish with the scalpel.

"Do these patches irritate you at all?"

"No." She moved her hands over her lap, smoothing the green skirt comfortably between her thighs.

"They don't ever itch or discolor?"

"No. I can feel them when I touch them, and I can see them in the mirror."

"They're nothing serious. Tiny nevi, not active. I can burn them off. There's one a little way behind your right cheekbone, the same thing."

"Yes, it looked the same as the others."

"It is. It's nothing."

It was nothing that she didn't know about. She probably spent a lot of time in front of the mirror. Men mostly didn't. There were a few cautious male patients, but not many; for dermatology was often falsely linked in the public mind to cosmetic surgery, women's business. Women being more intelligently, and decisively, aware of themselves.

He scanned the lines of her jaw and the sides of her neck, there were a few baby hairs and a mole under the lobe of her left ear, no more than a natural beauty spot.

He flipped off the light. "That's it. You're clean. There's nothing in your track record which is going to suggest that you'll have any trouble, as long as you look after yourself as well as you're doing already."

He said all this as her eyes opened and struggled with the daylight – the police have arrested someone, he thought – as her lips relaxed to show her teeth. She rested her hands on the arms of the chair, her nails sheened with a neutral varnish. "Good," he said, as her eyes focused on him, "that's good. Living in Europe doesn't do you any harm. I wish that half my patients would spend more time there. They would save themselves the cost of all those hours spent lounging around the pool without being covered up."

She was pleased.

He said, "It sounds so puritan, doesn't it? Like something my grandmother would have said."

"Mine too. But it can't be helped."

She stood up, half a head shorter than him. She reached her hands behind her and made to scoop up her hair, which wouldn't work because of her jacket. He helped her off with the jacket and laid it across the chair.

He asked her if she normally wore her hair down.

"Not always." Then she held up her hair and he checked her neck, which was clear, and he told her so. There was a perfume, and the scent of her body coming up from beneath her shirt collar, just as always, but momentarily stronger. He backed away, angrily confused. He thought of calling Julie into the room. And then he thought that *he* was the offender, that it was his fault, and that everything was normal. He had strung himself up on his own preconception. Just as he had done before: the man they had arrested was – wasn't he? – white.

"Okay," he said. She unfastened a necklace of colored beads or stones, lighter green than the skirt, and placed it on top of the jacket.

"We'll just", he said, "run a check over everything else. If you'd like to go behind the drapes and undress, Diana." She waited until he had finished speaking, and then as she walked across the room, beginning to unbutton her shirt, he turned away and entered the four nevi on her file, and looked down at her purse, which was on the floor by the side of the chair, a shoulder purse made from a light tan, western leather, supple at the sides and ridged into seams, the strap not soiled from wear. He watched her step out of the shoes. He went across and drew the drapes. He heard her lay her skirt across the arm of the chair. She drew the drapes back. As he turned around, she straightened her underwear, dark green, across her buttock, withdrawing her thumb from beneath the elastic, so the underwear fit like a small patch of skin.

He averted his eyes as she turned to face him.

"Okay. Legs a little further apart."

He stood beside her and ran the pads of his fingers over her torso, frisking her for points of dry skin. The skin at her flanks goose-bumped, a ripple passed through the abdominal musculature. The underwear was minimal, and decorative; cut far lower than was necessary, unless she wanted him to check her Caesarian scar. He asked her.

"Would you?" she asked.

He did, carefully.

"Fine so far."

Fine, and exuding health. Healthy. He looked at the brassière, which was expensive, and pretty, as were the briefs. Finely decorative. He knelt on one knee, beside the bikini line. The skin on the inside of her thighs, near her groin, was smooth, very little different in texture to the sheen on the material which covered her pubis; so she must prefer using a depilatory cream to shaving. He kept his thoughts objective. Her left hand hung protectively, close to his head. His fingers brushed quickly up from her left ankle to her groin, and then down from the top of her right thigh; he was conscious of the shiny material which pouched, tightly, her vulva. He stopped at her knee and smoothed scar tissue.

"A childhood accident?"

"Range-wire, when I was eleven. My knee went sideways into it."

"Ah yes, I remember. On a bicycle. Ouch."

"You have a good memory."

"It's more selective than I would want." He finished the right leg and straightened up. "Stay off the bicycling, and you should be fine." He handed her her skirt. "A-okay, Diana."

"I'm relieved." She smiled.

He stepped back and drew the drapes.

He laughed. "It's good to see someone without a problem."

"It's a pleasure to hear it."

"We'll treat those nevi, when you're ready. Back in the chair." He crossed his arms, let all visions of pouches sail through his mind, and smiled thankfully at their departure.

When she emerged from behind the drapes, he turned to a cupboard and reached out the flask of liquid hydrogen. "Just the same as usual: a small pain, like a burn, although we are of course freezing them. Then it will scab in a day or two. And they will be very sensitive to any sunlight, so wear a hat. Try not to touch or rub when washing. You've had this all before, Diana. Still, now. Very still."

He withdrew the swab and applied it quickly to the four nevi, and replaced the swab in the flask, and sealed it. Everything was now so automatic.

"All done." He handed her a tissue, which she took to dry her eyes.

She reached down for her purse and put the necklace inside. She didn't say anything, she must still have been in some pain.

"Sit for a moment. There isn't any hurry."

"Is this the end of your day?"

"It's the end of my week. We don't get any emergency calls for skin. I might do Saturday mornings once in a while. In September usually, after vacations. It's much better to get checked over regularly, but some people really like to save it and get alarmed. Some patients need to panic."

"You treat them for panic?" she said, raising an eyebrow.

He laughed, wondering at his sudden levity. "Yes, sometimes. Hey, I can understand it, I'm the same way."

"You panic?"

Yes, he had panicked, he had lost control. But now they had arrested someone. It was finished. He was unburdened. He could forget. Nothing had happened. Nobody would know.

He wanted to talk with her, but there should be an amicably impersonal release from the examination. Thank God for the examination room, with the chair, and the cupboards, and the table, and Laurie's framed photographs of Colorado. They constituted a sterile, sober setting.

"Me? I worry. But I don't worry about worrying. Every patient has a right to worry. And with cancer, you'd be irresponsible if you didn't." She must feel relieved, he knew, everyone was relieved when they got a clean bill of health. He remembered the lunchtime conversation with Bill.

How did Bill get from "palate" to sex? Crudely, he guessed. Sex was crude and sudden. Just a simple mistake. Once, during a televised football game he had been watching, the wide receiver had tripped, unmarked. He had, according to the commentator, "entered a self-tackling situation". Crudely.

"Has the pain gone off now?"

"Yes."

She stood up and slipped into her shoes. He helped her with her jacket. She would leave. It was too abrupt. Like a roller-coaster.

"Can I ask you something, as a regular patient?"

"Of course you may, Paul."

"Do you ever feel vulnerable being examined?"

"Oh . . . sometimes. Or scared."

He tried to consider. "Maybe that's it."

"I'm scared by what a doctor might find. When I come in here I'm scared what you might find. Vulnerable isn't the right word, is it?"

"Maybe not."

"It's embarrassing. Sometimes. Not particularly in here. If it was, then I wouldn't come. Is this a worry for you?"

"I wanted to check with all my patients. It's an issue for any doctor."

"I can see that." She paused. "If you want to go back a step, then I can say definitely that I don't feel vulnerable when I come in here."

She was playing now for a sense of humor. "I suppose that the other thing", she said, "is does it embarrass *you*?"

"Oh well . . . it shouldn't. Not by now."

She was watching him. To his surprise he realised that this was something of a flirtation. She said, "Is it something either of us should worry about? Most doctors never talk about it and when they do, that's when it's trouble. It's worse trouble than paying the bill." She paused, and then said gently, "Which I'd like to card; I don't have my checkbook with me."

He looked at the small red blisters which were forming on her forehead, and glanced across her eyes.

He said, "I apologise for bringing it up."

She smirked, not unkindly. "So . . . are you in any trouble with a patient?"

"No. Not at all."

"I wouldn't have thought so."

"Thank you. You've had two children? Both by Caesarian?" She was well preserved, and he wondered how well Laurie's body would shape up after the birth.

"Oh," she said, "yes, I have. They are six and eight years old now. Two girls. Is that what you want to talk about?" She considered him, and seemed to make a decision as to his worth. "I can tell you that the last two months of pregnancy are the worst. You feel tired and big and ugly and somehow out of control with yourself. You don't sit in the sun, it's uncomfortable. And your husband behaves in ways that are just incomprehensible, so that you wonder why you would want to have another child to care for. It's nothing to worry about."

"Yes?" He wanted to know.

"But it has its ups and downs. I remember", Diana Caviatti said, "when I had my first pregnancy confirmed, I met my husband for lunch. He was over the moon – well, with a name like Caviatti, you can guess that he would be. And then he got his entrée fork stuck in his mouth, it just fit exactly into his bottom palate and stuck. He began to panic. I wondered what was happening. My God! – "

"Really! What did you do?"

"I don't know what happened, but the fork just came out. I worried that he might asphyxiate."

"Sure! You would."

Her eyes questioned this story, there were glimmers of the long-past episode, but she laughed. He guessed that she had told the story many times before, to friends, and that she wasn't sure whether or not he was interested.

"As I remember," he said, "Laurie and I had nothing so dramatic. How could that have happened? The fork just stuck there, that's strange. It's unusual."

"I said to David, if that's what fatherhood does to you, I'm glad I'm only going to be a mother."

"And what did he say?" She was beautifully dressed.

"David?"

"Who else?"

"Who else?" she said simply.

"No, I'm sorry, what did David say?" They both laughed.

"Oh, oh, David said that he was really pleased that I was pregnant, and at least for now we wouldn't have the hassle of birth control. He said that." She waited for him to say something.

He didn't know what to say.

"Well," he said, "I guess there are restaurants and restaurants. I'll bet you never went back."

She thought for a moment, and then she said that he was right, they never had been back to that restaurant." She smiled and shouldered her purse. "You know, men don't talk. It's a great advantage women have, so men make the next mistake of talking to *them*. Women can talk personally without any involvement. Don't make the mistake of going to another woman."

"I haven't."

She looked at him warily.

"Well, I have," he said, "talking with you."

"Yes." She said. "But that's anyway within the doctor-patient relationship, which has very strict codes of practice. So they tell me." He opened the door for her.

"Thank you for understanding."

"It's my pleasure."

"Diana, I have something you may like to try out."

"Yes?" she said warily.

He reached into a drawer. "This is Retin-A. It needs a prescription, and it's been tested. This is strong stuff, Diana, so you must follow the instructions. It's a non-toxic restorative cream which burns off the nevi skin and will open the way for new skin to form. Try it, just on the nevi, maybe once every four days. But if it gets sore, then leave it alone. Use it wisely."

"Ok-ay." She pursed her lips. "Thank you."

"You're welcome."

Exuberantly he followed her out, following her ass in the sways of the long green skirt. "Julie, four items on Mrs Caviatti's bill." He looked down at the statement. Destructions Fac Premal 1 thru 4. Diagnoses: Nevi check; History family mal neoplasm; Keratosis, actinic; Nevus, compound. He handed the statement to Julie, who would cost it. "Alice, Mrs Caviatti will pay by card." Around $350, he calculated.

She opened her purse.

She said, "Thank you, Paul. I'll try out the Retin-A cream." Alice started humming to herself.

"But please," he said, "read the instructions carefully. Is your car near?"

"Yes," she said, "it's outside."

"Which way you heading?" Alice demanded. "I hope it isn't downtown 'cos there's trouble."

"I'm going to Malibu."

"That's all right then. Dumb people don't appreciate a car like yours, ma'am."

"Well . . . " she said, "I suppose that they don't. Lucky people do."

Alice smiled at her. "I do."

She smiled back. "Thank you. I'd like an appointment in six months. Just to get checked up by Doctor Mathiessen."

"He needs checking up on. His wife's having a baby, first in the line."

He couldn't believe this protectionism. "I told Mrs Caviatti."

"You may have told her, but I'll bet you didn't announce it enough. The doctor's a quiet man. He gives me the creeps sometimes, he's so quiet."

"Thank you, Alice."

"You're welcome. If you sign here, Mrs Caviatti."

She did so. He watched her signature extend, a strangely erotic, removed moment, she central to the group of women.

"Six months?" Alice said. "Would you like any time on any particular day?" She rustled through to the empty pages.

"No. Friday at this timc suits."

"Suits fine, ma'am"

"Okay," he said. "I'll see you in six months, Diana. Spend some of them in the shade."

"You too, Paul."

"Bye now."

Julie escorted her to the outer door. Diana Caviatti held her purse in her hand on the way to her car. He watched the way she walked, happy to detain himself within the dark gathers of the green drapes.

When they had come to LA, Laurie had found work. And had lost it within a year, through no fault of her own. Business was down, associates were laid off, and she hadn't been there long enough to make the leap upwards for safety.

In the confusion she had taken a few clients with her. She had set herself up as a political consultant. The consultancy went fine, but she pulled for an inexperienced politician who never got through the mud-slinging. She had recognised that she was more of a liability than a help, coming as she did from out-of-state, fraught with naivety.

For a year . . . fifteen months? . . . she had work, enough certainly to justify her moving off Paul's p.c. and setting up one of her own in the bedroom downstairs. Her father guided some business her way, and her own dedication to personal attention kept her clients loyal. Two days a week she went into her old firm to use the Westlaw facility.

Then Paul became aware that jobs seemed to have disappeared.

It wasn't an issue between them. Laurie was still ambitious, but she didn't like the work. She said that it felt like she was forever going into a room on her clients' arms, as a token, as the representative of a small legal matter which had been already wrapped up. (Paul thought, They could have escorted a lot less intelligent, and more wrapped-up, consultants into the room. Let them find that out for themselves.)

The truth was, he thought, that Laurie didn't like fighting. She never ran from an intellectual fight, she shone in legal research, but she didn't see why she should push her own personality forward into the front line. She believed, and felt, that her battles should be bloodless.

Maybe this was because of her good looks. She was aware of her looks, but she didn't want to use them, nor have them used against her. They were a private weapon, only to be used against him, and only when she was confident of the outcome.

No, she didn't like a battle. She fought by coldness. When Laurie fought, a terrible austerity sealed her eyes.

It had taken him a long time to realise how far such a lack of expression drained her, this bleak stating of her will. She kept it going for days, long after he had ventured on some dispute or other and had more or less forgotten the basis to his challenge. Meantimes she waited coldly until she was absolutely certain that she had exhausted any competition from him; and then she was simply tired; not confused, not pliant, but would spend the victory day napping. While he tried to get her attention by worrying about her, and his, morale.

Single-minded? Yes, he thought so, but, God, who knows?

When jobs dropped away, she had said that she thought that she might write a book, that she had it in her.

She did have most of a book. Her determination didn't surprise him. Bits of the book he had seen on her screen, set in three parts, or three subjects. Family. Law. And something clipped, to him nebulous, about being a woman. Which part, she said, she was just fiddling with; she didn't like it, she thought that it was full of clichés, there wasn't any point in finishing it. It should probably ground the first part of the book, and then influence the law part.

Not only had she written the book, but she was critically suspicious of it. For him, it was much easier to understand her suspicion than it was to understand what she had written. She was some way above what she had written, bloodlessly interested. It seemed that way to him.

Now that she was pregnant, she visited the word processor as a guest, not concerned to finish her book until she had considered its shape. She gave no sign of being proud of her creation. It seemed to intrigue her from time to time. She didn't fight with it. She gave herself no deadline.

Paul wondered how much the book was a friend, to her. Laurie didn't make friends easily.

Maybe that was Los Angeles.

Maybe that was part of the scheme of things at Seventeen Seventeen. Maybe that's how Seventeen Seventeen was.

Or maybe that's how Laurie, and he, had become.

THREE

Friday: 5p.m. to 7p.m.

He watched the flash of leg as Diana Caviatti got into her car and tucked the skirt in under her thigh.

"Dream on," Alice murmured.

"Alice . . . " Nonchalantly he rebuked her.

"It's late."

"Yes. And it's Friday."

"And there's trouble." Alice pulled her purse out of the drawer.

"Still? What kind of trouble?"

"Messin'. It's on the TV. We didn't have nothin' else to occupy ourselves. They occupyin' themselves all right. You stay out of South Central tonight, and tell your friends."

"Okay, sure. Do you know what started it?"

Alice stared at him expressionlessly. "Do you want a list?"

He shrugged. "No. Is it a race disturbance?"

"People disturbance."

"Yes. Excuse me, I apologise."

There was no point in delaying any longer. Julie had tidied the examination room and was already out of her uniform, happy to leave. The lab staff went home at noon on Fridays.

"Is the lab locked, Julie?"

"Yes it is, Doctor Mathiessen."

"I'll get my things."

He switched off the screen and the air-conditioner and picked up his briefcase, slinging his coat over his shoulder.

"Are the cupboards all locked?"

"Yes. And the examination-room door."

"Okay. Alice – everything off?"

"It is."

"We'll meet by the door."

They went outside, and he activated the security systems. Already, with the heat, he was sweating as he strode through the door. They moved away. He locked the door.

"Right. Okay. Have a good weekend, Julie."

"You too."

Alice stood patiently.

"Big trouble?" He asked.

"It's been comin'."

"I'm sure it has."

Everything came: earthquakes, fire, flood, mudslide. After the serial killer of unknown bent and the gang blow-out, now came disturbance. Now came the arrest of a man who was supposed to be the manifesto murderer. It was hard to grip these things. Newspapered terror arrived in blocks nowadays, there never wasn't a weight of news. If Alice hadn't have been with him he would have gone back inside and switched on the TV, and then maybe he would have known what to feel.

But Alice lived off South Central.

Dimly he tried to consider the bigness of trouble, weighty enough to make Alice drag her feet on a Friday.

"Alice, why don't you take a cab home? I'd feel better if you did."

"I don't know."

"You have a nice car, why risk it? Are they burning cars?"

"I seen one or two, maybe."

"Then take a cab. Your car will be safe up here. And get a cab on Monday. The office will pay. We'll do that. This is sensible. We'll do it."

Be practical. Approach these things one by one.

He took the keys out of his case, unlocked the door and beat the security alarm to the front desk. Get things in some kind of order. He called a cab and charged it to the office. Five minutes. He deliberately ignored the TV. He retraced the locking procedure.

"It's hot out here. We'll sit in Laurie's car."

Ten minutes passed.

Neither wanted to talk. Fridays limited any interest to a self-conscious desire to avoid condescension. They waited, air-conditioned.

When the cab came, he walked across with Alice.

He said, "If you have any problem, anything at all, you call me at home, okay? You promise me?"

"Home is home. That's not work."

"You call. Anything. Any trouble."

"If that's what you want."

"Try to get away this weekend, if you want to."

"Where to?"

"Anywhere."

"Without a car?"

"Take a cab and pick up the car."

"I might go to Chicago."

"Not in a cab, you won't. Call."

She wouldn't. He knew that. She had her pride. He waved as the cab drove off, and felt that it was a foolish, white, thing to do.

But it was the end of the week, the end of the goddamned week. He didn't want to be a doctor, he didn't want to be a white, he didn't want to be anything. They had made an arrest. He slammed the car door shut.

He slipped a CD into the player, reversed the car out of his parking space, and pulled forward to the end of the lot. Two cars drove by, an Acura and a high-series Beamer, and then he took his place in the slow drive to the hills. The rap was Heavy D and he didn't like it much. He liked some of it, sometimes wildly, but it wasn't a favorite. Wildness wasn't a favorite with him, he got hung about with suspicion. He felt his own falsity of wildness, come Friday, come home.

He wouldn't tell Laurie about the arrest.

He ejected Heavy D and put on Madonna; and considered Diana Caviatti dancing, and how many fine sets of clothing were hers. This was Diana Caviatti music, in retrospect. The rhythm. Oh, he and Laurie had danced to it, they each had mastered it, neither knowing what it meant outside their own sense of performance – when Madonna was cute and chubby – "Cos you make me feel, yeah you make me feel –

> Like a virgin, touched for the very first time
> Like a vir-ir-irgin . . ."

Should he tell Laurie about the arrest? Maybe. But how? How should he be? It was over and finished. He should be matter-of-fact. It had never been important. To her, it had always been nothing. He should tell her tomorrow, when it would be Saturday. Not on Friday.

It was hot outside the window, cool inside the car; there was regular Friday traffic.

In the darkness, underneath, dark green satin, like a pouch of skin. Diana Caviatti's hand, relaxed yet protective, on a level with her pubis. White hand. Long, sheened nails.

Slow down. Get off the freeway.

Turn left, away from the hand.

The CD ended, and he ejected it. There was silence in the car, apart from the whisper of air-conditioning.

Up the hill, across the side of the hill. And onto Jerome.

Burned weeds curled out of the crevices in the dark cream

concrete, smeared with rubber and stained with oil. Up the mound, a smooth concrete driveway treated with weedkiller, pristinely taut, shimmering like skin in the heat; the house hanging protectively above the dark green lawn, which was decoratively trimmed, and edged, and sprinklered glistening wet. 1717 Jerome.

He got out of the car, and took with him his coat and his case and his daydream of Diana. The garage doors came down behind him. Indeed his golf shoes still lay by the freezer. He smiled ruefully. He entered the house by the door which came out halfway up the interior stairway, then he walked through the hall past the open dining room to the kitchen.

"Hi," he called to Laurie, "how was your day?"

"Oh . . . good," she said. "How was yours?" She offered him her cheek, which he brushed with his lips.

"It was a Friday . . . "

"I know that. I'm not completely comatose." She smiled.

"Oh. Well, a couple of patients didn't show up."

"That's a nuisance."

"Uh-huh. It may not have been their fault. There's some trouble in the downtown area. They re-scheduled. Apart from that, it was just a Friday."

This was the maximum amount of information which would interest her. Occasionally he acted out some drama, or gave his patients a little character, which had used to make her laugh, when they had both wanted to ridicule the grotesquery of LA. These days she really wasn't much interested, which he reasoned as being a good thing. Since she was no longer working, it would be a bad sign if she had started to hang on to any small bits of entertainment which were offered by his working day.

"I'm going to take a shower."

"Okay. Do you want me to fix you a drink?"

"Oh . . . " he considered. "No. I don't think so. Can I get you one?"

"You know, I don't think I will."

"Maybe later."

"Maybe." She flipped through her magazine. "Leave your shirt and anything else by the washer, Paul."

"Sure. Any calls?"

"Just my mother, and George (her father) came on and said to say hi."

"How was your mother?"

"Pretty good. It was early evening, they were going out somewhere. And Helen Matson called to ask if she should bring anything tomorrow night. I said no, and then she gave me a list, so I said yes. It seemed like the path to least resistance."

"To what? What does she want to bring?"

"Really I can't remember."

"Laurie?"

"It all sounded good. I left it to her. I said 'nothing too spicy'. I never can order anything from a catalogue unless it has a picture. It sounded like a list of ingredients."

He laughed. "Did you work out a menu?"

"Oh sure, I worked out about six menus. I don't know, I didn't feel hungry. I guess that it's not surprising, considering that I just raided the refrigerator before she called. I don't want to think about it."

"How do you feel?"

"I feel fine. Go shower."

She put down the magazine beside her on the couch and looked at him. "You look handsome."

"I do?"

"Yes." She picked up the magazine again. "It's a pity that I ate all that food."

"You look good, too," he said.

"Thank you."

"Maybe I'll take a beer."

"Paul . . . "

"Okay okay, I'll shower." He called from the door. "Shirt by the washer?"

"Yes."

"Did my blue sports shirt get ironed?"

"Yes."

"Great. I'll wear it tomorrow night."

"Take your coat through."

He came back for his coat, and caught sight of his case. He should pick up the case and leave it in his office, but he didn't want to. He preferred kitchens, he liked the kitchen to be a center where bits of the periphery of life could be brought in, and dumped down, and chewed over. They had imported their dog Buffalo with them to Los Angeles and it had lived on the couch; but the dog, old anyway, had died, and the couch had gotten stylish in order to stare down the small TV which had taken up residence across from the kitchen table.

He left his case on one of the tall stools by the side of the breakfast counter. There was a jug of pens on the counter and two pads of jotting paper, and now, lower down, his case. He took his coat from the back of the stool.

Their bedroom was tidy. He threw his coat over his chair and himself onto the straightened comforter, smelling detergent and cleanliness. He looked up at the four track-lights, miniature. You could create straight and sharply confined beams of light in the darkness, almost like thin pillars, between which ran mystery, like a game.

It wasn't dark yet, outside. The afternoon ochre was settling heavily, well beneath the bedroom window, in the trough of Metropolitan Los Angeles. He couldn't see it from where he lay. Like a sulphurous mist of urine.

Not for some time had they played.

They had no porch. He would have wanted to take a bottle of wine out onto the porch, and sit. In the warm and fresh Colorado evening air, with wet hair, and his feet on the rail: the only knowledge being that he had more than enough money to cover the rent, and enough money to go out late somewhere, meeting and talking with friends in a bar, partying slow. Maybe. But they had no porch.

When they had first moved into 1717, their main project had been to make the house sexy. By having sex in as many parts of it as was possible. Such was to have been the colonisation of 1717.

And thus, from east to west, they had colonised: the master bedroom, the dressing room (and closet space), the bathroom, the kitchen, the second bedroom (closet space, painful) and bathroom, the office (yes!), the hallway (on castors), the dining room, the living room. Halfway down the stairs, one night, late, the door to the garage still open. The downstairs bedroom – when it was the guest room – and with languor when it was Laurie's room. The deck, which separated one level from the lower half-level on the outside of the house, and the patio which extended into the hillside.

They colonised roughly, and frequently not so roughly, some four and a half thousand square feet. They did this with some spontaneity, some strategy, and more ingenuity. They were flexible. They were playful. They were determined. At this time Paul saw a lot of rug; and he saw exotic woods from many parts of the world, on walls, on floors and fascias, against his and Laurie's skin.

The house had withstood the challenge. Seventeen Seventeen remained daunting and unimpressed. They had tried everything with sex. Everything.

He had wanted a porch. Laurie had wanted a pool. So they had a patio. No-one had a porch in Los Angeles, not a safe porch. He had been ridiculous in holding out against the pool. They should have had a pool while it was part of the house construction. He should have taken it while it was offered. But he had refused.

They had talked about it. He had been mulish about it, he had been financially cautious about it, he had been concerned about their over-exposure to sun. There had been no good reason at all, save that he wanted a porch not a pool. He wasn't able to explain it. Laurie didn't ask him to.

Fridays. He had gotten into the habit of taking a beer into the shower, and Laurie too. Later on she had taken to showering before he came home, and looking clean and pretty and appetising over a cocktail, having had the time to do things with her hair and to choose what clothes she wanted to wear. They either went out to eat, or sent out for a delivery, and the game lay in the waiting and the deliberating over which appetite to satisfy.

They had started to spend time on cocktails, and ended by finding their way more directly to the bedroom. Then there came to be never any sense of celebrating the weekend; instead they began to deliberately obliterate from their senses his working week. Fridays they started to argue. They drank and argued and sent out to the world for argument, which served as foreplay to their embrace of sanctuary within the bedroom, under the thin beams of light which silently picked out the surfaces of hair and skin. He knew all about her body, she liked to show him everything about her body, things which even surprised her.

Fridays they drank. Once or twice they had tried going back to drugs, heartlessly, without nostalgia. For they liked arguing. They had gotten arguing right down to the consummatively precise insult: – she was a tight-fisted neurotic (why else didn't they have any friends?), and he was a selfish coward (because he sat around waiting for people to call up).

Silence. And when the bedroom lights were switched off, maybe they'd maul each other brutishly without getting anywhere.

More often they had made each other whimper, forgetfully and gratefully, in sexual release, late the next morning. Mothering hell but did she look sexy with smudged mascara and faded lipstick after a night's unconsciousness. He had known all about what to put on her body.

Now, with the baby inside her, she talked factually about her body. And about things which he couldn't see. He wanted to be allowed access to mysteries. But she knew mysteries which wouldn't see light or daylight. Shc didn't want to talk mystery, there was no mystery, she didn't care to pose it. He wanted revelations; but there was nothing of her that he could reveal to her, or for her. He was on his own. Their lovemaking had adopted the strenuous languors of a pietà. More often than not he now lapped at her assiduously, striving for some communion, while her fingers pattered through his hair, comforting him with her pleasure.

But he found himself thinking, while he tried to adore her. He found himself thinking. He no longer lost himself in her, and she no longer surrendered to him. Their loving had become an art form, at most an event.

FOUR

Friday: 7p.m. to 11.40p.m.

In the shower, he closed his eyes against the spraying, hot water. He opened his mouth, let it fill and then spouted the water out against the tiles, in an arc.

He carried the towel with him, past the closets in their dressing room, into the bedroom. Laurie was in her underwear, looking through a drawer. He startled.

"Hi, darling," he said. She half-turned and looked at him, surprised.

"Well, hiya."

"What are you looking for?"

"Something nice." In her drawer. "I can't decide."

"Uh-huh."

He bent to pick up his shirt, which he had left lying on the carpet, and he laid it on the bed. He rubbed his head with the towel, glancing at her. When he had rubbed his hair no drier than the towel, he dropped any pretence and looked at her, watched her as she stood with one foot crossed over the other instep, flipping through her panties.

He thought, We're not this old. We just aren't! Really. This isn't *us*. This is just so damn unfair. What's happened to the happiness? This isn't the way we are! We're not this old.

He was thirty-six.

Laurie, thirty-two.

They weren't that old. He was in shape. She had, as he saw,

the same aura of adolescence; that sweep of long blonde-brunette hair to her shoulder blades. Washed; and it would never lie down, mattress-hair she called it. She was often angry at its unruliness. Her back was elfin thin, still. Her butt fuller, but muscular; the cleft deeply wedged between her buttocks. Strong, peasant calves. Fragile forearms.

"Let me look at your back," he said. "I haven't checked your skin recently."

"Sure."

She left the drawer open and faced him. He remembered the photo of her, taken when she was twelve, part of the family group Christmas card. She and her younger sister wore calf-length plaid dresses, dark green, with the long white linen and lace yoke and cuffs. Daughters of founding fathers. With fragile wrists, and forearms tanned against the lace.

Her face hadn't changed. Or, rather, it had changed back from when she was in Colorado. Her face had been thinner then, more lines around the mouth, determined. Now her face was the same as in the photograph, more childlike, puppyish, the lines were lost in a radiant skin; her cheeks were fuller, the bones not so much of a striking outcrop. The lips were the same, wide and fleshy, her top lip larger than her bottom lip. Her mouth never sulked. Her mouth was generous, its sensuousness lay in the lascivious breadth of her smile, not in any contrived pout. Her mouth suited ice cream.

From this distance her eyes were wide and thin. Mongolian. The mean Mongol, he called her, in darkness. Feline, slit. Close-to her eyes held the warmth of an old peasant woman, kindly but protective. He called her shrewd, but the shrewdness wasn't in her eyes; the shrewdness lay embedded in her generosity.

She could be generous with insults, shrewdly – when the ice cream mouth became smeared with cruelty and her eyes narrowed against any reflection. She was not beautiful in anger. Part of the game, in their arguments, was their certainty that his wounds would be far deeper than the scratches which he left on her. He hated it when she was not beautiful, when her honesty undermined his own.

She lay face down on the bed. She gathered her hair and directed it off her back, to one side.

"Okay."

He ran the pads of his fingers across her skin, shoulders, waist and buttocks; down her thighs and calves.

"Yup," he said, kneeling on the edge of the bed. "A-okay."

She propped her chin on her forearm.

He said suddenly, what was on his mind, "They arrested some guy, for those murders. And the manifestos."

She tensed. He saw it in her jawline and shoulders. He wondered what kind of tone he had put into his voice.

"Huh," she said, and that was the end of it. She went quiet. She didn't want to know.

He stood by the bedside. "Well . . . " he said; throwaway, sinking into silence.

"I'm sure glad that's over." Her voice fluttered with disdain.

"What do you mean?"

"I'm glad that's over. That's all. Having my skin examined. I hate it when you go clinical on me." She stared innocently at the wallpaper over the top of the bed. "Anyhow, I want a strong vodka tonic. If I close my eyes I can see one."

"I'll fix us one." He said.

"Uh-huh. Promises."

"One won't hurt."

"I know. None of my family have ever regretted alcohol. The baby had better get used to it."

"What then?"

She didn't answer.

He said, what he ought to say, "Do you know how beautiful you are!?"

"How beautiful am I?"

"Very."

He stood up, and went to his own drawer. "You don't believe me?"

"Yes, I believe you. I don't know how to take it though."

"Take it as it comes."

"For granted."

She rolled over onto her side and watched him. He wanted to look at her, to describe her to himself, but he was nervous. Her eyes narrowed, her small breasts were leaning into the comforter. She slewed the right leg across her other thigh, in both concealment and disclosure.

He said, "Do you want that drink?"

"No." She sat up; and swung her hair out of her face, her legs across to the edge of the bed. She walked to her drawer. "I want to go out to dinner."

"Sure. Where?"

"Not downtown."

"No."

"You heard?" She pulled up a pair of black underwear.

"Yes. Alice was worried. I got her a cab."

"Oh, you did? You know, you're very considerate."

He didn't know how to take this.

She said, "Fix yourself a drink, honey, and go sit on the patio. Let me get dressed."

He pulled on pants and a shirt, took a beer from the refrigerator and went out through the kitchen doors. He leaned on the deck rail, and thought about her.

He wasn't sorry that Laurie had quit looking for a job. She wasn't a big spender, and if she wanted to spend money there was a sizeable trust from her father, and his own income. He didn't spend money either. They kept themselves out of town. They were out-of-towners, temporarily misplaced porch people. And not worried about it. They were intact, and some of the Seventeen Seventeen plan was to keep it that way.

He tilted the bottle and swallowed a half-mouthful of beer.

Down below, in the grey yellow sunset, he watched fires; small pinpoints which he could trace back from the inky pillars of smoke, like bonfires burning cleared brushwood, except that it wouldn't be brushwood. It would be trashcans, or dumpsters, maybe a car or two; urban clearance.

No, he didn't care whether Laurie worked. He cared that she might care that she didn't work. But it wasn't a problem for her now, and wouldn't be, with the pregnancy. Afterwards, who knows? They might not even stay in Los Angeles. Laurie had been raised in rural suburbs; Paul imagined nothing but that she would want the same for her own child. Or children. They would move out, rather than in. Neither of them was tied to the city. Only work tied him.

But then maybe skin cancer would become so widespread that he wouldn't have to make a daily pilgrimage to any metropolis. There would be plenty of work in Colorado, Wyoming, anywhere. While the less susceptible Hispanic races would inherit California, the wealthier Anglos were already moving northeast. In a few years he might upgrade his clientele merely by moving back to where he had started, although he would have to keep a check on real estate prices; they didn't want to take a beating on the property market. There would be a right time to sell and get out, before the east stopped rushing west and the west started rushing inland.

The sky was soaking up night.

Some days he was seized by an undiluted panic at millennial chaos. Fear took him, and the fear didn't break down into pieces so that he could get it into proportion. Fear and then sadness at his own weakness and vulnerability.

It was getting dark now. The fires got lost among the fermented light from street-lamps. Noise of sirens clattered tinnily out of the bowl of droning traffic.

The first of the security company's patrols came slowly up

Jerome. It reached 1717 and stopped in the driveway, headlights playing on the front of the house. A pattern of light fell through the glass over the front door, onto the sealed redwood floorboards. The Jeep turned, and reversed. Its lights picked through the shrubs out front, and then it pulled away slow downhill.

The baby's room would need thick drapes, maybe shutters.

He heard the sound of her shoes on the deck, and he turned to look at her.

"Is this skirt all right?"

"Yes," he said, "it looks good."

"I thought about the grey silk?"

"No, you look good."

They went away from the city to eat. They had no reservation. They ate in a restaurant styled like a Spanish cantina, which was, peculiarly, occupied mostly by English immigrants. Mostly technicians from the movie companies. Laurie was surprised to learn, as Paul had been, that there were a dozen cricket leagues in the Los Angeles County area. Leagues, not teams. Paul wondered what the rules were.

Laurie allowed herself a glass of red wine. When they got home she said that she wanted to cook for Saturday.

As they were getting ready for bed, she said, "Do you still like my breasts? They haven't changed shape at all, not yet. Do you think so? Do you think they're heavier?"

Later she said, "Come inside me, sure you can, it's not going to hurt the baby. I want you to come, don't come just yet. Look at me. Touch me. Look at me! All right, all right; it's all right. It doesn't matter."

He reached away and turned off the light.

Laurie had had friends in Colorado, and girlfriends from her childhood back east. They called each other at least once a month and exchanged news. Paul had met them and Laurie lunched with them when she went home. They had come out, separately, to vacation in LA, leaving children behind, staying in the house, staying up late and talking. (In need of a pool, okay, it stuck out a mile.)

Friends from Colorado had come, initially, with reluctance, more out of duty. Porch folk stranded high and dry without a porch.

When he and Laurie had arrived in Los Angeles, she had more contacts than he did. Old friends, old boyfriends from college. She was interested in seeing them. None of them had anything to do with law. Laurie had gone through a cautious process of calling them, talking on the phone for hours: whatever happened to . . . ? . . . is he still alive? . . . and she married . . . ?

All that good stuff.

In due course they came to the house, and got fed, stayed late, and talked. Laurie talked; she worked hard as a hostess, being house-proud, being husband-proud; being generous, let alone being well-dressed; as beautifully dressed as the house.

So these guys had come and eaten dinner and the rest, with or without partners. Laurie made no point of fussing about that. A couple of days later they'd get a call to go somewhere or to do something together, and Laurie would turn it down flat. Sometimes she wouldn't bother to call back. There might be a reciprocating dinner invitation. Laurie wasn't interested. She didn't get around to calling back. So Paul did that, not knowing whether he had hesitated enough, or whether to open another offer, or what. Laurie never wanted to know.

Early on, she had once asked over someone from her firm, and when they didn't show (flu bug) she never asked anyone from any law firm ever again.

Apart from the embarrassment of making the excuses over the phone, Paul didn't care much about it. At that time there was enough entertainment in colonising the house.

So they met people at the Country Club, up the canyon.

Maybe they sat around after tennis. Maybe they snacked weekend lunch together with some people. Maybe they barbecued on the patio with some people they met, after these people had looked round the house. And they all drank wine together, outside, and looked out over Los Angeles. Once every two months. A couple of times with the same people.

The Deanes had got invited twice. During the Christmas holiday, annually.

He couldn't understand whether Laurie wanted friends or not. She teased him about his acquaintances, and in her own head she drew lines between friends and acquaintances which he couldn't understand. What did acquaintances have to do in order to become friends? What line did they have to cross? How far did they have to travel?

They had no friends. This was what she said. He didn't know whether he should encourage her. Maybe they ought to have friends. Maybe it didn't matter. It could be that they didn't have any energy for friends. It could be that they didn't fit into LA, or it could be that they had showed that they didn't care to fit into LA. It could be the damned house; that they didn't fit into the house, or that the house didn't fit anywhere.

At first he had been grateful. He hadn't wanted an exhausting social life, he had wanted to come to terms with the house.

But then he worried. A lot of his business might have come from being sociable, or might have gotten lost through unsociability. The dinner party circle – with a beautiful wife and new-in-town charm – that was the best way of picking up clients. He wondered why Laurie refused to react. Isolation did neither of them any favors. He was baffled by her.

Uneasily, with a feeling of betrayal, he sounded out Abe's opinion. Abe's opinion was that what you lost by not having a socialite wife you would gain by contacts through your children's school. He shouldn't worry.

He was less self-sufficient than Laurie was. That was the

problem. Or maybe he didn't have any friends and conveniently identified the fault as being with her.

Was she difficult?

She made people nervous. She made *him* nervous. You knew that when people came round it wasn't going to be careless. It would either be a triumph of her will, or it would be clear that she wasn't having a good time.

So, it was difficult.

For maybe two or three months he had hinted and then suggested that Bill and Helen come over for dinner, without any response. Then finally he had figured out a date and had more or less invited Laurie to come to a dinner which he would cook and arrange.

He would have felt happier with it this way.

She wanted to be involved? – Well, okay, that was natural: fine.

Paul wasn't so great a cook. But the main thing about it was to be invited round, to get together, have a few drinks and meet with people.

Well it wasn't that easy. Laurie was sure that Bill and Helen wouldn't want just to sit over an untimed steak. She would rather do something . . . she'd think about what.

You don't have to.

No no I want to.

You know I was going to . . .

I really don't mind.

So would Laurie triumph? And how much resentment would Bill and Helen feel? Would this be their only visit, and at what point in the next evening would this become clear to all of them?

FIVE

Saturday: 8a.m. to 12.45p.m.

Saturday, a perfect morning. A fine day, as should be.

An initial switching off of the programmed security system, announced by an intermittent beep.

For Paul: the sour smell of love arising from the bed. There was nothing like the high pungency of this smell; a smell of usury and of friction and of abandon, a fetid and spent purity to greet the bright new day.

Laurie asleep: sluggish and jowled. Sweat risen on her chest and mostly in the hollow of her neck.

He was heavy-headed, considering that he hadn't hardly drunk anything last night. He left her asleep.

And it was pleasant in the kitchen, silent for him, lying stretched, his eyes leaning back into his skull with tiredness, along the couch in the kitchen. Waiting for the coffee machine to start choking. And when it did so; lying, listening to the coffee machine with his hand inside his bathrobe holding the swollen stem of his penis, and there being the first narrow scree of sunlight coming through the windows onto the western wall of the room. Which was clean. No dust on the sealed wooden floor. White kitchen chairs with cushions. A blue gingham cloth on the table.

He withdrew his hand and smelt the high rotted love like a taste. It was like the dampened cinders from a dead forest fire. Momentarily – now superseded by the smell of coffee.

Good strong coffee.

He opened the sliding doors and went out onto the deck. He still smelt coffee, what with the steam rising from his cup even in an early morning heat. He put down the coffee cup on the deckrail. He smelt cinders, still, like Old Hickory barbecue sauce; and there were plateaus of smoke, like fungi on the bark of the cityscape, rising into the LA sky.

He showered in the guest bathroom, so as not to wake up Laurie, then he went back into their bedroom and pulled on jeans and a polo shirt; he found his old pair of loafers in the garage. These were his chore shoes, Saturday. With his heels slapping in and out of the rim – the leather was as stiff as jerky and bleached from California beaches and Saturdays, and Colorado softball mounds and Saturdays – he took out the garbage from under the sinks and beside the toilet bowls and loaded it into the bin in the alcove at the side of the house.

The same with the piles of weeds from the small terraced garden below the deck, which the construction company had carved out of rock and covered with bark-and-seaweed-based humus. Laurie grew flowers and shrubs. Some vegetables. She liked to shape and trim and prune. Fridays a woman came to clean house, but Laurie didn't want to employ a gardener. She liked to work with her hands.

She didn't much care for clearing away. She expected him to do that. She took it for granted that he would do that. It was the way things were. She wasn't lazy about it. She thought that he should do it. There was an element of righteousness in the chore, which would be best suited to him. It was one of the lines which she drew.

He some of the time understood, although the principle was a little woozy.

Okay, this part he couldn't figure: on a Thursday, afternoon maybe evening, the toilet bowls had to be cleaned. Before the cleaner came Fridays.

So maybe, *maybe*, you could understand this. Maybe Southern Californian housecleaners had their limits. Paul didn't think so, but it wasn't worth any dispute, there were more provoking arguments on a Friday night. Cleaning a toilet bowl was no big deal. He had agreed to do it. He did it. He did it Thursday nights, after his shower, before dinner.

One week he forgot to do it. Laurie didn't say anything, so Paul had assumed that the cleaner was picking up the slack. For two months he hadn't bothered with this chore, until, one Friday morning, he had yawned into the bathroom and found Laurie, six weeks pregnant, up early after being sick, cleaning the toilet bowl.

Jesus, he hadn't known about this. This wasn't how he had thought. He wasn't even sharing the chore, he'd kind of presumed . . . he'd . . . well . . .

Laurie didn't give a damn about cleaning the toilet bowls. She might prefer drinking coffee and reading legal opinions, but she didn't mind doing the toilet bowls.

Should he do them?

If he wanted to. If not, she didn't care less about doing them. They had to be done, right? So she'd do them.

Nevertheless she wouldn't – ever – take a garbage bag outside or clear garden mess.

He did that. That part of the world was his. On principle. On Saturday, and usually on Tuesday or Wednesday. Definitely early Saturday, sometimes while she was drinking coffee and reading the paper, sometimes, as now, while she was sleeping.

Then he would awaken her with coffee, as he did now.

"Hon?"

"Hmm?"

He put the cup down on the bedside table.

"It's nine-fifteen."

"It can't be."

"It is."

He sat on the side of the bed, when she had struggled up to lean against the backboard with the comforter tucked under her arms.

"Okay," she said, "okay, I'm conscious." She pushed the sides of her hair back behind her ears. "Are you going?"

"Soon. Does that fit with you?"

"Sure. Can you pick up those few things?"

"I have the list."

She yawned. "That should do it."

"You'll be okay?" He stood up.

"I'll be fine. You'll be back – "

"Around three."

She nodded. He took a change of clothes out of his closet.

"There's nothing else you want me to do?"

"No."

"Okay." He bent to kiss her. "Love you."

"You too."

"See you around three. I'll call."

This was Paul's Saturday. He took *his* car, the Mercedes which Laurie used during the week, and he drove to the Tennis Club. This was Paul's perfect Saturday.

With Laurie's pregnancy, his attitude towards this day had undergone a change. He no longer suffered anything much of a hangover since they didn't drink so wildly. So he was no longer stricken with fury at Laurie's apparently willful trashing of the Mercedes during the week.

Some weekends he had heaped every piece of paper and article of clothing and pen and hairband and cosmetic, every piece of discarded junk mail and flier, into a grocery bag and had hurled it into the kitchen before leaving the house. He didn't understand her deliberate untidiness, her contempt for his car. He still didn't understand it, but since the pregnancy he allowed it. Saturdays now he collected together the main trash and piled it in the back seat, and called at the car wash, and went to the club.

At the club he drank a fruit juice, while looking out at the lappers in the mostly empty pool.

The Men's locker-room had four rows of lockers. Paul had recently been upgraded to a wall-space locker, 153 out of 200, which gave him more room to transfer clothes and shoes from his sports bag. At eleven o'clock the locker-room would start to fill; Paul got there by nine forty-five now that he had given up purging the Mercedes of Laurie's spite.

He had time to drink an orange juice, to look out at the pool.

There were two lines of four basins in the locker-room, each basin with a stand of shave-cream, deodorant, soap and after-shave. Also a jug of hair combs in sterilising fluid. The green carpet was changed annually, the off-white walls and ceilings were painted triennially. The carpet was vacuumed daily at eight-thirty and four-thirty, and there were never less than a dozen freshly laundered white towels on each of the four tables at the ends of the lines of basins. The soiled-towel hamper was removed every hour on the hour.

There was an unspoken rule that no-one should ever produce a serious, critical comment in the locker-room. There was no rule about discussing business, but it was generally held to be permissible only within the four square yards which separated the inner swing-doors from the first pile of towels. Even then, such a discussion was restricted to hearsay. Such hearsay might be tinged with bearish or bullish speculation, but any mention of figures was deemed to be morally on a par with passing wind or displaying any vulgar superfluity of either jewelry or emotion.

On the other hand, apparently careless and jovial remarks – such as "We've got a little trouble with Such-and-Such County Board" or "You might like to talk it through with So-and-So" – such cheerful chatter suitably decorated the environs of the soiled-towel hamper.

There was never any need to read anybody's lips in the locker-room. "The place sucks," said Abe, many months ago, scribbling his signature to Paul's application form. "I love it."

Paul's love was already fully subscribed to Laurie, but the locker-room got his full appreciation; as a haven.

People had gotten to know him by sight. People said, How's things? Their families went to Abe when they needed to, and they would transfer to Paul when Abe retired. Paul was respectful and easy to get along with, talking Colorado and his family, real estate and Laurie and now the new family which they were starting. Abe had waited for six months before introducing him; Paul gathered that he had managed to fit in. He might have been a little less serious. But he had done well to treat the movie crowd cautiously, thereby picking up as clients several lower execs who proved to be less temporary than the creatives.

The movie business bored him shitless. Movie people were licensed to bring business out of the four square yards, and they sprayed it over every inch of the locker-room carpet and sent it flying up to the ceiling. Then the inner doors swung shut behind them and their attitude floated up against the skylights, and the atmosphere in the locker-room was again benignly humdrum.

Creatives never came in Saturday mornings. Pitching deals constituted a no-no on Saturday mornings. Saturday mornings were the lappers: thirty, forty, fifty laps of the pool for middle-aged men and women who relied on a regular pumping of the heart more than on the vagaries of adrenalin. Saturday mornings were lawyers, brokers, managers, and older ladies who bobbed through their exercise classes in the shallow end of the pool without endangering their perms.

Saturday mornings were not many doctors, strangely. Doctors did Saturday mornings at home with their children. Paul would start to do this, soon. This was the way of things. Doctors' wives came to lap and bob or to play tennis and eat lunch, and do whatever there was to do in the Women's locker-room.

He had no concept of the entity of the lives of female doctors, none whatsoever. Both he and Laurie used a woman general practitioner. She was friendly but Paul had never seen her socially. She had two young children. She was often on call Saturdays. One Saturday, when Laurie had woken with a fever and a rash, he had called her, and she had driven to meet them at her surgery. So that was maybe how female doctors with a family arranged their lives. Part of the attraction of the Men's locker-room was that nobody ever thought about things like that out loud, if at all. There were no women in the locker-room. By mutual consent, women merited a one-sentence enquiry.

In the future, Paul would almost certainly spend Saturday mornings playing with his baby. On the rug in the bedroom. Or maybe there would be a new area in the kitchen, like a play area, Saturday mornings.

He gazed at the pool. The remaining orange juice was now tepid in a plastic cup. He had no thirst. He turned and dropped the cup into a waste bin, and went to the locker-room.

Ten in the morning. It was only when he put his newspaper down that he saw the headline. "MANIFESTO ARREST". There was a small column, at the bottom right of a front page which otherwise dealt, scrappily and hastily, with the disturbance downtown. Jerome got the early edition at weekends.

He went back across the locker-room and took two towels, making a couple of greetings and an enquiry which needed no detailed response, not to a disrobing skin doctor. He locked the newspaper away. He wrapped the one towel round his waist and hung the other up outside the empty steam-room.

Someone had used the steam-room earlier, but the steam had cooled and condensed. He reset the timer.

He went outside and filled a paper cup from the Alhambra stand, and tipped the water into the small pipe which enclosed the thermostat. The steam-room was fine for squeaky clean tiles and smooth oak bunk benches, but the thermostat never allowed enough steam. The room was moist, barely warm, hygienically dank. He pulled shut the door. The metal balljoint clattered.

He climbed the bottom bench and sat in the far corner of the room, up high; his towel was already laid out. Water in a pipe somewhere behind the tiles gurgled. The steam tap spat and dribbled. He removed the towel from around his waist and draped it back over his shoulders, so he could lean against the colder tiles. The steam tap hissed into life. He adjusted his scrotum, for comfort, and sat back.

Across the white tiled floor the steam gushed, at first a shy and neutral gas, then rising with aggression, inquisitive, clinging to the walls. His body was hot, and dry.

The steam gushed persistently. Small pricks of heat sprung from his arms and thighs. His scalp itched.

The steam welled up around him. The room darkened into grey and he was hidden in his solitary purging.

Within a minute he came out. He saw that there were still people in the locker-room; and he showered, and he returned to scald himself lightly and to sit in the sheens of dribbled oily sweat. Nothing and nobody came to disturb him. He considered Laurie, some of whose oils must be slipping off his groin, some of whose love slipped off his shoulders.

Three times Paul poured cold water down into the thermostat and emerged each time to rest for a few moments in the locker-room, until someone came in. While the steam resurged behind the glass door. He sat with a towel around him, and a towel over his head, like a boxer, as the moisture dripped onto his copy of the *Times*.

MANIFESTO ARREST

The District Attorney's office yesterday
evening charged John Paul Stanton (42)
on suspicion of multiple homicide.

Assistant DA Elisabeth Weissman
identified Stanton and said that the
arrest related to some of the homicides
"which the press and national media
have arbitrarily grouped under the
heading Manifesto Murders".
Ms. Weissman, 34, refused to answer
any further questions. (C2)

Ten forty-five. No-one else in the locker-room and no noise from the hallway. Why not? The front page of the *Times* subheaded "Incidents", but they were at South and South Central, miles away.

Paul followed Stanton. He turned to Section C, Page 2. Water dripped from his hair and darkened the page, he watched the blot spread into a stain.

MALE CHARGED ON MANIFESTO MURDERS
Staff Reporters Jeff Grogan and Ernesto Silvero
Los Angeles, Friday. (A1)
The DA's office will today charge John Paul Stanton with fourteen counts of homicide. Sources close to the arrest would not comment on possible links between Stanton and the Manifesto Murders, saying only that "there is an ongoing investigation developing". Mayoral spokesperson Rashid Dominguez issued a statement saying that "there are no clear reasons whatsoever for linking a man suspected of multiple homicides to any data which has been grouped by the media under a single headline."
Stanton (42) will be charged in connection with the deaths of:

William J. Baxter Jnr, President, Wells Fargo Bank, November 1993.

S.P. Turner, Fred Weisz, S.Yoro, Ms. Adrienne Piesset in the executive jet bombing, February 1994.
Professor Hugh Demello, Chair of Quantum Physics, UCLA, March 1994.
Joseph Mill, Exxon Corp., May 1994.
Mr and Mrs Sam Kiesco, May last. (Bashka Kiesco chaired the State EPA Board.)
Gretch Bonner, Berger-Usello law firm, September last.
Dr. Luke Rabik, Head of Research, Swan Cosmetics, September last.
Timothy A. Hubris, VP Hung Software, February last.
Dr. Suro Ky, Grace Laboratories, February last.
James Liebermann, Realtor, March 15.

Liebermann. That was the name. It was madness that he had made any connection. One night.

He didn't want to think about it. Nothing had happened. He had been scared. He had been crazy and unhappy, about Laurie, about everything; without Laurie. One March night.

He read quickly:

Assistant DA Elisabeth Weissman affirmed last night that the police were not able to establish any connection between the deceased.
FBI spokesperson Maria Hearney refused to comment on reports that the FBI had further information on double killings in July and December last, and unsolved homicides in November 1993 and March 1994.
(LEISURE: MANIFESTO L42)

Still no-one else.

Paul spread out the Leisure Section across the padded bench.

How scared he had been. He must have been crazy, completely out of his mind.

None of it mattered, not now. None of it would ever matter. It mustn't matter. He had been scared about everything. Everything had built up, and that was why it had happened. But it didn't mean anything. He felt relieved; but not intensely so, he didn't want to feel that way.

(L42 MANIFESTO)
Staff Writer Ernesto Silvero
The "Manifesto Murders" have been so-called from the political tracts which were sent to this newspaper in the days immediately postdating a number of otherwise unconnected homicides . . . unsigned, and no recognised political groups claimed responsibility . . . demands stated by the author or authors were not financially based . . . assertion was for "a vital morality of violence" as a means or a tactic for "exposing and righting the moral imbalance sanctified by a corrupt techno-industrial society" . . . exhibited a compact rationality of argument but spiralled into an incoherent . . . scientists and top level business executives constitute the main part of the death toll. But doctors and environmental protection representatives have also been targeted. This is in line with the manifestos' bitter rejection of both establishment apologists and left of centre protest movements . . . a contempt for political activists, . . . and both gays and gay-haters. The "we" of the authorship has never been able to fix on a defined "them". There appears now to have been just a killer and his victims.

In the manifestos, a rough path was forced through the philosophical notion of dualism – the admission of both good and evil being inherent . . . a defiance of the binary code which underpins techno-computerised thinking. Symbolically, the manifestos were submitted after dual killings . . . the murders of Mr and Mrs Sam Kiesco, Mrs Kiesco being much respected for her work with the Environmental

Protection Agency, Sam Kiesco being retired from the board of South Western Oil Explorations.

The author interpretes the status quo in terms of black and white, such a fixation proving advantageous to the manifestos' incitement to pass judgement on, and sentence, victims who would otherwise seem to have been chosen at random.

Whether or not these manifestos are applicable to the man who stands charged with the murders, it is impossible not to condemn the demonic mayhem which pretends to both expose and expurgate such a contrived Nature.

What? What did this mean!

This was on the "IDEAS" page.

What was "contrived Nature"? Wasn't everything contrived? And how could it be expurgated?

Only in the Leisure Section. The facing page was given over to Irish and Ethiopian cuisines, under the headline "Out Of The Closet, Into the Oven".

The locker-room doors swung open.

Paul took the towel off his head, and re-assembled the newspaper. He went back into the steam-room. Apart from losing his driver's license, the whole nightmare was over. He surrendered to the feel of the hot moist vapor, letting it surge down into his lungs, sweating the toxins out and away.

At noon Paul unlocked the door to the office and let himself into his room. Inadmissably happy, he re-classified some minor data under new file headings.

This was Paul's perfect Saturday, back to normal. A little work pleased him, it shaved the indulgence off leisure. Alice's car remained parked in the lot.

PART TWO

Laurie

SIX

Since adolescence it had surprised Laurie that she had always managed to avoid trouble. Serious trouble, that is. Okay, she was rich and white. Not seriously rich, but comfortable, moneyed. She doubted that her father was seriously rich – according to the laws of astronomical wealth which were currently drawn up by magazines. However, you could say, with some safety, that she had always been in a position to buy herself out of trouble. But she would never have felt happy with buying herself out of trouble. She would have hated it as an easy and insulting way out.

She had never been in trouble.

One reason for this, she surmised, was that she *was* trouble. And therefore, maybe, trouble didn't trouble her: like poles repelling each other. Maybe her own magnetism saw her through; for trouble never had laid a finger on her. Perhaps if it had, she would have been less wary.

Laurie wasn't so blinded by comfort that she believed the world to be a fair and charitable place, nor did she believe that fair and charitable people got on well in the world. It disgusted her just how many people suffered misfortune or unfairness.

Unfairness might occasionally have happened to her, but misfortune, or trouble, had warily passed her by. This caused her to be uneasy, at times guilty, and very occasionally bitter. She couldn't figure out why she was bitter or where the bitterness came from. You could say that sometimes she resented the fact that nobody had any good reason to feel sympathetic towards her.

Never being in trouble was a mixed blessing: nobody ever felt sympathetic towards you. People were reduced to seeing her as strong, willful, and determined. Essentially chilly, with warm and oddly exhausting bursts of heart.

Maybe the reason she had never got into trouble was that people were scared of her. As a child she was precocious. Quite innocently she could cut people down to size. Conversely, her older sister retreated into being a demanding slob, who got what she wanted by having her feelings constantly hurt.

Laurie didn't like being strong. At quite an early age she was convinced that she was evil. This was ridiculous, when she looked at it now, but she still wasn't convinced that she wasn't evil.

Sanely, she refused to feel guilty about herself. She chose sometimes to dislike herself, and withdrew. She analyzed herself, she thought about herself, she was occasionally repulsed by herself. But the problem was that her withdrawal was only into severity. She would stay, wrapped up in severity – quite solitary, no-one knew about it or shared it – until that severity became a source of pride, and then she would throw herself vengefully out into the world.

The severity was more self-contained when she was a child. As a child she had never wanted for anything; but her mother was a busy socialite, her father a sociable businessman, and her sister was always indifferent unless Laurie attacked her with venom.

She was not a neglected child. She would never claim to have been a neglected child. If there was anything wrong with her family – and there certainly wasn't, according to Laurie's loyalties – it was that she wanted more, not that they gave less. The self-absorption was her problem. She hid it. Her pride wouldn't let her show it. Her pride would push her out to battle with her sister.

And once puberty hit – early – her pride pushed her out towards men. At the age of fourteen she started sleeping around.

She fell in love with their eyes, especially sad eyes into which she would charge, wanting to bring happiness.

She caused jealousy, suspicion and turmoil. She would not be refused and she would not be possessed. She hated caution. She, suddenly unreserved, hated the reserve in men, how they held themselves back emotionally, their fears and their pettiness immune to her.

Most men – men who had gotten themselves involved with her – simply saw her as attractive, passionate, teasing; and cruel. Both her female confidantes, to whom she had resorted after male lovers had gone sour, had said that she had problems; which courteously avoided using the same passionate-teasing-cruel rationale. (If there was one single reason why Laurie refused to dabble in lesbianism, it was because she hated all the womanly respect. It seemed that no one woman should ever hold another woman in contempt. Laurie was contemptuous of most people, including herself.)

She had too much intuition, and she risked using it. She really ought to have hit trouble, especially in her late teens and early twenties, provoking men, never leaving them alone, loving men until she realised that she could do no more for them: doe-eyed boys, bewildered husbands, miserable debauchees, room-mates who thought they got along well until she came between them.

She frightened lovers. She served them well, loving their blind surrender to ecstasy. She learned the different sexual likes and tastes which men had and which she could give to them. What they did to her often bored her; she liked to control herself. They complained that she wanted it all her own way, but this wasn't true. She liked the falling in love, she liked to discover men and reveal them to themselves, which they didn't want. They never quite trusted her, they simply wanted to surrender occasionally, or otherwise to bargain themselves away from difficulty, to take the easy way out.

Several times men had hit her, out of exasperation. She knew well enough to quit. Maybe her intuition had kept her out of more serious trouble. She never relaxed in a relationship, she was always alert.

Until her late teens she had never been sexually faithful to one man for very long. Then came two relationships in which she wasn't the first to be unfaithful. One of them had broken her heart, she had never thought that the man could be so stupid; viciously stupid.

She had found herself pregnant by him, which was no part of his – or her – plan. He wouldn't believe this. He thought that it was deliberate, and she wondered if he had ever trusted her. He accused her of using the pregnancy as emotional blackmail; and it was left to him to mount an aggressive defense which was so childish and obstinate and hysterical that she wondered what on earth she was doing with someone who so desperately needed to reassure himself that she was such a bitch.

She had dithered, perversely, for three weeks, with the idea of not having an abortion. She considered keeping the baby, who was – as chaos raged – the most straightforward and innocent part of a huge mistake. She became comfortable with the idea of being pregnant. She became determined to keep the child.

And then she had miscarried. One night, after yet another bout of raging recrimination, on the toilet. She gave birth to an indeterminate mass of blood and tissue.

She didn't wait to see her partner's reaction. She didn't bother to tell him. She padded herself up well, left him a note, and drove to the hospital where she checked herself in for the D and C.

She had taken a vacation with her parents, in a house which they rented in Cape Cod. When she told her mother what had happened, her mother said only that the baby 'wasn't meant to be'; just as her mother might have said about her relationship, of which she had always superciliously disapproved. She never told her father. She didn't know whether he knew or not, but he walked with her every day, for miles along the beach, and wouldn't let her sink into sadness. Her father didn't like defeat. She was his favorite.

The next time she was betrayed, it didn't disturb her heart. This second long-term lover had always been a sneaky creep, forever proclaiming to be in love with her. Charitably and indifferently she had been faithful. He had got her to agree to this, and she couldn't be bothered to disagree. They had both agreed. She suspected that he would sneak off. Sure enough, he did; and was too cowardly to tell her what she already knew. She seduced his best friend in their bed, and broke his pride. He was stupid too, he didn't understand or try to understand. He fled into self-pity.

His best friend had threatened to kill her, she remembered. She was a bitch. She had laughed, because it was absurd, and funny. Just holding the gun he was so ridiculous.

When she had walked out of the apartment her hands were cold and sweaty. She had gone to a bar and gotten drunk and slept with someone else. For days everything had seemed ridiculous. Then she went back to her parents' house and was ridiculously miserable.

She went to law school in Colorado. She had decided, some time before, that if she ever found someone with whom she wanted to have a child, then that baby would be meant to be. It would be discussed and it would be deliberate, and she would make certain of it.

Saturday: 9a.m. to 12.45p.m.

Laurie waited until Paul had gone. She heard the garage doors come down; the Mercedes made no sound. Paul always coasted it downhill, part saving gas, part playing a game of seeing how far he could get without engaging the engine. He only ever played this game in the Mercedes, never in her car. He said that the Mercedes cornered better. Laurie's four-wheel Isuzu was so top-heavy that nobody in their right mind would attempt to freewheel corners.

It was just a dumb thing to do anyway. Paul always needed some game or other.

She didn't begrudge him that.

After the first ten weeks of this pregnancy, Laurie had never felt nauseous in the mornings. But she didn't like coffee any more. Since she had known that she was pregnant, she liked tea: Earl Grey tea, fresh and not very strong, not left to settle in a teapot. (The second serving out of the teapot was stronger and more bitter, and made her feel queasy.)

Paul had paid attention at the begining. He hadn't known anything about tea, but he had made it, before leaving the house, for her.

One Saturday it had been too stewed. She hadn't touched it. She was crabby. When he asked her what was wrong, she had said that the tea was disgusting. He had gotten hurt feelings.

So he went back to bringing her coffee, and he didn't care whether she drank it, or not, or what she did with it. And she couldn't be bothered to say anything about it because it really didn't matter and wasn't important. The smell of coffee still made her wake up, and she was quite happy to go out to the kitchen when he had gone, and then to make tea for herself the way she liked it. He knew this, she supposed, because he always called her when he reached the office, and that was always when she had her half-empty cup in front of her and was enjoying the start of the day.

Saturdays he never called until midday, when he told her who he was having lunch with, or, if she made encouraging noises, who *they* might both lunch with.

Today she might have felt like playing tennis, or doing something. Which was a nuisance, because she couldn't anyway, what with preparing for the dinner party tonight. And being five months gone.

She smelled of sex. And was aroused with remembrance, of him. Last night's sex had irritated her. He had used her. He hadn't taken advantage of her invitation. She liked him to use her, but not for himself, coldly. What was wrong with her invitation? That dumb Manifesto thing. Again! Pushing her aside. Shit, the signals he gave out were so contradictory, what was she supposed to think or do? Be real!

She thought about turning over and getting a hold of his pillow and going back to sleep. Instead, because of the smell of the coffee, she left the bed and put on her robe and brushed her hair back, out of the way. Then she went into the kitchen to make tea.

When the water boiled, she put tea in the warmed pot and poured the water over it.

Paul had left open the sliding doors to the patio. She wished he wouldn't do that.

She might have gone back to sleep in the bedroom and the doors would have stayed open. Anyone could have walked in. Any murderer. Any rapist. Any homeless bum. Anyone could have walked in. They could be there in the house right now, having watched Paul leave. Paul could be such a fucking idiot. So irresponsible. They weren't back home now.

She thought of calling him on the car phone, she turned to go to the phone hanging by the cupboard. She wanted to just yell at him and scare the shit out of him. And serve him right.

But was there anyone in the house? Of course there wasn't. She would have known immediately. She would have known. She would have felt the intrusion.

And then, Laurie, you would get the gun, and you would creep round the house with your back against every wall. Alone, like a crazy. For maybe a half hour. Scaring yourself shitless.

God, and she thought Paul was the only one who liked games?!

Nevertheless, she stood by the teapot and imagined how long

it would take, and with how many paces, running, for her to get to the drawer by the side of the bed, for the gun.

About long enough for the tea to brew.

She poured it into her cup. And watched, and smelt, the scented steam rise.

The perfume was always unfamiliar. Coffee was always familiar. It's okay.

She persevered. So, Laurie, you stand alone in the kitchen. The sliding doors are open to the patio. You don't know whether the intruder is inside the house, or outside the house. Do you lock the doors? Do you lock yourself and maybe him inside the house? Or do you run outside where he is maybe waiting?

Which would be more scary?

As a death, inside would be scarier. She imagined it. The intruder would have all the time in the world to stalk her. From room to room. He would have as long as he pleased to watch her and her fear. The mental torture would be his pleasure. He could watch her. And do anything he wanted.

There would even be Paul's photograph, of him ready to go hiking in Colorado, on top of the dresser, for her to try to watch, in the terror and the filth of someone else crossing their bed in order to kill her or to cut her with a knife or to rape her.

She shuddered. It would be better to get it over with quickly.

So, Laurie; start over. Running outside. And the shock. The shock of someone else. The sudden certainty of not being able to get back into the house ever again. That heart-stopping moment when the real is nightmare and vice-versa.

And then a sudden death without being able to leave any kind of a message or protest, or any chance of being able to talk, or plead, or argue. Shock! And quick regret, and death. Her own death.

She would have no time to say anything to the baby. No single word of apology or comfort. Not one moment or confession or word of love, nor any consolation. No soothing. No privacy between her and the baby. No white lies, or promises, or soothing farewells.

That would be worse. That would be losing the baby. For ever. Worse than any physical pain that anyone could inflict on her. She would lose her baby for ever, eternally.

My God. Stay with me, stay with us.

When she attempted the formality of a prayer she saw how ridiculous she was being. The sliding glass doors were still open. Anyone could still have come in while she was off on this morbid paranoia.

Laurie, you should have picked up the phone and yelled at Paul. Close the door on all this fear. You are *so* stupid.

She scribbled a reminder on the notepad. She picked up her teacup and walked cautiously through the doors out onto the deck. Putting her teacup down on the glass-topped table, she took a chaise and pulled it across the patio, past the rail, to where the pool would be, sheltered by this shoulder-high wooden fence. She arranged the chaise and got her tea, and got a book, and sunscreen; and she sat with her back to the city, facing the locked gate through which she could see the garbage bins and her father's land and the hillside beyond.

She didn't open the book, nor did she apply the sunscreen. Laurie finished her tea, locked the doors, and went back to the bedroom. She flushed the coffee down the toilet bowl and then showered to get rid of her smell. When she opened the doors again, with her hair tied back severely to encourage its shape for that evening, she still noticed the smell, a smell of sex, retained. Some sunscreen initially concealed the smell from her but she noticed it at odd moments, and felt insecure, as though she was, in spite of herself, like a bitch inviting trouble.

She hated cooking.

At eleven o'clock she closed her book. She felt uneasy. She showered again and soaped off the sunscreen, soaping herself thoroughly. She dried, and looked at herself in the closet mirror, the front of her body and then from the side. Her body was changing. Her breasts weren't much larger. Lower down there was no spare flesh but her belly had begun to protrude. It might be like being occupied by an alien. Was that why Paul didn't like her body? But he did, didn't he? She just couldn't get him to say anything. It still felt like her body, young. She was filling. She was meant to be this way. Why shouldn't Paul desire this?

The thought of having a child didn't scare her. It wouldn't be an alien. The thought of having a boy unnerved her slightly. She didn't know what boys were like, or what they did. Individual boys she knew about, but she didn't know about boys in general, the guys together, what they were like. She had never cared for ('the guys'). Whenever she had gone out with someone, she had always made sure that he got rid of "the guys", the crowd. If her lovers were infatuated with her, it wasn't her fault. She had wanted no "ball-buster" humor, no "pussy-whipped" talk.

She didn't know if she could cope with having a boy. And if the child was a girl – what would she say to her? What *could* she say to her? "Be lucky"? "Stay out of trouble"? "Get married and be happy or unhappy"? "Say no"?

Say no. All the time say no. Even to yourself?

Laurie knew that she could cope with having a baby. She knew that she would be a good mother to a baby.

Paul would be a good father.

She had used to like cooking. Paul liked cooking when he had the time. She had liked cooking, whether she had time or not. Nowadays she hated cooking and serving up food as though she was dressing it, as though it were sexy.

She avoided these dinner parties and foodies; she didn't like to watch people eat. Now it had gotten so total. Now you served food which was pretty and overdecorated, and all the conversation was about food. It was like being a hooker at a tastebud convention.

Laurie got dressed.

She couldn't delay any longer. She couldn't think anymore.

She went into the kitchen and switched on the TV.

She couldn't still smell, could she? How could she still smell? What had they done last night – nothing, not for her.

They were running a report about the disturbance in South Central. Laurie got the salad onions out of the refrigerator. As she bent down she thought, What *is* this smell?

She put the onions on the chopping board. The smell irritated her so much that she got irritated by the TV, and turned down the sound, and changed channels.

And then she suddenly thought, Oh my God I must have forgotten to turn the gas off and the kettle is burning up, Laurie how can you be so *dumb*!

No, the gas was off, the kettle wasn't hardly warm.

She sniffed, and she walked around the house, sniffing, the odour getting fainter and fainter until she came back to the kitchen. She thought that she would get rid of it by opening the sliding doors. She opened them, and she was relieved that the smell was coming from outside the house. There was no smoke to speak of. Just the smell. And a fire somewhere down in Central.

She called Paul's office and left a message on his answering machine, asking him to add air-freshener to the shopping list.

When she had finished the onions, she filled the sink with water and soaked the salad greens, out of their Safeway bag. The pictures weren't doing much on the TV. Having television meant endlessly fleeing the crappy garbage which it screened. Channel-surfing reduced her to anger and depression. She found a younger James Garner in an older Rockford Files and settled for lying on her back, pretty much like the salad.

Momentarily it crossed her mind that she should send out for dinner. Sushi over cocktails, and then Thai. Too spicy?

But then she might put her energies into making her grandmother's apple tart.

She liked James Garner. He had a kindly face. A lot of irony in the face. Kind of mock-weary like Bob Mitchum. Or William Hurt. She hadn't seen William Hurt in a movie for a long time since. What was he doing? Off being a father?

James Garner got hit in the face.

She resented it, and surfed. She came back on a commercial break, stayed on the channel, killed the volume and got up to wash the salad.

It was too early to wash the salad. It would be limp hours before they arrived.

She would, for sure, send out for sushi; at least.

Paul wouldn't be angry. He knew that she was not into cooking anymore, and he didn't expect her to do it, generally.

Today he expected her to cook.

Everyone knew that she couldn't cook. The Matsons must be dreading the thought of coming over.

She stirred the salad greens round the sink, gently, with her forefinger, and took the finger out and tasted it.

She felt lazy, suddenly heavy and discontented. Tired. She didn't want anyone to come round. Still less did she want to spend the afternoon cooking.

She felt sick, with a nervous anticipation.

Quickly she ran through the possibilities.

If she didn't cook then Paul might be disappointed, but he wouldn't be angry. Because she was pregnant. And because she might sulk, and then the dinner would be a disaster. He deserved better.

If she shrugged off how she felt and pushed herself through the whole thing of cooking, then she would be tired and nervous and irritable. The Matsons would do their best to compliment her, which would make her more irritable. Helen, who apparently used to cook professionally, would talk about how difficult it was. Then she would joke about what a lousy mother she was to her two children, which would annoy Laurie because Laurie didn't care what a good mother should be and knew that she would do it by instinct.

Ever since the pregnancy had been made public, it was all that people wanted to talk about. She didn't want to talk about it. Everything had been said to them; she and Paul hardly ever talked about it.

She loved him.

Laurie, let's face it, you love him. If he doesn't know it, that's his problem. Nothing else matters. You might as well forget everything else.

But with this baby, everyone she met kept wanting to give her confidence. Why? She didn't like it, all this trying-to-be-scary about having a baby. Or else it was like she had gotten a fantastic career break and they were glad and envious and excited, which was neat, but weird.

James Garner had gone. They were screening *Bonanza.*

Not *Bonanza*; no way.

She dialled and ordered a Sushi Mixed, to be delivered at six-thirty. When Paul came home they could decide what to call in for the entrée.

She went to the garage and pulled out two bottles of Moët and put them in the refrigerator. She closed the sliding doors, and left the salad soaking and went and lay down in the bedroom.

SEVEN

She had the best love in her life with, and from, and for Paul. The deepest and most durable love, for her.

He was good-looking, in his way. She didn't like handsome men, whose looks had been reflected back into vanity, or who had become set into handsomeness. She didn't mind handsome men who didn't know that they were handsome, except that after a certain age they would have to be stupid not to know it, or horribly coy in pretending not to know it.

Paul was intelligent. And he was sensitive. She hadn't been sure about the sensitive: there were so many people who were sensitive *to* things, not *for* things, people whose main concern was the state of their own sensitivity. Paul balanced it, except when he wanted to display weakness in front of her. It was one of his games, and one of the games which they would have to drop when the baby came. Paul was strong enough, and she could make him feel stronger and be more confident.

They had had fun playing around, and pleasure, especially for her. He was never afraid to experiment with himself, with her. They had the best love in the world.

He *was* good-looking. None of her friends had thought so. They still thought that he was insignificant, she saw. They had been surprised when she had said that she and Paul were going to be married. Most likely they were surprised that she was going to get married at all, never mind who to. Although, still living in the place where they had come from, her friends would have expected her to settle eventually for some rich and significant guy.

She had asked Paul to marry her.

He had said, Why? What does that have to do with love?

She said, Everything.

He said, Okay. Then let's get married, just as long as the two don't get confused.

Later he had asked, If I had said no, would you have left me?

Probably. Who knows?

It was lucky I said yes.

You might have gotten one more chance.

I don't think so, no. Luck doesn't happen twice in the same place.

After their engagement, she had been bewildered for a time. They were engaged. Their affair hadn't been going on for long enough. She seemed to have lost control. What was luck? She never had thought about having luck, and certainly had never thought about being controlled by it.

It had really been touch-and-go for a while. Their affair stopped. It just ran dry. Sex was clumsy and embarrassing. For a while she had thought that they were getting into some weird brother-and-sister thing. They talked about the most boring subjects. She had felt like crying out in protest.

She did cry, but at herself, by herself; for what, she didn't know. She didn't understand any of it.

But nothing else had appealed to her. She had never had a moment's doubt that she would marry him. She became acutely scared that he wouldn't marry her.

Then her pride and her (old?) character had surfaced. She became bored with herself. She tested him. While they were making love, in a lubricious pause, she told him about how she once had skinned her knees when a man had been making love to her from behind on a floor.

She was shocked by the effect.

Why did you tell me that? he said. And she really didn't know. She knew that she had made a mistake.

Quickly she had said, Because I trust you.

He had sat back. He had grilled her: What for? What do you trust me for? What reaction do you expect me to have, with all this trust? Do you want jealousy? You can have it if you want. Is that what you want?

You *are* jealous! She tried to sneer it away.

And you're tasteless.

Boy, that had been a mistake. She knew that Paul had never forgotten it, even now. She never again talked about her sexual experiences with other men. He had been the first lover who had ever cared about that. She didn't know whether it was good or bad.

But, because he had reacted so strongly, she had never told him about her miscarriage.

A year after they were married, in a good-humored mood for both of them, she had teased him:

"Would you have liked to have married a virgin?"

"Hell no!" he answered straightaway. "I know when I'm well off. Sex is great."

Babies shouldn't kill that. She wouldn't let it happen.

She would have liked to have been a virgin, for him. Or just younger, less knowing. There had been so much wasteful loving.

She didn't love Seventeen Seventeen Jerome, but this was not unusual for she never loved any house while she was living in it. If she looked back at the houses and apartments in which she had lived, she suffered a nostalgic love which attached itself to *her* room and the people whom she had liked while she had lived there. She could rarely recall any particulars, unless they had interfered with the privacy of her own room. She was generous in giving, but she didn't like sharing. She accepted that she shared 1717 with Paul. This did not offend her because 1717 had been given to both of them.

But right from the start, although she had wanted to be married to Paul, she did not accept that "marriage" was a shared gift. Marriage, she determined, should be worked at, and worked for, by both individuals. When they were introduced to anyone, she never called Paul her husband; she always said, I'm married to Paul. One of the reasons she disliked going out to social gatherings – a small but dense reason – was that she resented being on someone's list and someone's lips as The Mathiessens. A Mathiessen evening made her heart sink like a stone. It involved being obliged to share, and both of them being taken for granted as indistinguishably shared.

She didn't worry that 1717 was bigger than both of them. 1717 was an investment; Paul and she were caretakers and trustees of that investment. She didn't find the house cold, she found it objectively pleasant and suitably respectful of themselves. She was not housey, anymore than she was wifey. If she got angry with Paul then she got angry, she never nagged. Similarly she never could be bothered to nag the house and never let 1717 nag her.

Paul was intimidated by the house, she knew. There was a sort of guilt in him which she found weak and absurd. She despised him when he allowed himself to be intimidated by anything. It seemed like a silly choice on his part, like a little private creeping away, a childish threat of weakness. It was a strange side to Paul: that he would then attempt to justify his display of weakness by stirring up a fight with her just so that he could lose it. Which is what had started to happen on the Fridays, at night, when they had binged.

Saturday: 1p.m. to 2p.m.

This was Saturday. Really it might have been any day, since she had given up working. But no, it was Saturday; she kept Saturday blank, free even from the check-ups and ultrasounds, half of which Paul knew nothing about. He had tried to talk her into a regular Saturday schedule at the Tennis Club, but she had tiptoed discreetly away from it without Paul complaining. God, she had cut back on working in order to safeguard this pregnancy, so she wasn't going to risk running around the tennis court in competition with, or against, him. And there was another risk – that she might beat him – which wasn't worth considering.

Part of the perfect Saturday lay in considering Paul from a safe distance. She might wish that he was here. Saturdays were missing him, thinking about him. All five foot ten of him and starting to spread.

Sometimes Seventeen Seventeen seemed empty, during the week, on hold. It filled up, Saturdays. They started again, in bed. Coffee, or tea. Paul being angry about the dumb car.

He could have put the down payment on the pool, asshole. He knew it as well as she did. Paul Mathiessen. Patio Schmatio. She got a rush out of trashing the Mercedes. They weren't that old that they had to have a Mercedes.

So get angry, Schmatio! It's good for the heart, all that hot blood pumping fast. Then play tennis, and go to the office so you feel righteous. And come home.

She had done . . . nothing.

Yet.

Besides nourish his child. Easy cooking, great cuisine. You wait till you can taste it. When my breasts get larger and more sensitive; and very, very sexy.

It's time to do something, Saturday.

Okay . . .

She straightened the bed and went through to the kitchen.

God how stupid she had been about the doors being open; not stupid, but stupidly panicky. She had just let herself go, like any hysterical idiot, reacting in the most stupid way. Like a victim. Was it being pregnant, or was it just spending too much time on her own in the house? Whatever it was, it was dumb. That kind of a victim mentality invited trouble.

She would have to get herself together. These mood swings

could easily tip into a panic attack if she didn't get a hold on them. She was just indulging herself. Get your priorities figured out, Laurie. You're pregnant, okay? Okay. But there was no call for the baby to take such a complete emotional priority. If it started controlling her now, then it would control everything.

Paul was the priority.

The kitchen-timer was not a priority and could go back in the drawer.

The salad: dried off, and put in a pillowcase in the refrigerator – a lesson from her mother.

Jazz on the CD player, low.

Call Helen Matson. 650 forty-seven twenty-two. On the machine.

"Helen, hi, it's Laurie Mathiessen. I'm caught up in something and so we're going to send out for dinner. If you and Bill have got any ideas, then call me back. It's just after one and I'll talk to you later. Bye."

Two Moëts, and Paul will pick up some wine.

Done. And the house is tidy. Just the table to set.

She cleaned the vanity in the second bedroom.

She thought about eating bacon. She ate a bowl of raspberries and most of a carton of chocolate-chip ice cream. She made fresh tea and called up the Maytag dealer to come check the washer which didn't stay on the program for Paul's shirts.

Saturdays she would have sat out on the deck. She liked waiting. She liked starting to feel better. Friday nights used to be excessive, like a surgery to remove the week. Now that the drinking had quietened down, Friday midnights had turned into Saturday midnights, almost without her noticing. A baby's priority.

Well she wasn't going to sit out on the deck now, not with that smell.

And she kind of missed Fridays. She missed the edge; sexy and exciting, before it had become a pattern of less sexy and more frustrating.

She decided. Sexy. And Moët. Stay up late. Be a hostess.

As she set the table in the dining room she felt the pressure of anticipation settle into its familiar channels, the blood tingling, a familiar ache.

She remembered something, and shut it out of her mind. When the table was finished, she took a glass of Alhambra down to the guest bedroom and switched on the PC.

"Book" – she inserted the disc.

She didn't know where to finish, with the book.

When she first knew that she was pregnant, she had felt angry about giving up her work; and with her book she felt – maybe, sometimes – slightly ashamed that it might be seen as an excuse for not having a job. The truth was, and she admitted it freely to herself, that she didn't want a job. Financially, she didn't need a job. And she didn't want one. She would have to work hard at keeping the pregnancy. But she didn't want this recognised, she couldn't tell Paul this.

She wanted to devote herself.

Maybe the reason that she couldn't finish the book was that she didn't like working with herself.

Could be.

But the writing itself was okay. It was something, while she was waiting.

Laurie remembered what had crossed her mind upstairs in the dining room, which was in the book. She downloaded it, and read through it.

When she and Paul had gotten engaged, his parents had begun to involve her in the family. Paul was one of four children, he was not an object of devotion for his mother. It surprised Laurie that the mother didn't even seem to have a favorite. She ran the family politically, she ensured that the financing and the love were evenly distributed, and occasionally refereed the jealousies with a sympathetic firmness. Laurie would never consider coping with four children and she admired the mother's practical efficiency – her own mother was far too conniving and scatterbrained to be a matriarch. But Laurie couldn't detect that Paul's mother liked, or had ever liked, Paul's father. Loved, perhaps; but not liked.

Paul's father had never been wary of Laurie at all, which had irritated her. She, after all, worked with the environmentalists, and he ran a lumber business. She occasionally put in a block tackle, Laurie-ish, but he never ran with the ball. He waited to listen, politely, and he considered what she said, and then usually Paul would clumsily divert the subject. His father paid no mind to her.

One weekend Paul was away, doing something somewhere, maybe it had been one of those pathetic job interviews on the east coast, and Laurie was invited up to the house for lunch, which got eaten, and Paul's mother had a back pain and went to lie down. Paul's brother and his wife went off to a game, and Laurie had found herself, with more alcohol inside her than she would have liked at midday, alone with the father.

She challenged him about the exploitation of the forests and the collusion between federal government and private business, the corruption which nobody could ever prove.

"Yes," he said, "I could prove it. If I thought that it would be a good thing to prove."

He then explained to her why he thought that it would be a bad thing; that conscience was much better left to U.S. companies because there would always be corruption, and in the U.S. it was more controlled. It was much better that the lumber industry had paid people inside the federal government, influencing policy, than that an independent group of legislators should find themselves under a larger national policy which might become part of any foreign trade pact.

"The great mistake you make is to think that lumbermen don't like trees. If they didn't, Laurie, they would put themselves out of business. The best business I can do is to have one company which buys wood, and another which plants trees. It isn't a matter of conscience. It's good business."

He had been authoritative. He had impressed her. His argument was perhaps plausible, but he hadn't convinced her. She couldn't imagine but that he had some doubts, which he either wished to forget about, or insisted on riding roughshod over. He wasn't generous enough to admit anything outside his terms. She saw that he kept his life in a series of compartments, and she had understood then how wearying this must be to Paul's mother. She understood the dislike, and she had never felt that she could trust him in the same way that she trusted the mother.

It was in Paul. Paul was part ways his father's son. Paul kept things hidden, sometimes evasively, sometimes protectively. There was a lot of his mother in him, the fairness and the generosity, but there was some of his father.

Which she had chosen to ignore, or forget, or forgive. Pass over.

Delete.

She cleared the PC screen.

It *is* strange, she thought. It's strange how I cared about the environment, and then I cared more than anything about *my* environment, with this house. And then I decide to have a baby, which I care most about. It *is* strange how life closes in.

And now, Saturdays, I sit here and talk to the baby.

Crazy. I'd better hope that it isn't a boy, but I shouldn't hope that.

EIGHT

At the beginning of March, by the time that she was three and a half months pregnant, Laurie had seriously wondered if she should, or would, stay with Paul. In January she had suspected that she was pregnant, almost immediately. Paul had been cautious, and even when the test results came to confirm her hopes he showed no warmth.

Worse, he didn't seem to want to have any reaction at all. He didn't want to know about it. He acted as if there was no room for this fact, and Laurie came to think that there might not be the emotional depth to him in which the fact could take root and grow.

He depressed her. He cut off her excitement, any excitement. He kept her at a distance. He seemed to imply that he was not a part of this event, nor what was to come. It was as though he nailed her enthusiasm to the wall and glanced at it sometimes with dislike.

She had swallowed her disappointment and her feelings of betrayal. She knew how he hated gifts. She read books and talked to friends back east and found out that most men didn't know how to react. So she told Paul how to react, she sat him down and yelled at him objectively, she told him what he was feeling and why, and she asked him to talk about it. He didn't have to talk with her about it, he should talk to someone else, anyone else. But he should *do* something. He should learn to show her some respect and attention, he should *love* her, for godsakes it was his baby she was carrying and it had been their shared decision to drop contraception and have a child.

Yes, of course she had known that she would get pregnant quickly. She had told him so. She had warned him dozens of times. Her mother and her sister both got pregnant at the drop of a hat. She was healthy and fertile; they had discussed all this, they had made a decision, together.

"So shape up! I, and this baby, are going to need you!"

He had apologised, absent-mindedly. Almost in sorrow.

And he hadn't treated her any differently. He simply had worked longer hours, as though seeing more patients and earning more money would constitute his own charitable status and provide a gift to lay before her. This attitude had just emphasised the gulf between them. It exhausted him and reduced her to solitude and bitterness.

When he was at home, he trudged resentfully around the house like a wounded butler. He drew attention to every little chore and got picky about the housecleaner, Maria, whose name he persistently and wilfully forgot. Laurie let fly at him again. They would need a housecleaner after the baby was born and good housecleaners didn't grow on trees; he never saw Maria, so he should just shut up about her; it had nothing whatsoever to do with him. If he couldn't be sympathetic, he should just butt out and mind his own business. Leave Maria to her, she would deal with Maria.

And she dealt with Maria, whom she liked. And whom she watched with her two-year-old, and she asked Maria questions and watched over the child while Maria worked; which she would never have told Paul, who didn't know that Maria was stuck with a child which she had to bring to the house; which was why Laurie cleaned the toilets before she arrived.

Several times it had been on the tip of her tongue to tell him, but each time she had thought first, Why should he care? He wouldn't want to know, or understand. He would want to feel deceived, and then he would make himself out to be the victim of yet another female conspiracy.

She had tried to feel neutral, she had tried to temper her anger and restrain her anticipation. But it seemed that, for him, any conspiracy would do. There were two murders in February, one of them of a doctor. Paul had pored over the newspapers and searched through the TV channels in his den. He became a serious-minded citizen, perplexed by the weight of the world, shutting himself away. Laurie couldn't see what on earth this had to do with him. He went out and bought back copies of the newspapers and murmured darkly about manifestos. She wondered if this was some sort of macabre mid-life crisis; there was a lot of self-important head-shaking and vacant expression while he stood staring out of the kitchen window. She ignored it, and carried on as normal, or in the way which had become normal for her, until she could stand it no longer and asked him what he thought about these murders.

She had allowed him to sit her down. He wanted to be serious. He put on his weariest tone of voice. He explained about the murders and the manifestos which had been issued afterwards. She stared dumbly at his pile of newspaper cuttings.

She had realised that Paul didn't know what he was talking about. The newspapers had no definite picture; he was putting together bits and pieces which were often contradictory, and was ignoring the most obvious fact that none of it had anything to do with him. He was insisting to her that *this* was the outside world, *this* was reality, all this violent death and crappy rhetoric which he wanted to show to her, which he wanted to pose at her, or pose against her. He was not even being realistic, he was being destructive. He was being sadistic, with a precise and maniacal bullying.

She had started to cry. And he, mistaking the cause but delighted with his effect, had hastened to reassure her that they were both safe, that they were both secure if they were careful, that neither of them should pay too much attention to what was happening at the moment.

To what? *To what was happening at the moment*?! She was carrying their child for godsakes!

She gave up.

She had felt so exasperated, and so unfairly sidetracked, that finally she had asked herself: Did she need him? Did she want him? Didn't she have enough to take care of, without his sulky assertions and negative self-pity?

She had known that she was right about him, that this was only one of the more dramatic displays of weakness on his part. But she didn't see why she should have to get into the old familiar ritual of a fight. Family would be three, soon, not two. There would have to be two mature adults, not one. She would need him, but only the best of him. And that would have to be taken for granted, not played for. She deserved better.

One Sunday she left Paul pretending to be asleep and drove to church. It was early, the building had been unlocked but there was nobody inside. Laurie walked around. She wondered at the solemnity of the building, and wondered why the building was so solemn. Somehow she had never equated solemnity with the west coast. She sat down, and the church began to fill, so she stayed for the service.

When she got back to 1717, Paul was furiously cleaning the fridge. She ignored him until he couldn't ignore her any longer. When he asked where she had been, she said that she had been to church. When, half astonished and half scared, he asked her why, she said that she had been to give thanks.

"Why?"

"Because I *am* grateful! *I* am! I'm not asking you to be. I wanted to show it, and share it with someone or something. It's no big deal. Because if I have to do this baby all on my own, then I will. I'm strong enough to do it on my own. And I'm lucky enough to be able to afford it."

Once again, he hadn't any clue how to react. He had tried to pretend that he thought she was crazy, that he had been misunderstood. She didn't care to offer him any further understanding.

Why should she? She was strong enough to do it on her own. If he didn't want to commit himself to the baby, then she didn't want to have to talk him into committing himself to her. She would rather go somewhere else, where the trust could be taken for granted.

She would go home.

Ever since she had picked up the phone and told them the news, her mother and father had urged her to fly back east for a visit. They wanted to see her, they were thrilled with the news, they wanted to be a part of it. She had promised to schedule. Their excitement was put on hold. She had delayed, waiting for Paul. Their frustration was evident. They had sounded her out about flying to LA, they wouldn't get in the way or intrude, they would stay in a hotel and visit.

She had delayed them, had waited for Paul to come to his senses.

Two weeks later he came to church with her, shy, like an innocent, as if to make it clear that he was going through some isolated spiritual crisis which she couldn't reach. She sat with him, and sang with him, and knelt with him, and prayed without him. The whole time she thought that he was being ridiculous. He had swung the balance in his – sullen – favor. They were behaving as though they had recently lost a child, blaming each other, not rejoicing in the joy of a conception nor reaching for what that conception promised.

Maybe they needed a break from each other. Maybe the immensity of the situation had made them static. Maybe there wasn't the energy in him to move forward.

She had thought: I can't withdraw from this one. Not this time. He may withdraw, if that's the only way he can cope with it. But I am operating not just for me but for a child, and the child isn't going to withdraw. It can't. And it's not going to get hurt by him. We need protection.

When they had got back from church and she had picked through the refrigerator to hand him a beer, she said: "Mom and Dad have asked us for Easter, and I think I'll go."

"What about Colorado?"

"Sure. Why?"

"The whole family will be there. We can do them all in one sweep. They want to see you."

"Well, then maybe we can arrange Colorado. Can we find a stopover flight?"

"Maybe."

"Paul, they want to see *you* as well. And I want to see them. It's just that I feel I need to see my family."

"They *are* your family."

"Yeah. Yes. You know what I mean."

"What's wrong?"

"Paul, I want some time out."

"From what?"

"From everything. Don't be an asshole, Paul. I don't want to fight. I want time out from *us*. You're not *there* for me. And you know it! I only want to go home for a visit, that's all."

"Running . . . "

She stared into his eyes, beyond the provocation and the useless defence. "No, I'm not running. Not from anything. We could run together, if you wanted to. But you can't even walk, and my parents have more pride in you. So I don't want to hurt their feelings, and I don't want you to hurt your parents' feelings. Something's wrong, Paul, and I don't know what it is. I don't want anyone else to know, that's all. Because then they'll start to ask me about it and I might just decide to tell them that there isn't enough. Between *us*!"

"Isn't there?"

"I don't know. For godsakes take this beer!" The bottle wrapper was by now slimy in her hand. "If I said white, you'd say black." He took the beer. "I say Massachusetts, you say Colorado. None of it is real, Paul!"

Twenty minutes later she had gone out to the patio from the bedroom and told him: "I'm going to spend Easter at the Cape. Really. I've told them that you might be tied up with work, so the invitation is open. I called your mother and left any arrangement open. It's all open, Paul, everything. Think about it. Decide for yourself. I'm not going to decide for you."

It had been hard to find a flight. Almost all the airlines were fully booked for the holiday period. She had up-graded to business class and resented the extra cost, which would give Paul another reason for prevaricating. She still believed that he would come with her.

Even after he had driven her to the airport and waited with her at the check-in line, she half-assumed that he would announce that he had decided to join her in a couple of days, or a week, or when he had wrapped up work for the Easter break.

But he gave no hint of any plan. He was efficient, he was funny. He had bought a present for her parents. He was affectionate. He wanted her to have a good time. She deserved a good time. She should enjoy herself, she should have a ball. He was insistent.

They had kissed, and she had gone through the gate.

For the next half-hour she was angry. Paul was a jerk.

Then she was deflated. Paul was back at 1717, and what was she doing but climbing into the sky, Laurie flying home.

But business class was pleasant. Several of the passengers in her vicinity were working on laptops, the older people were reading. There was a quiet and comfortable lull, undisturbed by gently ministering flight-attendants. Laurie kicked off her shoes and relaxed to the softly seeping sway of the air-conditioning as the flight headed away east, cocooned from all earthly worry.

And her family had come to her like a balm. She hadn't realised how tired she was, how preoccupied she had been. At the house on the Cape she slept long and deeply, her mind drugged by the sounds of the ocean, muffled crashes and the sighs of surf as it fanned across the beach, the same undertow of sound dragging her drowsily through the day. Her father was happy for her, he looked at her and she saw that he thought that she was beautiful, and that was his happiness; her mother laughed in amiable mockery but was careful not to break the spell. They let her do as she pleased, which was little enough, and more than enough to keep her happy. She had never before felt how much she meant to them. And realising this was, for her, not at all oppressive; it was a confirmation of herself, without the edge of pride pushing forward to open old wounds. She wondered placidly: Am I a different person? How has it happened – has anything happened?

Her father went through her stock portfolio with her, like he had used to go through her grades, and everything was satisfactory, like an easy dream. There were a few rough fringes but nothing that couldn't be smoothed out. He wanted to add to her dividend income, there would be additional expenditure coming up. She said that she had it covered, on budget, anything extra should go to his grandchild's name.

"Yes," he said, "and no doubt it will, from your mother and from me. But you know, Laurie, parents need presents as well. Babies are much happier with giftwrapping paper, as I recall. They are a gift to which you always give, for the rest of your life. You'll find that every once in a while you'll want to take a break, you and Paul."

She hadn't thought about Paul for nearly a week. They had talked on the phone, nothing more than a ritual, twice: he from the office, she from a comfortable chaise, ready to hand him on to her mother or father. She saw that her father's hair was almost all grey. Her mother had said that he was thinking about retiring, but of course with several projects that were interesting him.

"Yes," she said. "I guess so. Paul's completely tied up with work right now."

"I remember that. Men have changed, I hear. I hear that they get much more involved with babies."

"There are rumors."

He smiled.

"Damn right," she said, suddenly angry. "Why shouldn't they? They have responsibilities too."

"Good. That's why both of you will need a break. I don't think that your mother and I ever wanted to have to figure out every little domestic arrangement. We argued enough as it was, without tripping over each other around the house."

"That's the way you did it, dad. It worked fine for you. And us kids."

"Thank you, honey."

"Every couple's got to figure it out."

"I have no wish to interfere with you two. My love, and my loyalty, is primarily to you."

"Oh that's . . . dad, I know. That's . . . "

"Good. As long as you understand, Laurie."

" . . . the same with me."

"So if you have anything to sort out with Paul, don't try and do it over a diaper or with family."

She said, "Okay." And she thought that maybe he was right; maybe she had been wrong. Maybe she had been the one who had withdrawn, if only into happiness. But he interrupted her.

"So your mother and I are each giving you a check for five thousand dollars, which is not to be spent on the baby or the house. It's for a vacation, from being householders and parents, you and Paul. Go somewhere. Before the baby is born. Get away together. Your mom and I should have done the same thing, if I hadn't been completely tied up with work."

She had been confused by her parents' generosity. It seemed straight enough, her father always liked being in a position to give and her mother waved any gratitude away. She was a great believer in busying giddy minds with foreign travel. And, much as her father had posed the gift as resulting from his own benign guesswork, Laurie felt that they were urging some sort of a solution on her, and for her.

She didn't want a vacation. There was nothing she wanted to see, nowhere she wanted to travel. Certainly not with Paul. She was having a vacation, now, from Paul. She couldn't imagine sitting down with Paul in front of a rug spread with travel brochures, having a conversation about hiking or reef-snorkelling. There was so much more that they ought to be talking about. They ought to be talking. They should be talking. She hadn't talked to anyone for a week or more, besides getting along fine with her parents.

She had felt uneasy, suddenly alone with a growth in her womb. But she had made herself not call him.

On Friday, Good Friday, there was a storm. A real humdinger which crashed up from the south, lashing rain and whipping the crests off those surging Atlantic rollers. Grey piled on top of grey until the sky was indivisible from the ocean and the mixture hurtled horizontal at the house, slapping windows and rattling doors and seeping in through the lintels. Laurie loved it when the sky was irritable and the wind lurched childishly against the house. All afternoon the storm built up its courage, swaggering in from the beach and sideswiping the trees. Darkness came early, the power went out and everybody went to bed to listen to the storm shriek its persistent victory. Laurie had called Paul and got the answering machine. "Hi," she said, "it's me. We've got this great storm. Love you. Listen . . . " She pulled the phone as far down the bed as it would go and held the receiver out towards the window, feeling an ache of regret at what he was missing. Later, she replaced the phone and put her pillows at the other end of the bed, and fell asleep with her head facing the ocean.

The next day he had called her at four. She had been along the beach with her father, picking through driftwood for sea-smoothed trophies and bleached treasure, with memories of years ago, her blue jeans stained and her face stinging from the wind, more tired and exhilarated than she had thought possible. Full of affection, she returned his call, from her room.

Was she all right? Yes, he had heard the storm. It had been on the NBC news. No, on the weather report, so he had known that it wasn't too serious. The house okay? 1717 was fine. He hadn't gone to Colorado, no. His family was fine. Hers? Great. Should he water the squash? Uh-huh. No, everything was fine. He hoped that she was having a good time, not chasing around too much. Well . . . give his love to everybody. He would call. Easter Sunday maybe? Okay. Yes, him too. (Love you.) Bye. Bye.

He hadn't said that he missed her. He wouldn't say, anyway. It didn't mean that he didn't miss her.

Laurie's sister came Saturday with her husband, an actor. Her sister sponsored the arts. Or their father did. Paul had called and had said hello to everybody. Laurie wanted to go home, back to LA.

She had waited another week, under orders to relax and obliged to do it gracefully.

She had planned their vacation.

All their vacation had gotten lost on the flight west, amongst wanting to see him. She had changed into her new clothes and had made herself up carefully. She had loved his shy hug at LAX, and his nervousness about her baggage and parking the car in the Loading Zone. She had kidded him into a smile and he had liked her clothes, and she saw him take his eyes off the freeway to like the way she looked, and it wasn't until she took his hand off the steering wheel and held it for a moment, clammily in her lap, that she had known, in the midst of her chatter, that he had had an affair.

Saturday: 2p.m. to 3.45p.m.

What was she doing down here, a month later, in her workroom? In the unborn baby's room, her child's room; with the crib which they had bought together, and the stuffed toys which she had brought back from the Cape. What was she doing?

She was saying, I have to get a grip, what am I doing? The dining room table is set. What are you doing, Laurie?

She inserted a clean disc, and named the new file 'Christmas'. Onto the screen she tapped:

A Merry, Merry Christmas to You All.

And over the next hour she wrote, edited, and rewrote:

> Well, we don't have any blizzards out here and so our Christmas thoughts and wishes are sent peacefully. We are still in Los Angeles.
>
> It has been a wonderful year for all three of us. Yes, three. Jane/John Mathiessen came down to earth in September, fine, healthy and with strong vocal chords to answer all our prayers.
>
> (INSET: date of birth, weight, appearance, hospital story, getting to hospital, family reaction, Mom still trying to lose weight, thanks again for all presents, etc).
>
> Now three months old, J/J lies asleep in our bed. It is mid-afternoon and Paul is half-asleep watching the game on TV, so I will probably never get a better chance to write.
>
> It has been a pretty good year for both of us outside of preparing for the main event and the main event itself. Babies take up a lot of time and so time has become more valuable and we haven't had to worry about wasting it. (No kidding! – and purrleese no rude remarks from anyone who thinks they know us well!!!!!)
>
> This year the environment has been kinder. There have been just a couple of small earthquakes and no flash floods.

Okay, so then there is a worry about drought, but out here life isn't the same without worry. We have learned to take worry as a fact of life and a major player in late twentieth-century speech patterns. This year, though, God has His heart in the right place and has handed us a little one, instead of the Big One. And we are grateful.

You always have to find something to worry about and I guess that we have settled into Southern California much the same as anyone else. Paul has great jokes about it which never look good on paper. Anyway, I'm sure that you've heard them all and we are still capable of laughing as much as anyone else. (As long as we don't wake the baby!!!)

So it's been good, and we've been blessed. Sometimes I look up at the sky, when I can see it, and count my blessings, which is a new attitude for me, and sometimes I don't just sit here and count them. There has been some real-estate development in the neighborhood, and there is now a small and friendly episcopalian church up the valley, which Paul and I started to go to on Sundays. We started to go there in February, I guess as tourists, but there was something simple and good and uncomplicatedly spiritual so we stayed and it has become a habit.

(INSET: what happens when J/J hollers in church.)

There are a lot of good people, even in Los Angeles County. Sometimes there are things that you can share and not have to bargain for, outside of the city, some kind of community outlook and values which have nothing to do with all the hyped inner-self stuff that we have here in extremes. From the church we have met people with firm dignity. Often this is more rewarding than entertaining at home, and I guess that we both at this time appreciate a sense of values which is not pushed at us by any interest-group.

Doctor Paul's career is doing well. He is still happy working with his senior partner Abe Deane and the practice has gained new clients. Abe is a strong anchorman while Paul is always finding new clients through his social activities. For a doctor he sure has high principles, and doesn't speak up for them enough.

With his agreement I have delayed going back to work for a while. It would have happened anyway for J/J's birth, but there isn't any need to hurry back. I was finding it impossible to feel positive about going in two different directions, and there wasn't any other middle ground, not even sentimentally. Paul worried about me sacrificing myself but I don't see it that way. (Nobody's going to make *me* do all the sacrificing, no sirree!!!) It's been a time to put other projects on the back burner and concentrate on keeping family ties together.

So in March I went back east to see everybody (Hi Guys!), carrying J/J who couldn't be seen by anyone (it didn't stop us both having a great time!). Paul stayed to bring home the bacon and to get used to the *idea* of being a father and this was the first time that we had been away from each other for such a prolonged absence. Maybe it's no bad thing. We now have a much stronger appreciation of each other and a fresher outlook fuck him cheap scuzzy shit

Filler:

April screwing around
May
June
July
etc. vacation? pre-natal class?
Men needing the *idea* of being a father while women . . . (boring?)
The house.
Anything major locally. Or minor.

Paul. And ask Paul? about Easter
End with baby waking up.

For now, all is well and Christmassy and peacefully settled. We hope it is so with you. All three of us miss you and still have plenty of room for travelers.
Have a Wonderful, Joyful Christmas
Think globally, act locally.
Love from all of us – Laurie, Paul, and

Laurie looked at her watch. It was a quarter of four. She filed the Christmas letter onto the disc.

She turned away and ran upstairs to the bedroom. She went to the closets and sorted out exactly what Laurie would wear, knowing what she, and Paul, liked.

NINE

She knew that he had slept with someone else. She knew it when she came back from the Cape.

She had set herself to ignore it. Trouble didn't touch Laurie. This was trouble. It shouldn't touch her, and it wouldn't touch her unless she caused it to.

When they had got back to 1717 she wound herself around him, until his indecision met her jet lag and she folded innocently and apologetically into sleep, promising tomorrow.

She had awoken at four in the morning, suddenly, a stranger to the change of climate and the harsh unpleasantness of her anger. She left him asleep, showered downstairs and felt sick, and sat at her desk.

Rage. It was rage. That stupor and the swirling bits of feeling and image. Her mind was like a kaleidoscope held numbly by the rest of her body. This was simple rage, she told herself.

For more than an hour.

She was so tired. She wanted to sleep. She wanted to be able to think normally and go to sleep, like after a fight, for a whole day.

Five forty-five a.m.

She had thought of watering the terraces, logically, before the sun came up. To kill time. But the noise of the running water might wake him, even though the shower hadn't.

Nor did she want him to see her watering the terraces, like a stupid, blithely contented peasant. She wasn't stupid! She was not stupid. She wasn't ignorant.

And her eyes, were her eyes narrowed?

She went to look at herself in the mirror.

A half-hour later she knew what she was going to do.

She had brushed her hair and, when she had heard him using the bathroom, she went upstairs. She stood in the bathroom doorway and disturbed him, and interfered with him as he was slow with sleep, dumb and easily aroused before he went to work.

When he had gone, she had lain in bed, resting, sleeping, eyes half-open, thinking. Occasionally she thought of previous times like this. And there *had* been times like this, though not with Paul. She had been betrayed before Paul. She still felt, and felt nauseous, with anger; but she was not overwhelmed by feeling. Objectivity flitted through the prances of chaos. She was most objective about Paul. She didn't want to know anything about him, she had a bellyful of him.

At two in the afternoon, she had got out of bed and called the office. She spoke to Alice. She said: "Hi, Alice, it's Laurie. Yes, I had a great time. Has Paul been behaving himself? He hasn't made too many passes at anyone in the office lately?"

Unperturbed, Alice laughed. "No, ma'am."

Laurie laughed. They were allies. "Good, then I'll talk with him."

So it was a joke, for the office. If Alice hadn't have laughed, or had taken time to answer, then she would have known that Doctor Mathiessen had officially gone a little lower than skin deep.

She asked Paul to pick up some groceries, then she went back to bed.

Let him suspect nothing. Let him be ignorant of her knowledge.

She had napped fitfully, overshadowed by a dark depression. She wouldn't allow herself more than two or three minutes with her eyes closed, and when they opened she stared straight at the clockface, hating the passage of minutes, hating the nearness of his arrival. She fought away the feeling that she didn't want him in the house. She didn't want to have to be normal, she didn't want to be how he wanted her to be; she couldn't imagine how he expected her to be.

What was *he* feeling? She was perversely interested. She wanted to ask him. Did he feel guilty? Did he like, or love, this other woman? Did he dislike *her*, Laurie? What had she done? Had she done anything, or behaved in any way, to deserve this humiliation?

Was she humiliated? She asked herself. She didn't feel humiliated. She felt soft and amorphous, and wondered how she would harden.

She had napped; it was too complex.

And when her eyes opened, she had wondered, *when* did this affair happen? What was I doing when it happened? Was I on a chaise staring at the ocean? Was it straight after he dropped me off at the airport? *What* had happened? How had he made it happen?

She couldn't imagine that she didn't know everything about Paul. He wasn't successfully secretive. He wasn't interested in women, other women. He had had plenty of opportunities before now. Women trusted him; he might be insignificant, but they trusted him. It must have been simply a sexual act, with a hooker or an unprofessional equivalent. It couldn't have been part of any relationship. Someone must have picked him up and taken advantage of him when he was in one of those weak moments, when he wanted to lose everything. Those moments of self-negation which she really hadn't wanted to know about.

Damn her, whoever she was. How could he be so stupid? How could he be so weak and stupid? Damn her. Once, twice, a half-dozen times? Was it still going on?

If it was still going on, then there would inevitably be an end to their own relationship, in the sense of living together. Never mind how she felt, he wouldn't be able to handle it. He wouldn't be capable. And she wouldn't live with his dithering misery. She wanted a straight answer, a decision.

But she didn't want a confession, or an apology, or creeping guilt which would drag on. She wanted no bargaining, no discussion, no admission. She didn't want to watch him pay with any tacky embarrassment which would demean them both.

The idea of a short, sharp vengeance had crossed her mind. She might hurt him back in the same way he had hurt her. A sudden and brazen retaliation. She could date one of his lunch partners, openly. There would be an explosion, and they would be quits, and they could get it all out of the way.

The fact that she didn't want to go to bed with any of his friends hadn't influenced her. There would have been no shortage of takers. Men were only too happy not to care. She had done this before and it had worked. She didn't bother to consider "what's the point?" The point was nothing, but was valid. If she hadn't have been pregnant . . .

Fact is, that when Paul finally arrived home, she had stumbled heavy-headed out to the kitchen and had made herself comfortable on the couch. He had asked her how she was, and grinned, and she had seen no reason to attack him or to demean herself. He hadn't been ill at ease, he had grumbled about work, grumbled his way through to the shower; he had come back to grumble about his grumbling until he got the attention from her that he thought he deserved, causing them both to smile.

Later, she had asked him: "So how has it been, since I went?"

He had said: "You know, Laurie, you were right. I don't know about you, but I needed the break. I didn't like to say it and maybe I didn't even know it. I needed the break to straighten things out. It wasn't that things were too much, but somehow they were all centered in you, like you were protecting them, and I couldn't get through without attacking you. You're pretty damn strong, you know. Thank God."

"Stubborn?"

"Maybe." He had smiled crookedly. "I don't mind losing this argument."

"Good. So did you have fun?"

She wanted him to play his part in concealing everything, she wanted him to lie.

"Fun?"

"Well I thought I'd find some empty bottles and beer cans, at least. You didn't have anyone round?"

"No." He had looked ashamed. "I don't know why not. I just couldn't be bothered. Anyway, everyone we know is married or living with a girl. I didn't want to get involved with any entertaining. I know, I know. That's one of the things I got straight. *I'm* the antisocial one."

"I was quite happy missing you. For a week or so. That was enough."

They had talked awhile longer and he had gone across to the other side of the kitchen to prepare dinner.

"I want a couple of days off," she had said, "then I want to start cooking again."

"Why?"

"I'll have to, anyway, for the baby. We *will* have to straighten some things out."

"Do you want any more help?"

"Maybe. But not really. I don't want anyone else in the house. If you could help, that would be enough."

"Sure I'll help. Of course I will. Are you crazy?"

What was the value of knowledge?

Laurie had asked herself many times in the weeks following her return.

Jealousy was out, it was just a waste of time. And she couldn't do anything with suspicion. She wasn't going to be a private detective in her own home. There was nothing to be suspicious of. There were no grounds for suspicion. Paul didn't behave suspiciously.

They had returned to the sanctuary of the San Batista church – the first, second and third Sundays after Laurie's return from the east.

Laurie had kept her eyes peeled, there wasn't a woman in the congregation whose modesty Laurie didn't scrutinise.

They had been missed. They were new members of the Church, but they had been missed, at Easter.

Paul hadn't attended service, not liking to be without his wife, his family.

They were recognised; Laurie chose to make them known, after the services. Herself with child, Paul with career, both righteous, the Mathiessens.

People paused to chat. They were an attractive couple, the slightly withdrawn young doctor, and the naturally radiant wife who gave her time to talk with the children and to admire what they were wearing.

She felt that he was happy at having her back. And there were no suspicious incidents, no suspiciously slick phone calls, no peculiar absences. She couldn't do anything with suspicion. It might have been useful had she wanted to put it to use. But if she admitted suspicion, the moment she allowed that she was suspicious, then she would live with fear and imagination, and in the search for proof she would lose all balance and capacity for careful thought. She would live at the whim of suspicion, without any defense. She refused suspicion. Downgrading to suspicion would drive her crazy.

Knowledge, the surety of her own intuition, now that was different. It was carefully under her control. It was her property. She had considered whether she should share it.

She had wondered whether she should tell Paul that she knew that he had been unfaithful.

She couldn't see how they would talk about it. In context with something? As an experience? They shared most experience. How and why should they share this one? It would be grotesque.

The process of establishing and representing what had happened would create a chaos from which they might not recover, from which they would never be safe.

What could she do with the knowledge? And it *was* knowledge; she never chose to question it.

Laurie had quickly come to the conclusion that the affair was better hidden in knowledge, and that the knowledge was better hidden in both of them. She would not let it loose around 1717. Any admission would harm and then destroy their relationship, this home and the future of their child.

So she chose concealment.

Occasionally, momentarily, such concealment made her bitter, but she knew a lot about herself and bitterness. She didn't sink. She didn't, for one moment, doubt her decision.

Paul's self-doubt was more likely to float to the surface. She watched him. Sometimes his mind would sail away from her in an uneasy swell of non-comprehension. His shoulders turned inward and his body shrank timidly with guilt. He had remembered something. He had remembered someone and saw her – this someone – vividly; and Laurie saw how defenseless he was, almost morbidly plaintive. On the verge of appealing to her for understanding.

At times like this, she rushed light-heartedly to cover for him, quickly teasing him with his worries about being a father, diverting his anxiety, assuring him physically, like a baby against her body. She felt a richness of secrecy; she was powerful, nursing discretion.

Of course, if she had thought that his affair was still going on, then she would have withdrawn. She would have let him bleat to the Mongolian steppes. There would have been no shelter. She would have swept him away mercilessly and vindictively, denied his scrabblings at her body, his adolescent eagerness.

There was this about his love-making: that he was trying to

search back to innocence. Whereas she wanted intimacy to spread like a storm, blanketing them both.

As if nothing had ever happened.

And then she could tell herself that she had merely been paranoid. No windows had been opened, no other person had intruded. Knowledge was a valueless commodity on such a closed-option market.

And on this most recent Sunday, Paul and Laurie had been introduced to the minister at San Batista, John Pearson, a studious middle-aged man who lapsed into bursts of good humor as he toured his congregation, but who mostly seemed relieved at the compliments which were given for his ministry.

"I like him," Laurie had decided on the drive down the valley, the windows of the Mercedes sealed shut to preserve the air-conditioning. "He doesn't smile the whole time. It's strange to have someone who doesn't insist on acting inspirational, don't you think? He's sensible. You couldn't imagine him running a cult, could you? He doesn't try to sell you anything."

"He doesn't have to," Paul observed, "he's sincere enough."

"One of the women there told me that he used to be a lawyer. Then he quit to become a minister."

"Why would he quit being a lawyer?"

"Mid-life crisis, maybe. Or maybe he wanted something more positive and got sick to death of law."

"Are you through with practicing law?"

"This isn't exactly the time to go looking for an opportunity," she said irritably. "Are you worried about money? Don't worry about money, don't worry about everything."

"Why the hell not?"

"Because you're not good when you're worried. It drives you crazy and you try to get rid of it by doing something dumb. Do you want a hard-nosed career woman?"

He glanced at her nervously. She shifted her hips in the car-seat.

"Oh, I can do *power*, babe," she said, huskily. He smiled and was embarrassed.

"Cut it out, you're pregnant."

"All the more powerful. You'd better believe it."

"Oh I do."

"And now that we're talking truth, you tell me, are you sick of skin doctoring?"

"Not at all." He was amazed. "Why d'you ask?"

"You'd have every right to get sick of it, why shouldn't you? It's not the kind of practice where you have the reward of any deep one-on-one patient relationship. It's much more casual; isn't it?"

"It's almost more bureaucratic than anything else. Checking up on people. Kind of boring."

"No." She was serious. "No, it isn't; not to me. You don't feel that, do you?"

"No."

"So we're not in competition, are we, about having this baby? Being pregnant, day in and day out, isn't my idea of excitement. My excitement depends on sharing it with you. Quit low-esteeming yourself. I'm not doing this for me. There's nothing boring about being a doctor and a father. We're yours. This isn't just a break in my career and it isn't an end to whatever you want to do. Don't get stuck on feeling that way. Be proud. You deserve it."

He drove silently down Jerome. He had forgotten to freewheel like he usually did. She felt his body relax and then tighten with suppressed emotion, it seemed like grief or a slow release from fatigue.

"You deserve it too," he mumbled, and he took a deep breath. He didn't look at her, and she kept her eyes on the road, to steady him.

He turned into the driveway and reached for the garage control.

"Your vacation", he said, "did us both a whole lot of good."

"My vacation", she said, "has changed nothing."

They sat in the car in the garage at 1717, with the garage doors closing down behind them.

"Great," he said, "that's great. Thank God."

"No," she said, "thank *you*. And me."

She was prepared to get out of the car but he reached for her and they embraced across the stick-shift, the car warming and unpleasant, light beads of salty sweat smearing across their top lips. She felt uncomfortable and she felt like laughing or getting angry, but she needed the bathroom and told him so.

After she had changed her dress for a pair of shorts and a shirt, she found Paul in his den, scanning through the Sunday papers. She had stood behind him and he had reached her arms across his chest, placing his cheek in the hollow of her elbow. "What shall we do?" he asked.

"Let's just do the same as we used to do," she had murmured. "The baby isn't here for another four months." Fingers crossed. "We'll get settled and then look around."

"Oh," he said. "I wasn't thinking of a world plan. I meant this afternoon."

"Oh, well, how about a light lunch and a siesta."

"Something slow."

"Uh-huh. Not *too* slow. Something mutually appreciative. And then a nap, maybe."

He had followed her out into the hallway, desiring her. Her shorts fit her like a glove, swollen as she was, and no amount of his investigation could have gotten his fingers down inside. It was like being a teenager; she laughed at his exasperation and backed away into the kitchen, relishing his predicament and pleased with his reliability; and she had suggested a Russian salad and then ice-cream, caramel pecan.

When Paul had finished a second glass of wine, she let him use the bathroom first, she being not quite ready. The shorts were too tight, vanity-tight; she wriggled them off and discarded them in the laundry room – supposing that she might never be able to get back into them, promising herself that she would have a darned good try – which gave her a moment's sadness and the impetus to lie in bed, close to him, and have him make love to her. She had thought suddenly: if nothing else, he is good at that. Then she had thought: he's kind, and decent, who knows what mental aberration must have gotten into him? I know that I love him, I shouldn't have gone back east.

Never leave them alone. That's what her mother had said. Never leave them alone. If you can't be anything else, just be a pain in the butt.

She had laughed.

"Laurie?" Paul's voice came from the bedroom.

"I'm coming. It's nothing."

"Laurie, did you ever run into a man called James Liebermann?"

"No. What does he do?"

"A realtor, and then some."

She straightened her underwear, let the T-shirt hang, untied her hair, and sauntered into the bedroom. "I was just having a crisis about not being able to wear those shorts again."

"Don't." He looked up at her. "You will."

"So what about this James Liebermann?"

"I didn't know him. I only know the name because he put funding into some hokey alternative-medicine clinic which set up in competition with Abe and me. It was a real cowboy outfit. We lost a couple of patients though."

"Serious?"

"Hell no. Holistic. The only serious thing about it was that Liebermann got killed."

"He did? How?"

"Just after you went away. He got murdered. Six weeks ago. They said it was more like an assassination. By the guy who always issues a manifesto. But no-one could figure out what this James Liebermann had got to do with it. Like it was with the Kiescos."

She kept stony quiet, while the anger built up in her. When he looked at her, wondering why she hadn't said anything, she said quietly to the ceiling: "Now what the fuck has it got to do with us?" Which he would have heard.

But she looked down at him and said: "That's terrible. Isn't it?"

"Jesus, I don't know . . . "

"Paul, you're *not* going to fixate on this stuff again, are you?"

"No," he had said. "I can't see anything to worry about. Not right now. Not with you. Nothing at all."

Saturday: 3.50p.m to 4.10p.m.

There was nothing at all to worry about. Not now.

Laurie looked at her watch. It was ten of four, Saturday. Laurie knew exactly what she would wear, what she and Paul liked. A black crepe skirt with elasticated waistband, a light grey silk shirt, black shoes with a slight heel; for him the blue sports shirt and olive linen trousers. She laid them on the bed and then, thinking about how it might be when they were both clean from the shower, she gathered the clothes and laid them over the back of (his and her) chairs. She straightened the comforter and tidied the bedside tables, sweeping junk into the top drawers. If she added a Bible the bedroom would be almost like a hotel room, free of debris and inviting the imprint of personality.

She walked quickly through 1717 and saw that the house was immaculate, ordered, and ready to be mussed. The smell of smoke had all but disappeared, leaving a light, acrid perfume, like saltpeter, not unpleasant. She went to the back of a cupboard for a scented candle, and lit it; usually the sweetness of sandalwood made her feel sick, but it mingled well with the dead smoke, both odours losing their edge.

She took the gleaming dry dinner plates out of the dishwasher and placed them on the sideboard. Paul would arrange glasses and bottles, whiskey, vodka, and maybe cognac. Beers were already in the refrigerator. She cleared out the stale ice, and the icemaker started to grind out fresh cubes. Laurie didn't much like the way they tasted but she couldn't for the life of her remember where the ice trays were. It reminded her to put three bottles of mineral water in the refrigerator, and Paul would decide whether or not they needed a full Alhambra brought up from the garage.

Napkins. She went to the dresser drawer. The top one was a little dusty, but she only needed four. She put the top one in the laundry room.

There was suddenly nothing to do, at five past four. She couldn't do anything else, except pat herself on the back for having decided not to cook.

Oh God, what about the dessert? What!?

There was just time. There was plenty of time, and apples. And, yes, flour, thank heaven. She got the recipe card from a small wooden box. Her grandmother's recipe. It never failed. She rolled up her sleeves and reached for a large stainless steel bowl. Where was Paul, what could have happened to him? Ten past four, and they had people coming round, where was he? He had invited them.

Enough sandalwood already.

PART THREE

Paul and Laurie

TEN

Saturday: 2p.m. to 6.30p.m.

It took Paul much longer than usual to get from the office back to the club. Saturday slewed to a halt.

He was running late by the time he pulled out of the parking lot. He had wrapped up the small bits of organisation which didn't really need doing and had ascertained that his desk was clear for Monday, the schedule familiar, the supplies in stock, every eventuality covered, including Laurie's call for air-freshener. Life wouldn't be too demanding. Which was a good thing, because he had promised Laurie to go with her for her scan on the Monday afternoon. He had locked up the offices, and walked across the lot.

He was surprised at the smell in the atmosphere, which was far thicker and more noxious than the usual polluted air. The offices were set in from a street of middle-income housing; they had neighbors on the one side, domestic rather than business. Their house was divided into apartments; Abe would probably convert the offices into the same set-up if business ever went bad.

Tenants came and went, the family on the ground floor had been there for several years. They all parked in the street, but no-one minded if they used the office parking lot for loading or unloading furniture on weekends. The family had a new-style station wagon, which the husband was loading up. Paul walked across, and said: "Hi there, are you going camping?"

"I don't know where we're going," the man said. "Maybe to

my sister's. We're getting out for a while, that's the only conclusion we've reached so far. My wife is calling around."

"I don't blame you," said Paul. "It looks like a good weekend for getting out of the city."

"Yep. I don't see any reason to stay around waiting for things to happen. If it hadn't been for the children I would have stayed to look after the apartment. I want to get them somewhere safe."

"Do you think that this neighborhood is in danger from what's happening downtown?" Paul wondered, incredulous.

"I don't see how anyone can tell. Once it gets going, you know. And I don't think anyone knows how it's going to finish. They don't have any idea. Have you been watching? They can't even find anyone to interview." He strapped down the lid of the U-haul container.

"No, I haven't been watching."

"You're not from around here?"

"No, not originally."

"Well, I'll tell you, this baby's building up to be worse than Watts. This one's spreading a whole lot faster."

"No kidding?"

"*I'm* not kidding. Why should I? And we don't want to be stuck here next to a doctors' office. No thank you."

"Because of the drugs?"

The man didn't say anything. He bent to arrange a cooler inside the car. Paul said: "We don't carry a lot of heavy drugs."

"Well they don't know that, and I'll bet you there's enough in there to get them interested."

There was. And there was nothing he could do about it. He said: "I hope you make out okay."

"You too," the man said. His wife came out, and she was pale with worry. Paul said hello, then excused himself.

There was more traffic around than usual. He stopped at a small grocery store, which was nearly empty. There was one guy on the check-out, and two men were unloading sheets of fiberboard from a pick-up. Paul collected what was on Laurie's list, and watched as the two men nailed fiberboard over the windows. It got dark until the interior lights were switched on. What was happening? What was going on here?

When he got to the check-out he said to the guy: "I'm sorry, but I only have a temporary driver's license, will that do to ID my check?"

The man said: "We're doing cash only, right now. We're about ready to close up."

"Okay", Paul said. "I think I have enough cash." He edged out the clean hundred-dollar bill. "Are you closing up for good?"

"Just until it's safe to stay open. I don't know when that will be."

"What do you think's going to happen?"

He looked at Paul. He thought one way; he thought another way; but he shrugged. "Nobody knows, right?" He looked down at a small TV set which was mounted next to the cash till, alongside the security monitor. The security monitor showed his own deserted store, the TV showed people watching a fire-bombed store. "That", he said, "is not far away." He handed Paul his change.

"Shit. How far away is it?"

"Four freeway exits. A half-gallon of gasoline. Which way are you headed?"

"The other way."

So was the traffic. Paul got back to the club late. He hadn't arranged to meet anyone for lunch. Whoever was there took from the buffet and sat down next to whoever else was there. But the club was quiet, there were no members in the dining room and no service outside the bar. Paul took a beer into the television room, where a half-dozen members stood watching silently pictures from downtown.

"It's too goddamned depressing," said someone after a while.

It was, to Paul, unbelievable.

There were small pockets of talk, which he half overheard. Someone occasionally left the room to make a phone call. Reactions ranged from impotence to incomprehension to military solution. Paul himself was amazed, as the coverage went on and on. He forgot about the time. Time rolled into a blur of incident. When he remembered to look at his watch he saw the time and walked quickly out of the club, past the deserted weight room and work-out machines, into a quiet daylight where everything seemed intangibly frail.

Laurie was up to her elbows in flour when Paul came in from the garage, clutching two grocery bags with the newspaper balanced on top.

"Are you late?" she demanded.

"I know. Sorry. Have you seen the news?"

"No." She turned back to her bowl.

"The riots?"

"No. I didn't put the TV on."

"At the check-out in the grocery store they couldn't stop talking about it. It's live on TV."

"You mean it's live, and on TV."

"Whatever."

"Who would want to watch it?"

"People who live near it."

"Uh-huh." She looked up, and out of the window. "So?"

"So no-one called?"

"No."

"No-one from the family, yours or mine?"

"No, why should they?"

"They might be worried."

"If we're not worried, then why should they be worried? You're not worried, are you?"

"I don't know."

"Well," she said, washing the flour off her hands under the

faucet, "let me put it this way: you can't have been very worried or you would have come straight home, wouldn't you? You wouldn't be the kind of person who would sit down and worry at the club, safely, with a group of other worriers, over a couple of drinks and a steam bath."

"I have the groceries."

"Fine. And we have nothing to worry about."

"I don't know. I'm not sure. Nobody's sure."

"Paul," she dried her hands on a dishtowel, "I don't want this to be like the murders. I don't want any of that crap again. It ended up being one big manifesto for *you*: Paul Mathiessen's worry. Now, do we have anything to worry about?"

"I don't know."

"Then I don't want to know. Put the grocery bags down over there. We're having people over for dinner and you're late. As it happens, you don't have to feel guilty because I'm just as guilty. I decided not to cook. We're going to send out. Is that okay for you?"

"Sure, that's fine."

"I just didn't feel like it. I'm making dessert."

"That's okay. Are we friends?"

"It was a bit . . . Last night. One-sided."

"Yeah. I know."

"We can do better than that. Are you scared of me?"

"Why?"

"Are you scared of me being pregnant?"

"I don't think so. Not now. Why?"

"I just wondered." She bent over the bowl, cussing the pastry. Behind her, he opened the refrigerator door.

"Oh," he said, "there is some news, for definite."

"Don't tell me: *you're* pregnant. You haven't been sleeping around, unprotected?"

He said: "Only with you, it seems. But this has nothing to do with us. They did get the guy."

"What guy?"

"The murderer with the manifestos. They arrested him and that's the end of it. It's in the newspaper."

She held her hands up out of the way. She took a deep breath and she followed him to the kitchen table.

"John Paul Stanton . . ." she read.

"White. Middle-aged."

"That's him? They're certain?"

"Pretty much. The Kiescos, Liebermann, and a lot of other people."

"Couldn't that be just the DA's office clearing up its records?"

"It could be, but it doesn't seem like it."

She covered the bowl with a clean dishtowel. "So I can take it that you're certain."

"Yes. They've got him, and that's the end of it."

"Good. That's the end, you promise?"

"Of course I do. It was a strange time, Laurie. I don't know what was going on with me."

"Nor did I."

"I know."

"But it's over."

"Yes." He looked at her enquiringly.

"Then I don't want to hear any more about it."

She switched on the oven. She spoke more generally.

"I don't understand how someone can kill a lot of people. I understand someone going crazy with a gun; but just deciding to do it to different people on different occasions, I don't understand that. I'm against capital punishment. It's the same thing. Manifestos are just one man's legal system, and both systems incorporate capital punishment. The system is crazy. It's good that they got him. It's one less dumbass middle-aged male on the loose. Two, including you. Put the paper away somewhere. Not on the couch, Paul, I've cleaned house. We have guests. Slice some apples for me."

"Think you can trust me with a knife?"

"Do you mean: do I think that I can trust you?"

He stood with the newspaper, looking for her to tell him where to put it. She didn't mean to be serious. She lobbed an apple across the kitchen at him; he caught the apple with one hand, but the newspaper slid from his grasp and spread across the floor. "Got it!" he called triumphantly. "You didn't think I would, did you?!" He was pleased with himself.

"Just trying you out", she said. Angrily, she went to the fridge and took out a tray of eggs. "Right?" And she lobbed an egg, high. He went backwards and was stopped by a chair, he watched the egg pass over his head, turned as it smashed against the wall and turned back quickly, forgetting shock as he saw another egg leave her hand. This one he caught, low down, the shell breaking in his hand, the albumen hanging in a glob before dropping to the floor amid splatters of yolk. "Wait!" He looked at her warily, anticipating more.

"No, that's all," she said. "That's not bad. Pass in intentions, pass in reactions, fail in priorities. You should have dropped the apple, it would only have bruised." She threw him a dishtowel. He wiped his hands.

"You know, there were hard-boiled eggs in the bowl on the shelf."

"Hard-boiled eggs take the fun out of life." She turned and threw one more egg which hit him hard above the ear, to his pained surprise.

"You see," she said, "With a hard-boiled egg, you might have gotten badly hurt."

In the bedroom at five-thirty, Laurie stands in her skirt, her neck arched back as Paul stands behind her, nuzzling her. The cold air from the air-conditioner fans across her belly. Laurie smiles at the ceiling. Her eyes are narrowed. Paul's hands reach under her arms to cup her breasts, she leans back against him and surveys the length of her body. It gives her a power and an immunity. Everything is ready. There will be no more surprises. She knows what she wants to know about Paul. She hasn't flipped, she hasn't let herself panic like she did when the windows were left open, and therefore she feels sure of herself. For all she cares, Paul's affair has been no intrusion, it hasn't existed and will not be brought into existence, not by her, and she will not allow it to escape from him. It has died and is securely buried.

His right hand detaches from her breast and picks a black speck off the skin over her stomach, then rests just inside the elastic of her waistband, the palm resting against her womb. She allows him this for a moment and then stands on tiptoe, offering herself to be stroked, already anticipating her own acquiescence. Her eyes close, and the bell from the kitchen timer shrills.

Laurie smiles wryly, and disengages, bending forward to allow Paul to remove his hand. She promises that it will not take a moment, she will not be a moment, why doesn't Paul go and lie down on the bed. No, she replies from the door, she won't take the skirt off, she'll keep it on. She just has to take the pie out of the oven, she won't be any time at all.

The pie is perfect, with the steamy, flannelly smell of apples rising through the caramel and cinnamon glaze. The warm air from the oven drifts around Laurie's breasts. She places the pie on the side to cool, closes the oven door, kills the oven and hangs up the glove on its hook.

She pauses to pluck at the creases in her skirt, freeing its sway. She likes the sexiness of discretion. The next time that she will arrange the skirt will be when she is sitting astride Paul, with him inside her, when she will lower her stare calmly from his and sit back, feeling him deeply and carefully within her, arranging herself and adjusting the hem of the skirt so that it drapes in a line across his navel, shrouding the meeting point of their bodies.

Anticipation is sacred, and Laurie knows well enough that sacredness can run harmlessly astray. So when she finds Paul not awaiting her in bed, but standing in front of the air-conditioner, naked and peering first at his stomach, then gazing into space, she approaches him demurely and kisses his shoulder, more inquisitive than intent on realising any sexual fantasy.

Paul is bemused. He sees specks floating in front of his eyes. He wonders if these floaters are a sign of age; but no, Laurie can see them too; and Paul is right, there are several tiny black specks clinging to the skin on his belly.

It's the thunderbug season. These specks are tiny little thunderbugs which get everywhere, even behind the glass on sealed picture frames. That's what they are. Laurie had better put a cloth over the pie.

You know, says Paul when she returns – by now she is considering whether or not to put on her underwear – I don't think they're thunderbugs. They leave a smear, like charcoal. You know what it's like, it's like when they burn straw, and the specks float across the porch from miles away.

Hon, says Laurie, they don't burn straw in Southern California.

No, Paul shrugs.

Laurie takes the matter in hand. She kneels and he watches her, holding her shoulders, uneasy at the coercion. He has time to reach for the remote control while Laurie draws the drapes. He watches on screen the fires in South Central. The camera pans back to capture unpatterned blotches of flame and a medley of black smoke plumes which lean crazily across the sky. A reporter stirs the brew.

Laurie turns back, disappointed.

Paul calms her. "I'll turn it off." He smiles ruefully, as though he has been teasing her.

"Just turn the sound down."

He does so. There is no sound, neither of them want sound. There is only a rasping swish as Laurie draws her black skirt across in front of the screen, her belly tanned, skin stretched tight, and the whiteness of her breasts hanging forward before she settles him within her and pauses to watch the confusion of senses trail across his eyes.

It is strange. Both of them feel that they might have a predicament; love is, but love is not going well for them. Sex might be something of a cure. They need love from each other. They must start again to appreciate each other. Sex must bring them close. They want to trust sex. It is of course full of pleasure, she is, and he is, concealed within her skirt, but the pleasure is soon enthroned in both their eyes, windows out of each frustrated sanctuary. Tiny cinders float across them from the air-conditioner, smudge against their nipples, black on red blush as they bite their lips and listen to the noise of the helicopters bobbing in and out of the body of the city. Their love-making is a strange defiance, mock ignorance near to exasperation. The Mathiessens are absorbed in the trading of sensation, to and fro, revitalising their economy of love. Together they defy the chaos which the networks decide to broadcast. Together they will triumph.

When they lie side by side, specks of burning city stuck to their sweat, Laurie feels in Paul a huge relief which rises almost tangibly from his body, like a prayer. As he falls asleep his muscles twitch, his body startles. He mumbles angrily at this interruption. He turns in a daze to face her, he sighs deeply. His top shoulder relaxes and slides inwards, his mouth loosens and his jaw drops; he whispers that he loves her, and he dozes.

Laurie lies on her back, eyes half closed, feeling that she has brought peace. She has claimed him. The black specks drift languidly through the air, indifferent and weightless. Laurie remembers visiting Pompeii with her classmates from high school, and seeing the centuries-old bodies set calmly in volcanic ash, shapes lying on benches in ruined houses. She bought a postcard, which is still in a box somewhere in 1717. It isn't the sort of postcard you could send to anyone. She had stolen more postcards than anyone else on the trip to Italy, and afterwards had never looked at the Renaissance again. Good days? Maybe they were; she wouldn't want to do them again, perpetually roller-coasting on flirtation. She wants this relationship to work. It must, and will, work.

Laurie starts to feel a little chilled by the air-conditioning. She opens her eyes and sits up on the end of the bed. On the TV screen there are soundless pictures of looting, people walking out of stores, ecstatically laden with stolen merchandise. Laurie sees frozen food, a broom; a dustpan, which amazes her. The looters look drugged with achievement. Even as she watches, a car pulls up, two men get out and saunter into the store and emerge each with a six-pack, and climb back into the car and drive off. Nobody in the crowd has bothered to steal the car, although most looters are badly in need of a car, the same as anyone with too many groceries to carry.

It is all kind of ridiculous. There is no structure. Some of the middle-aged women need help, they can't carry what they've stolen, they drop packages out of their arms. No-one pauses to help them. And two young boys are having a difficult time with a vacuum cleaner, neither of them can decide which part to get a hold of, they don't discuss it, and finally they just give up and drop it and go back inside the store.

And here comes a woman with two overflowing bags of canned food, who has lost one of her shoes, and it must be her delirium which protects her from the pain as she trudges entranced over the broken glass from the storefront. Just crazy. Why doesn't anyone tell her that she's going to end up in the hospital? Why doesn't she leave the groceries with her friend and go back and steal a pair of shoes? How long is it going to take her to get to a doctor? There is no structure, no thought.

Laurie shakes her head and is suddenly pissed at these little black specks which pirouette through the artificial twilight in the bedroom. She turns off the air-conditioner, and there is slowly a silence of warmth, a stirring of perspiration from her skin, which is not unpleasant because it feels like reality.

Laurie wonders at the dustpan. Why a dustpan? Godsakes, she had lived in that rooming-house in Boulder for more than a year without a dustpan, no-one could be bothered to get one, album covers were just as efficient. And would that woman bleed all the way home with her bags of petfood and soup and beans? Why didn't she get a ride with the guys in the car? Why didn't they load up the car?

There is something missing. It is a comedy of errors. Who would want to watch it on TV? There is something missing. Maybe it's the sound, maybe it has to have a commentary, maybe an endless jargon would flesh out patterns of coherence, like in sports programs, the corporate construction of trivia into significance, as relayed through a sublimely inane anchorperson.

Ten bucks' worth of food for an infected foot? The woman should have an ambulance. Laurie is tempted to pick up the phone, but she hasn't seen any street names. There is nothing she can do. She, too, is missing.

And then it strikes her, what else is missing. There are no police. There are no police anywhere, not in any of the camera shots. There are no police, no store attendants, no check-out staff, no baggers, no traffic cops, no gas station attendants, no fire department. There is no structure, no shape for the TV to show. It is all as formless as the air inside the bedroom, the random movements of the little black specks.

Laurie opens the drapes. It is a hazy, early evening; Saturday foreshortened, without a sunset.

She walks to the other side of the bed, finds the remote control, and shuts off the TV.

"Paul," she says brusquely.

He wakes immediately, his shoulders rise to lift the burden of sleep.

"It's six-thirty. The Matsons will be here in an hour. I'm going to shower off."

The skirt is creased and soiled, and she throws it onto her chair. Paul sits up and feels like the whole party is over. Everything has gone pretty well, considering. He feels like he should be able to call up Bill and Helen, and uninvite them. But it has been such a good, clean day and everything has been solved, he and Laurie are together, so there must be a tax to be paid somewhere. Bill and Helen and dinner. On his way to the shower, as Laurie is leaning forward towards the vanity mirror to apply her cosmetics, he rubs her butt affectionately.

Standing under the shower, with the hot water beating down on the nape of his neck, he remembers the riots. What should they do? What *could* he and Laurie do? Seriously.

ELEVEN

Saturday: 7.30p.m. to midnight.

They are running late.

Bill called up on his mobile. Some of the freeways were closed, others were gridlocked by stationary traffic. They might not have come at all, but as they had done more than half the journey Bill figured that they were committed.

"This is a *major* urban riot." Paul couldn't sit still, and stomped from kitchen to den to bedroom, where each of the televisions screened different coverage. "This is big, Laurie, this is out of control and spreading. This is a firestorm. Most all the channels are covering it. One of them just runs the pictures with classical music, it's like a Soviet funeral. It's like *Apocalypse Now* only more solemn, it's like a kind of requiem mass. Nobody can do anything about it, not a damn thing. People are getting shot out there."

"More than usual?" Paul was getting on Laurie's nerves. "Or instead of usual." And she was begining to get on her own nerves.

"This thing is serious," he insisted.

"I believe you."

"And nobody can do anything about it," he stated once again, for nobody's benefit.

"Does that mean we have to have it on every single television. Are we asking to be a part of it!" He stared at her resentfully. "All right," she said, "I don't want to know that I can't do anything about it. Are we supposed just to watch all this? Is there any kind of a decision we have to make? Do you have any ideas?"

"No. And in the middle of a riot what is it that white liberal lawyers do? Have ideas?"

"They act intelligently. They bring to the attention of worried white doctors the fact that they are not in the middle of a riot. They live on the hillside and they are surrounded by too many televisions. Hon?"

"Great. Sure."

"I can't even hear myself think."

He wandered off and killed the sound, first in the bedroom and then back in the kitchen. From the den a sporadic commentary bubbled through the sudden, fatuous silence; reminding Laurie of the golf matches which her father liked to watch in his study at home. But there was no sound of applause, and presumably no wide expanses of green fairway. She started to worry, it was contagious. She told herself to think, clearly. They were out of the trouble. Their dinner guests were still coming. They were not dealing with Apocalypse Now. There was no need to be afraid. She would not let them surrender to panic. She would play some jazz. Something heartfelt, melodic. The Biff Smith CD which Paul had given her last Christmas.

It was dusk, and as Laurie looked out of the window over the sink she saw wide beams of white searchlight thrown down to the city, presumably by helicopters; lights and orange fires were both muffled by rolls of black smoke. She could see them more clearly now that it was getting dark, and she saw how far they stretched.

It was horrifying. It made her feel sick. Night was coming, and she hadn't realised the extent of the fires. During the day they were patchy, but now, spreading out and spread across, they were a unity. It was like a war, but it couldn't be serious, not here, no. Not *here*, surely. On television. With television lights. With no sound over the vacuous, eerie silence: just the sudden, bubbling, skeetering noise of a helicopter passing overhead through jazz into the bowl of the city.

It had spread. Laurie could see through and into the falling darkness. The city was not so much punctuated by flame as breathing through flame, like a collapsed torso prodded by white needles, its head in the hills, its legs sprawling away towards the ocean.

She turned on the faucet. Cold water streamed noisily into the sink and down through the Insinkerator, a comforting and freshening noise, practical. Laurie forgot about Paul. She imagined that there was a vast reservoir of water up in the hills, which would burst and sweep through the fires like a gigantic storm, bending trees and sweeping debris away. And that she might be able, tomorrow, to walk through the whole of razed Los Angeles and pick out bleached mementoes, tangles of bits and pieces to keep as treasures, to wonder at how things got so tangled up together.

"What – " She startled at Paul's voice. " – are you doing?"

"Nothing." She felt guilty about forgetting him. She turned off the faucet.

"The gun is loaded, on safety. It's back in the drawer."

"Oh, okay." Somehow it had always seemed loaded and she hadn't ever considered that it needed loading, not in her calculations, when she might have needed the gun. "Okay. Why?"

"Because there's no good reason for having an unloaded gun."

"Unless there are children around."

"Right. But there aren't."

"Paul?" She didn't want to crap on him for his practicality, but she couldn't let him close this way. "Paul, what do you think is going to happen?"

"Here? Nothing. I don't know, but I don't think anything will happen."

"Should we check the fire sprinklers?"

"Hell no, it would ruin the furniture."

"But the fires have spread. You were right. I'm sorry. I just didn't want to mind it, not from the TV."

"There's probably something more intelligent to do."

"Yes . . . " She thought, and again looked out of the window. "You know, why don't you go find a map?"

"So we know how to get out . . . " He mused. "Leave the house?"

"Maybe. It's only a house."

"Do you want to pack?"

"I wouldn't take much. Photographs, I guess. You?"

"Sure, I'd take me if you didn't. But we might as well go together, don't you reckon? Save on gas."

She smiled. "You're such an asshole."

"Always?"

"Sometimes. Get the map. We know how to get out of here anyway. That may not happen. But you could track by streets how far this thing *is* spreading."

"That's not a bad idea."

Well, she breathed, it'll give you something to do.

At a quarter of nine, Laurie opened the door. Here were Bill and Helen, dressed casual, for dinner. Helen carried a gift of Korean starters. They were good. Laurie didn't like to eat anything too spicy, she got indigestion too easily at this stage of the pregnancy; Helen understood, and Laurie should try this, or this, and this. She herself would just smoke a cigarette, if that was okay with Laurie. She would stand outside on the patio. She was used to it. Bill wouldn't let her smoke in his car. They had come in Bill's car, so slowly that she might have gotten out and smoked a cigarette on the side of the freeway.

Paul laughed. He was pleased that they had arrived. He had felt isolated, up here on Jerome, with Laurie, watching everything burn. He was begining to scare. Stopping on the side of the freeway to have a cigarette brought the world down into focus. He asked Bill: "Is it safe to do that?"

"It's uniquely safe," Bill said, "you'd have to be out of your mind to do it at any normal time." Many other people were doing it, standing and watching the fires from the safety of the freeway.

"I don't mind if you smoke in here. I don't mind. Paul used to smoke cigars. Let me find you an ashtray. You can take it outside if you want to, but neither of us cares, really. Paul, do we have an ashtray?"

"It looks like we're going to have several hundred thousand square yards of ashtray," Bill said.

Paul laughed. "Like a scotch?"

"Sure."

"Over ice?"

"Sounds good to me."

"We have champagne," Laurie said. She couldn't find any ashtray, she handed a bottle of Moët to Paul and put a saucer in front of Helen.

"Champagne?" Paul desisted. "I don't know if this is the right time to celebrate. I don't know if this is . . . " He looked to Bill, who glanced at Helen.

"I would like some champagne," she said.

"So would I," said Laurie.

Paul filled glasses, and Helen said: "To your first baby!"

They drank, and Laurie suddenly remembered that the sushi had never been delivered. She explained, and she asked them what they wanted to eat.

From the den Paul called up five places, and either they hadn't opened up or else their delivery drivers hadn't come in to work. Voices asked him if he was crazy. He felt crazed. Time was moving right along. Eight, ten minutes. The others were talking in the kitchen. Bill came and refilled his glass. The champagne went to Paul's head. Bill leaned against the door frame, sipping scotch. Paul started going through the Yellow Pages. He drew blanks. He passed on street names to Bill. Bill fetched the map in from the kitchen table, and the marker, and the shaded area spread, like a bruise. Bill said: "I know that place, that's near . . . ", or: "You remember that restaurant, we ate there when . . . "

And Bill said: "That's Helen's area. One store on that street, another on the next block. The warehouse is right there."

"Helen's business!?"

"The family's."

"Hadn't you better tell her?"

"She knows. Tell her what? They're all down there with guns, all the men are. The Korean side of the family is pretty tight. They know about this kind of thing. The women are all over at our place with their kids. CBS may have it as a riot but to them it's a war."

"You're kidding!?"

"Undeclared. Naturally."

"What about Helen?"

"She's the management. The guys work for the business. That's how they get to live here. It's family."

Paul had never thought about Helen. He knew that she was half-Korean, married to Bill. She had something to do with a food program. He had placed her as a peripheral TV producer in cable, occasionally harassed, handsome, mixed-breed intelligence; he hadn't known anything about her.

"What are we going to do about this dinner?"

"Shit, I don't know. You got any eggs?"

Paul tried to think. "Yes, usually."

"Omelettes are okay by me. Helen likes them."

"Doesn't it piss you off that you can't get food delivered during a war?! Jeez, they can do it in Bosnia. How come they can't drop haute cuisine into California? Why the hell do we pay taxes?"

"I don't think that it's going to do Helen any good to see this stuff on TV."

"No." Paul shut it off. "I'm sorry, Bill. Thanks for coming. You should have taken a rain check."

"Hey, I wanted to touch base with something normal. I would have cancelled if I'd have known how bad the traffic was going to be. Half the people out there were driving back into the fringes to see what they could loot."

"Like *commuting*?"

"You'd better believe it. Whole families: Mom, Dad, and the older kids. And these guys banged up against all the white exodus traffic leaving town. Freeway overload, buddy. Once they shut the freeways down then maybe they can get the National Guard in."

"Laurie and I thought about leaving. What d'you reckon?"

"Sure. But I can't. I'm married to it. Helen won't budge. She started here. Her people don't go back, you know. I might just die with a bunch of Korean hors d'oeuvres on my lap."

"Is Helen, like, sensitive about being Korean? Do you guys talk about it?"

"No. We never talk about being American either. Helen's a businesswoman. The racist hassle comes from people who aren't good at business. She's good."

She was petite, and beautiful. Laurie thought so. Maybe this beauty came from her composure, and maybe it was in her manner of being polite, with a warmth that was naturally mannered.

They talked children, babies, bodies, interests in reading, families; nothing unsafe. There was no carelessness about Helen. She was sympathetic without being presumptuous.

Laurie was both grateful and relaxed in her company, and then maybe just a little bored. She was not bored with Helen. Helen was unpredictably intelligent and interesting. What Laurie felt were the stirrings of a boredom with herself, and with her own involvement in the pleasing formality of the occasion. She felt frustrated. The lines on Helen's face indicated no worry, nor even any concern that there were lines. Helen was balanced and worldly. She sat comfortably, with her back straight, one leg crossed over the other knee, hidden by the wide calf-length skirt; no jewelry except for a gold wedding band, and the perpetual cigarette resting between painted nails. Her dark, grey-brown eyes were not of the soothing mud variety but richly alert, despite an obvious tiredness. She reminded Laurie of Paul's father, twenty years younger but the same compact generosity, the same consideration, here an unpatronising maternalism.

And why, conversely, did Laurie feel such a struggle with defeat? *Did* she feel defeated? Why? What was the defeat? Boredom, her old weakness of boredom? That she didn't want to be herself. That she was just, somehow, slipping . . .

She refreshed Helen's glass.

"So will this riot affect you badly?" she asked.

"We have everything insured," Helen said. "But it will affect everyone badly. Homes, and businesses. We will protect what we can, but it will cut down on investment."

"Helen, what would you do if you have a child in the house, and someone breaks in? What would you tell a child to do?"

"I would tell the child that the things in the house don't matter, because they are insured, and so everyone should lie still. From the statistics, I don't believe that many unrelated intruders attack children. They aren't threatened by children. Adults threaten each other, don't you think so?"

"I just want to go on being optimistic, you know?"

She felt childish, but didn't care.

"You should be optimistic," said Helen. "Pessimists are asking for trouble. Always be optimistic."

Uh-oh. When Paul and Bill came back into the kitchen, Paul saw that Laurie was a little high. This was okay because he was a little high also. He liked it when the house was full of people. Well, when they had guests and Laurie looked good, in the way she moved around, knowing that she would be observed. Sometimes he missed the way she had been, in those lawyer days. By contrast, Helen looked graciously immoveable. Paul preferred Laurie, who rolled her eyes suggestively as she passed.

"Omelettes," he said.

"Bathroom."

"I'll make them."

"Sure," she called, walking briskly towards the bedroom, the sealed wooden floor creaking beneath her shoes.

"So how's the pregnancy going?" asked Bill.

"Great," said Paul.

He felt suddenly at a loss without her. He wanted to shake off Bill and be shut away with Laurie. Instead, he went to the fridge and got out the second Moët. He opened it over the sink, glancing at the fires which angrily splotched the regular starlight of street-lamps. South Central was a swamp of black around islands of flame, burning out. No power. There was still power nearer to Jerome. It was impossible to imagine the whole city black, like some dark basement out of which anything might crawl.

"South Central's out," he announced cheerily. "No lights."

"Nine-thirty," Bill observed.

"I'll do these omelettes. Helen, we're eating an everything omelette."

"I'd like that."

Inglewood and Downey suddenly teetered and went black. Paul stared.

He turned away and carried the champagne and the scotch over to Bill, at the kitchen table. Helen sat with an expression of distant amusement. "Helen? Bill, take care of this, will you?"

"Glad to."

Paul put a skillet on a low burner, and poured some oil. He was chopping onions when Laurie joined him, leaning her head against his shoulder. "You're sexy when you're cooking."

"It's like the *Titanic*," he said, thinking of the lights flickering off in the sinking areas of town.

"It *is* kind of quiet. Should we have some music?"

"Sure." He smirked, the sting of the onions getting to his eyes.

"I like Helen," she whispered. He wondered if she was trying to soothe him.

"Good." He turned and dumped the onions in the hot oil and ten seconds later the smoke alarm went off.

Ten-thirty

Apple pie, and no more of the city was lost to blackness. The fires were closer, weren't they?

The night was hot but they agreed not to use the air-conditioner. Helen saw no reason to smudge the furniture. So the dining room was overpoweringly insulated; the candles burned perfectly upright, fluttering only in accord with conversation. Having liked Helen, Laurie talked with Bill; Helen, designated driver, talked with Paul.

Helen. Paul wanted to fill gaps. Laurie didn't like business, he did. He wanted to understand, and to show that he understood. Importing. Storage. Work force. Advertising. Cash flow. Distribution. Loans and investment. Percentages. This much Paul understood. Helen's skin was aging, but there was nothing wrong. The darker skin could handle sun – a genetic and racial aptitude.

Bill. Laurie wanted him not to short-change her, for Paul's sake. He was cute enough, nothing special. He was serious, with an annoying adolescent humor to get the seriousness out of the way. He had eyes for her but he really wasn't very interesting when he came on. He couldn't flirt to save his life. Laurie imagined that he could be lousy and vulgar, given half a chance;

but she couldn't imagine that chance being given by Helen. She saw dissatisfaction beneath his veneer of well-being. She preferred Paul's worry, which in its own way stopped her from becoming as complacent as Helen might be, behind a desk – across the dinner table, as Paul threw softball questions at her shell. Paul was good at taking an interest.

Helen's family. Korean? Or half-Korean. Korean-American, yes. Paul was interested. Helen's mother had moved over here with her father, had married him. They had started importing from Korea. With his army money, and her work and her family. He lived in New Hampshire now, he went back to his home town. He was a supervisor in a shoe factory. Blue eyes, and quiet. Taciturn. Different. Her mother was still married to him; the family paid into a pension fund which he didn't know about. Helen had been to see him in New Hampshire, in Manchester, which didn't suit her. She had seen him more recently in Boston. They had thought about doing some business, but it wasn't his way of life, which she and her mother understood. One of the reasons she liked the United States was that there was no pressure towards any single way of life. There was the fundamental freedom to work at whatever you wanted to do. Truthfully, she couldn't understand why there were no Afro-Caribbean restaurants in a cosmopolitan place like Los Angeles. Did Laurie know of any? But Laurie was talking with Bill.

So much for Bill. Paul was the one who had had an affair. Which she herself knew about. She deduced that Bill didn't know about it. Bill would be an average "several affairs" guy, needy and irresponsible. Helen wouldn't consider it. It wasn't business. Helen made a lot of money, Bill would only commute to any other bed. Bill would have told Paul over lunches about hot little numbers, most likely agency nurses at his practice. They would go for his lean jaw and all that piercing eyes stuff, and the free cosmetic treatment for themselves and their teeth, and maybe their children's teeth. One of the things that symbolised America, that represented America and the individual according to Bill, was the smile. Really? And strong teeth. That was his, own, philosophy. For real. Bill *had* something there. He had thought of writing a paper for one of the dental journals. Screw orthodontistry – fill Bill's glass. Some more pie? She would stick to water from now on.

Helen. The name. Paul was interested. Some more apple pie? Okay. So she had the choice of her own name – her mother's family name – or the American name. Why did she choose "Helen" instead of the ethnic original? So there is no such thing as a static identity, she didn't believe in it. Yes, he could understand that. It wasn't like an attempt to avoid . . . anything? She didn't *look* ultra Korean, like Koreans do. Okay so it wasn't a negative, rejection thing; it was positive to go forward. Sure, you could call yourself anything you liked. No? But her *brothers* changed back?! Why did they do that? The whole thing is strange, that whole thing of shame because of being half-Korean *is* strange, you know, Laurie? Why is that?

The tennis club, Bill? No, she didn't go there very often. It was Paul's hang-out. She wouldn't step on the guys' territory. Anyhow, this pregnancy would kill tennis for a while. Paul had picked up some business over there and, she hoped, nothing else. "Hell hath no fury . . . " Who got free skin treatment off of Paul? She might run a check, but how? Not through Alice. Who would like some coffee?

"Paul, would you fix some coffee?" She stood up.

"Sure."

"Great pie, Laurie."

"Why, thank you." And smile, fine teeth; she wouldn't change her dentist.

Helen looked exhausted. They all looked tired, Laurie thought, glancing at herself in the mirror in the hallway. Doesn't Helen ever go to the bathroom? She heard Paul call.

"Hey, it seems to have died down."

"They've been going at it for twenty-eight hours." Bill's voice.

"Maybe it's over."

"Or they've run out of gasoline. I wouldn't bet on everything being over."

"You think it's just gone into darkness?"

You dumb jerk, Laurie thought, listening to it all. With Helen sitting there worrying. She's the only person we know who's caught up in this. It's her business, you jerk, and who knows who might be firing a bullet at her brothers!

"You know what else happened today, or yesterday? They got the manifesto guy."

"I heard. I never understood anything about that."

"Uh-huh."

No-one else cared. What was it with Paul and this manifesto guy!?

Laurie finished up, did her lips and hair, and walked back to the dining room.

"I don't envy those guys," Paul was saying. Coffee steamed in mugs.

"Paul, we have demitasses, you know. It doesn't matter. What guys?"

"The National Guard. They've set up base near where Bill and Helen live. They're going in tomorrow. Maybe they've gone in already?"

"I don't think so, but I sure don't envy them."

"They're not there to be envied," Helen said. They're there to do a job. We pay them like we pay the police, and neither they nor the police have done *anything*, other than leaving people to kill each other." Said with a contempt and an anger which silenced her husband.

Paul muttered a "No . . . " into the silence.

Laurie sipped at her coffee. "What about Alice?"

"She hasn't called."

"It's been really kind of you to come." Laurie held both Helen's hands and kissed her. "I admire you. I feel like I should apologise for everything."

"Nothing is your fault." Helen smiled. "I would rather eat an omelette than anything else. And it's been good to get away from home. Especially to see you so well." She walked with Laurie down the hall.

"You'll be all right getting back?" Paul said to Bill.

"For sure."

"You can stay if you like. There's room."

"I noticed, but we'll take off. Hell, I only have to pick up the car phone and there'll be a four-wheel drive full of gun-totin' relatives at the next corner."

"I'd better phone the security company. They can be a little jumpy at late-night visitors. They'll get your car registration on their radio."

"Are they Afro, Hispanic, or white?" Bill grinned.

"I don't know. Mixed. Equal opportunity."

"Well, I'll try and find a place for lunch next Friday, if there's anything left standing. I'll call you. And thanks. We should do it again."

"Soon."

"Our place."

"You got it. Bye Helen."

He gathered Laurie in against him and looked up at the dark hillside, not a star to be seen, a smell of smoke different from the scent of oak or pine. He waved as Bill's car went away down the street. "I have to call the security company," he said. "Maybe check the news. We must be the only people who have spent the evening ignoring everything."

Paul closed the door behind them, and bolted it. Laurie walked on into the dining room. Paul went to the den and called the security company. He surfed the television, which showed wall-to-wall black sitcom and soul concerts. There was one incoming call on the answering machine. Laurie's father growled from the east: 'Stay out of trouble and you'll be fine. Blacks don't like to climb hills.'

They were out of trouble now. Paul opened the bottle of cognac for himself.

Little of the brandy got drunk. Laurie thought that the best thing about having people over to dinner was talking in bed about them when they had gone. Paul was just glad that the invitation was over. Water retention – now was that a Korean trait?

Paul forgot to tell her that there was no answer from the security company, but neither of them were sufficiently awake to notice the lack of headlights patrolling across their bedroom ceiling.

TWELVE

Sunday: 2.35a.m. to 2.45a.m.

Paul woke up suddenly. His body felt as though it hadn't slept and didn't need any sleep, as though he hadn't exercised enough during the day. But his head was thick with sleep and a logjam of alcohol which hadn't yet begun to break up.

He wondered what had woken him, if Laurie had snored. She did this sometimes, in her pregnancy, and disturbed his sleep.

She lay, turned away from him. Her breathing was quiet and regular; his watch showed nearly twenty of three.

If Laurie had stirred, then he would have reached down under the covers and teased her groin. She would have spread easily from sleep, she liked being taken from behind when she was half-asleep, and there was no talk and sleep would follow after him. Laurie liked that.

But she didn't stir, and Paul knew that he was only teasing himself.

The idea, however, had him awake, and would pester him.

Then he wanted a soda. He couldn't get the thirst for it out of his head. He could go into the kitchen and sit with a cold 7-Up. And the riots. He *ought* to get up, to check things out. Why had he woken? – to check that everything was as okay as he and Laurie had decided it was, an hour ago.

Quietly he slid out from under the comforter. He felt for his sweatpants, and walked across the carpet to the bedroom door.

They had shut the bedroom door. That was a habit; it had become a habit, Lord knows why.

Laurie was out. She didn't move when the door brushed across the carpet. He had suggested they get a carpenter in, to shave the bottom of the door so that it swung easily, but she had wanted to keep the sound as it was, to serve as notification that the door was opening. He guessed that she wasn't too notified this time around, but he left the door ajar in the unlikely event that she awoke and wanted to know where he had gone. She always wanted to know where he was. He liked that. And she might come looking, and – who knows? – they might go back to bed and take up where they had left off.

The lights in the kitchen near scraped every thought out of his mind. He fumbled with the dimmers, and needed that soda. The refrigerator light wasn't too subtle, but condensation rose quickly on the outside of the can and beckoned. He poured the 7-Up into a glass, and drank down half of it before it had settled. Both the taste and the coldness were good. He burped with a satisfying, noisy violence.

She was sound asleep, sure enough.

Paul looked out of the window over the sink and, sure enough, there were fewer fires, and they seemed to have retreated. Helicopter searchlights concentrated on the blacked-out area. In some parts the power had been restored. Things weren't normal, but they were getting there, back to being normal. Some different Saturday! The dinner party, the riots. What was it Laurie's father had said – "Blacks don't go uphill"? The man was a fucking racist. An okay guy, but Jeez . . .

Things were okay. 1717 was A O-kay. He and Laurie were doing great and getting along fine.

One soda, and then church tomorrow. Ten-thirty, today. Wake whenever. And give thanks.

Would the riots ever have gotten close?

Who could tell?

Maybe, like with a forest fire, it would do a lot of good to get things cleared out.

It was kind of a shame that he couldn't make the steam-room on Sundays, though. Especially after a dinner party. But the church was good, Laurie was right. Church was something they did together. And maybe . . .

If things were quiet, maybe they would go down and take a look at the riot area, from the freeway. Take some photographs. Maybe Laurie would get a good picture for the office wall. Frame it, and have a forest burn-out picture on the same wall. The nature of things. And new life, as green baby pines started up out of the cindered forest floor.

He let the faucet run, and washed his mouth out, rubbing his gums with his finger. He killed the lights and, already thinking himself into bed, ambled down the hallway to check the security alarm.

Opening the box, he saw that they had forgotten to set the alarm. He cussed himself.

He tapped in: 0034. The warning tone might wake Laurie up. But it didn't. The red standby light flashed.

He was tired now, and he cussed again. The circuit was broken somewhere. Hunt the fucking circuit at three o'clock in the morning?! What the hell had Laurie left open this time?

He switched the alarm off. He thudded back into the kitchen and saw that the windows were closed. The next place to check was the basement room downstairs, Laurie's room.

He didn't bother with any lights until he reached the stairs far away from their bedroom, by the door leading to the garage. He flicked the lights on, and went down.

The door to her room was open and there was a neonish grey light. She had left the word processor on. Paul sighed. And presumably during the afternoon she had been out under the deck to water the plants. Uh-huh. Sure thing. The french doors were half open, the lights of Los Angeles pushing an orange glow up against the acrid-smelling gloom. Paul went across and closed the doors; and locked them.

Waywardly inquisitive, he went to look at the word processor He read the last page of her Christmas letter, the "wonderful, joyful", not quite knowing what it was.

He heard a scratching sound, louder than his heart. It wouldn't matter if the word processor stayed on all night. It was made to stay on for days. It shouldn't matter.

The shuffling sound didn't come from the machine. Paul turned, and in the light cast from the screen he saw a black guy, crouched by the easy chair, the palms of his hands held up, empty. Paul turned back towards the door: he looked for a paperweight, a baseball bat, anything; but there was nothing with which he could defend himself.

He froze.

"Paul?"

"Who are *you*?" he demanded; but even as he said it he knew the answer.

"Mel, man . . . Mel. You know *me*."

Paul stared. He closed the door to upstairs. And the only thing he could think to say was: "Why?"

Sunday: 2.47a.m. to 3.02a.m.

"Babe . . . "

"You can't stay here," Paul whispered. "Anything else. Anything. Maybe I can take you somewhere. Anything. Do you need money?"

But Paul saw that all his offers met only with contempt. Mel – how Paul hated that name – cast his eyes superciliously at the ceiling. His top lip twitched, his mouth made a dry, sucking noise, over and over again. Paul couldn't tell whether this was deliberate or not, this lizard-like act, this sudden clicking of his tongue which rattled the silence like a dice-shaker.

"Money? Not money. I need somewhere safe."

No noise, Paul prayed, please God make no noise. This has all got to be rational, this has all got not to happen. Please. Please. This can disappear.

He had shut the door, and the ceiling light was on. Laurie would not be able to see the light from their bedroom, but she might see it from the kitchen. He followed Mel's sneer around the walls, watching it smear across his and Laurie's framed California prints, gallery pictures of beach scenes in strong colours, restaurant posters of chillis and peppers and tomatoes, and on the crib Laurie's collection of stuffed animals, old and valuable bears, sentimental and personal bedmates, and brand new friends which they had bought together for the baby. At which this man, this Mel, hissed his disdain.

Paul felt sick, and weak to his stomach, and embarrassed, and desperate.

"This is Laurie's room," he pleaded, as though neither of them should be in here, as though there was the chance that Mel might decide now to bow out gracefully, like a gentleman.

"I should say so. May I have something to drink?"

Paul obeyed. Paul went to the bathroom and ran a glass of water, and handed it over to Mel, and retreated smiling, with a painful, convivial falsity; while Mel sipped.

"You see, you can't stay here," he said encouragingly. "You wouldn't want to stay here," he said with authority. "It would be hellish." He smiled. Just a little complicity, maybe, just a little and Mel would surely understand.

"She here?"

"Yes, she's asleep upstairs."

"Oh, baby, so she doesn't know. And now you're going to say to me: she doesn't know *what*? Isn't that right? She doesn't know *what*?"

"Anything." He could hardly speak, through the rush of blood to his head and the sick dread fermenting underneath.

"Oh, come on! Laurie is no part of this?"

Don't say "Laurie"! Don't use "Laurie"! "She's not any part of what happened."

"That's the truth, sweetheart. No part of *what.*" Mel smiled. He whispered: "Wake up, Laurie . . . "

"No – what's the point?!"

"Man, will you stay calm?!"

"You can't stay here. It would destroy us. It would destroy everything. Don't you understand? Please understand, Mel . . . anything, anything else that you want . . . please. Please . . . "

When Paul looked up, he saw the glowing kindness expressed in the man's eyes. It gave Paul that same feeling as it had done before, when he had met Mel, that everything would be all right. That Mel was not a bad man, not a threat. That however incapable and clumsy and fucked-up Paul was, Mel would make everything all right. Mel would take away his feeling of nausea and his worry. Mel would understand when he understood nothing. He didn't understand anything. Mel would understand.

Sunday: 3.04a.m. to 3.13a.m.

"How did you come here?" Paul whispered. "Isn't there a curfew?"

"Oh yes."

"I mean here. How did you know this address?"

"I have your driver's license and here all this other plastic. You aren't the first married man I slept with, but you have to be the most careless." He handed Paul his card wallet. "It's all there."

"Thank you."

"Check it."

"I'm sure I don't need to." He put the wallet away, out of sight, in the pocket of his sweatpants.

"You are one sure human being."

"Sometimes."

"And that is why you didn't call? Not once."

"I'm sorry."

"That is what I assumed."

"I'm sorry, Mel."

"It happens."

"Does it often happen like that, just once?"

"May be."

"And only the one time, like now. And then it's finished. It's just something that happened the one time and that's all. Like nothing. Like it didn't happen."

"I hear you, man. 'And no hard feelings'; right? No hard feelings?"

"That's not it. That's not the way it – "

"Sure . . . "

"Can you understand?"

"I understand, all ways, lover."

Sunday: 3.13a.m. to 3.21a.m.

"You can't stay here . . ."

"You have a baby?"

"No. Not yet. It's months yet."

"Seems that way. I said to myself Paul doesn't have the baby yet, it's too quiet in here. I don't smell diapers and all that shit. You understand what I'm saying. It's peaceful. Everybody sleeping peaceful."

Sunday: 3.24a.m. to 3.40a.m.

"You can't stay here!"

"I understand you, Paul. I understand you. It's too dangerous for you, baby. I understand this shit. Man, I know how you are, I know what you're going through. I understand how you're feeling, Paul. I can see that. I can understand it, man! I do. You look tired, lover. I know what you're going through. I understand. Shit just happens."

"You know, I just feel that – " How would he force Mel to leave?

"Tell me what you feel. You tell me what you feel and I'll tell you what happens, you know what happens? You understand that people are killing each other all over this town? You know down there? You remember down there? You understand that the LAPD show pictures of Afros to the Hispanics and pictures of the Hispanics to Afros, and they say Hey, get these guys, shoot these guys if you see them. They say Give these guys a hard time! You don't like the Koreans, you give them shit, man. Hey, you Koreans, shoot these niggers! Understand! Sweetheart?"

"You have proof of that?"

"Bay-bee!"

"How do you know?"

"Understand, anybody can kill anybody down there. And they're doing it!"

"Jesus . . . "

"Bang!"

"But you *can't* stay here."

"I understand, man, I know where you are, no hard feelings."

He thought of waking Laurie. He thought of telling her. He thought of calling their home number on the mobile so that they could respond together to an imaginary call for help. He thought of having Mel go round to the front door. He thought of them letting Mel stay for the night, through the curfew which Mel said lasted until eight in the morning.

He told this idea to Mel.

And again Mel's superciliousness spread across the room. There was no deal.

Shame chased him down every blind alley, like a vengeance. There was nowhere to hide.

"I understand you, lover. I know how hard this is for you, right now. I want to help you, Paul."

There it was again, Mel's kindness; that "kindness", condescending and triumphant, that "understanding" which was so debilitating.

"How? I have my wallet and I'm grateful, believe me. But how would you help me?" Paul asked, weary and unnerved.

All charity went.

"*You* came to *me*. As I recall. You don't recall? I got no time for all this Queen Jerome. If I open my mouth, what are you going to fill it with? Shit . . ."

"Listen – "

"Do you have something that you want to whisper to Mel?"

"You can't stay here."

"One time. May I use your bathroom? I would hate to defile your garden. Allow me to run that by you, oh please." He sauntered to a statuesque stance before the window, lithe and tall and muscular. Paul remembered his body, with shame. "Is that what you call it, your 'garden'? I see that it is. I would just abhor any such intrusion on *my* garden, angel. So where *is* the bathroom?"

"It's in here."

Paul obeyed. He opened the door and switched on the light.

Mel smiled graciously, and watched him. Paul caught the lightest scent of cologne as he came closer. "Hey, Paul . . ." Mel said, "I was an ugly kid too, when I was young. We all get to grow into ourselves." He went on into the bathroom, leaving Paul with the scent and his body-smell – of polished, locker-room allure – which Mel drew with him behind the sliding partition.

"No peeking . . ."

Sunday: 3.35a.m to 3.42a.m.

Laurie found herself awake. Her stomach was heavy, like she had swallowed a block of lead. She could kill for a glass of water.

She didn't want to be awake, and didn't want to think about what to do; but the weight pushed heavily against her diaphragm and she would have to sit up, and stand up, and go into the bathroom for something to deal with this indigestion; which she might probably manage to do without opening her eyes too much, and maybe without switching on the bathroom light; so sleep wouldn't escape.

All this procedure she followed, and came back to bed where there wasn't anything of Paul other than his smell on the pillow. She snuggled and tried to doze. She still felt lousy.

She lay on her back, aching for sleep. Her legs shifted restlessly and she was glad that Paul wasn't next to her and couldn't be disturbed. She needed to burp, but that too had gotten stuck.

She gave up. She might at least go out to the kitchen and complain to Paul, who was presumably staying up drinking; and she needed to walk around with this darned indigestion, and talk and bum some sympathy.

She put on a T-shirt and pushed her hair back.

The kitchen was dark. There was only the noise of the refrigerator. "Paul?" No light came through from the dining room.

He hadn't done this before. Maybe she had been snoring, and he had gone to sleep in the guest room.

She liked the dark. She didn't want to be startled by light, or by him.

She switched on the lights in the hallway. She half-expected to see him sitting in the lounge.

She didn't. She saw him running silently up the stairs from the basement, a-ways away down the hall. "Paul?"

He came closer. He was bringing something, she saw. Like he was bringing something. "Paul . . . ?" He came, very quickly, closer, bringing a wave of fear. "What's – "

"Get the gun."

"Where . . . ?"

"Laurie, get the gun, quickly. Don't make any noise!"

She turned and ran. She thought, Get the gun!

Feet too noisy?

Quickly!

She thought, There's someone in the house.

Across the bedroom carpet. No noise. Screw the noise.

She thought, Downstairs.

She ran across the bed. She pulled open the drawer. She got the gun.

She thought, Why does Paul look that way? Why isn't he flipped out?

Back across the bed.

She thought, He's flipped out.

She ran down the hallway, a long run, hardly any sound.

She had seen this before. Like in the Olympic relay race. It all screws up at the changeover, the baton gets dropped.

There was no Paul. She ran towards the stairs.

She thought, Keep the gun, hold it right, keep the gun.

Slow now, slow at the top of the stairs.

Round the outside. Maximum visibility.

Hold the gun out in front, both hands.

Slowly. Quietly. Go down.

Don't let the movie run away.

At the bottom of the second flight of stairs there was Paul, by the half-opened door.

More light, suddenly, in the basement room. There was someone in there.

Paul was saying: " . . . got to go *now*! She's coming. Now!"

He turned and saw her. He mouthed silently, Give me the gun! His mouth wide open.

She motioned Paul out of the way, pointing the gun at him. She reached him. He opened the door – why!? He had his hand on somebody's shoulder, pushing the shoulder away – why? She pushed past Paul. She saw the intruder, she saw that he was black. Paul said: "Give me the gun, Laurie." The black, she appreciated, was a good-looking guy. Cute. Handsome. He had his hand on Paul's arm – fighting?

Then coming forwards, his hands out: "Hey . . . Pau – "

She shot him.

The decision scared her. The noise scared her, the confusion.

He was scared. He was wild in running. Dangerous now, crazy.

Paul jumped back, he was holding his hands up to his ears.

Laurie saw in Paul's eyes nothing, nothing for her. He was looking at the black man. She screamed at him: "Say something!" He was looking at the black man with sorrow. She screamed at him. "Do something!" He looked forlorn with sorrow.

And the black was definitely fighting now. His body leapt gigantic onto the chair by the french doors. He screamed filth and hate. He kicked over the chair, crashed a table lamp to the floor. And she shot at him, once again; twice. Until 1717 was motionless.

Sunday: 3.42a.m.

Three times. She had fired three times.

The noise ran up against Paul and passed through him; and slapped against the wall and toppled back through him, crashing repeatedly, stunning him. The noise swept from side to side, breaking against the walls, falling back upon its own echo, tilting the room with its momentum. At one moment the left side of the room, with the easy chair, with the body, climbed and reared. Spots and smears of blood lost their hold on the white wall and reached down towards the carpet. Then the noise swung, and the storm rushed, and the stuffed animals on the crib climbed high with placid and grotesque smiles.

Paul reached out an arm to steady himself. His hand was numb and the fingers were numb as they closed on the bathroom door, and the door itself was still part of the tilting room. He looked at Laurie, but she was not saying anything. He thought that she had said something, he was sure that he had missed what she said, and that he was deaf, or dreaming; and his next thought was that when the dream ended they would be separated.

All this came. Thoughts came like nightmares. The noise sagged into a deadweight of silence which filled his head. He felt top-heavy. Silence seeped from his ears. The room should stay still, like a waxwork tableau. Nothing should move. No-one should say anything. Laurie should be able to stand motionless, as she stood, with both her arms out in front of her, holding the gun. Her arms should never get tired. Neither of them should ever say anything, neither of them should ever hear anything. The silence should stay.

The silence condensed, like steam. His eyes closed. He bowed his head.

PART FOUR

Paul, Laurie and Mel

THIRTEEN

March.

He had decided in March that Laurie was leaving him, and he could see that it would be right for her to leave him. He couldn't find a way to care for her; he couldn't think how to care. He couldn't feel any caring inside himself. Perhaps she was right to leave him, because perhaps she had exhausted him. He had nothing to offer her.

Laurie had been two months pregnant. It was March, which shouldn't make any difference. He had neither the will nor the desire to go away with her. Not to his family in Colorado, not to her family in the east.

He was, dimly, capable of wondering why he was so depressed. He did know that he was being unfair to her. He didn't want to be cruel, he had no intention of being cruel; and he couldn't understand why his own unhappiness should amount, in her eyes, to cruelty. He wasn't mean. It was just that he wasn't anything; he knew this and could only apologise, and it hardly surprised him that his apologies didn't amount to much, not in Laurie's eyes.

Laurie didn't take up the offer of any apology. He was unable to react to her analyses, which, as far as he knew, might be right. He thought that she would, and should, let him be. It would be logical, and justified.

He wished her no harm. On the contrary, he wished her every

wonder and happiness in the world, as should befit Laurie with the wonder and happiness of her first baby.

He didn't wish her the gift of his own melancholy. He didn't want to shift that onto her. He wanted to keep his unhappiness to himself, and to deal with it; he didn't want to discuss his unhappiness with her, he didn't know how to discuss it. He was so exhausted that he couldn't begin to think about it, for himself. He didn't want it to be contagious, he wanted it withheld. Definitely withheld.

Her reasoning – about his becoming a father – was probably right, and it would be wonderful if her reasoning worked like surgery, or even aspirin. But these reasons for his unhappiness, they in no way touched upon him. The depression did not consist of reasons. It consisted of him, and the consistency hardened whenever he was with Laurie. God knows why. Paul didn't understand why. When he said that he loved her, he wasn't lying. He was trying, but there existed no love that he could give her; there seemed to be no love that was worth giving her. She was contained, she was self-sufficient.

Therefore he set himself to contain his own unhappiness. He was sure that he dealt with it very well. For the most part he lived with a feeling of eccentricity. In his mind he succeeded in divorcing himself from the depression, in his daily life it was as though he lived near it, as a neighbor. Occasionally he would come across this neighbor and treat him courteously; one of those acquaintances with whom one would never do lunch, for fear of succumbing to a needless and capricious examination. In this daily life his unhappiness never showed itself. Paul was light-hearted, and almost independent. Paul watched himself with a kind of giddy joy, in his daily life. He seemed to be making the right moves. He seemed to be mature. He was successful, with a fine home and an attractive wife, with the prospect of a family. Things didn't get to him.

Laurie got to him. She dug out his neighbor. She teased this unhappiness up from behind locked doors, she went out of her way to make it socially acceptable, decreed how it should behave and how it should dress. And so his unhappiness became gauche, and clumsy, and a figure of fun for as long as she chose to be entertained by it. Sometimes Paul felt that the larger part of himself was picked out of a cage like a household pet, at Laurie's whim, to amuse and irritate her. God, sometimes he envied such an attitude, even when he was painfully at the butt end of her jibing inquisition. Her own happiness struck at him and caught him off guard, he couldn't match it. He wanted to protect himself but was defenseless. For, once out in the open, his unhappiness followed her around like a ball and chain, dogging her every exasperation.

He was exhausted by her. He was entirely sick of himself and the way he undermined her.

March; not that it made any difference, not in Los Angeles.

What was the difference?

He needed to find a reason that would satisfy her, something that would prevent them talking about himself, something on the outside that would leave the inside alone. Something about which he could pretend to worry, and which both of them could believe would sooner or later go away.

Paul was attentive to specialist medical journals, but he rarely bothered to digest what was written in the newspapers. He contented himself with scanning the headlines and reading the opening paragraphs, which enabled him to join in whatever topic of conversation his patients might care to bring up, thereby soothing the awkwardness prior to an examination. There were endless opportunities for worrying about the world, but the correctness of worry couldn't be allowed to overshadow the benevolent efficiency which his patients required of him. Pessimism cornered no markets.

In February there had occurred two murders: of the Vice President of a Software company, and of a doctor. Paul had noticed the reports, his initial reaction being one of anger that Vice President Timothy A. Hubris had merited constant upper-case entitlement while doctor Suro Ky, whose name and reputation Paul appreciated, was despatched in lower-case. These days, a Vice President was at one remove from a telephonist; every single company was clogged with Vice Presidents whose only claim to social distinction was that they were able to code-dial each other direct.

Once over his anger, and then some shock at the violent killing of such a leader in medical research, Paul had wondered why Timothy A. Hubris should have been linked with Doctor Suro Ky. He read the article, and then the feature, and then the Sunday analysis.

"Who is Doctor Suro Ky?" Laurie had asked, when he handed over the paper.

"He's a brilliant man. He's head of research in skin cancer at UCSC."

"And Grace Laboratories."

"I don't know. Why does that matter? Have we got stock in Grace Laboratories?"

Laurie looked up. "What's eating you?"

"The guy's dead."

"I know. I'm sorry. I didn't know that you knew him. Did he mean a lot to you?"

"No, not really. Maybe." He stood up. He tapped his fingers on the kitchen table. "Laurie, I don't know who's doing this thing."

"Nor do the police."

" – these manifestos, all this pattern of killings."

"Do you know any of the other victims: Mill, Demello, Rabik?"

"No."

"Then it isn't a pattern. Maybe it is, for the LAPD, but not for you. Paul, there's nothing in it for you."

"Okay, maybe not."

"Bashka Kiesco got killed. I ran across Bashka Kiesco a couple of times, so what? It isn't any pattern for me. Why should it be?"

"But the guy thinks about it, Laurie. He has a pattern."

"It doesn't mean that *you* have to think about it." She went across to the stove. "If you think that you know anything about it then call the LAPD."

"I don't know anything about it, except what's in the *Times*."

"Then leave it alone. Forget about it. It's not our – your – problem."

"No," he said lightly, "it just gives us something to talk about."

"Well maybe we should find something less horrible to talk about. You've started to fixate on these things. It's so useless."

"Would you like some tea?"

"I'm *making* some tea."

"Great. Then I'll have a beer."

"Do that."

Later she had said, "I am sorry for the guy you knew."

He had replied, "It doesn't matter. There was no big buddy thing." And at least she hadn't questioned his state of mind.

Paul had never, not once in his life, met Dr Suro Ky. But he found himself looking up Suro Ky's papers in the journals, and reading them, and talking with Abe Deane about the murders.

"Yup," said Abe, "there's someone out there sure enough, some asshole with an axe to grind. There always is. Life's full of 'em. They have to market their bullshit somehow. Someone should publish a complete edition of this guy's political thoughts to add to all the other bullshit around. Pens and bullets make the same lack of impact on the system these days. Sooner or later they'll make a movie about it, starring some other asshole with good teeth and better skin who'll send me a couple of freebie tickets. I can't hardly wait for the credits to roll."

Paul set himself to wait. At that time they hadn't come up with the dual-killing theory, not in black and white. He waited to see what would happen.

"I think it goes in twos," he said to Laurie.

"Okay, so tell the LAPD."

Paul waited to see what would happen, whether Laurie would leave him.

He waited at the airport, stood with her while she checked in, handed her the present for her parents. He wanted her to go away. He wanted her to have a good time. Neither set of lips was warm, as they kissed. He waited until she had gone through the gate, and then he stood, waiting.

He didn't know what he felt, although he tried to decide. It was a Friday. The departure building was crowded. There were rushes of purpose, past him and around him. It struck him as bizarre that all these people were probably going somewhere where they would be well-received, where they were expected and would be warmly greeted. There were thousands of ties, like elastic, drawing people towards each other, from hundreds of miles away. A massive dispersal into joyful compartments, great happiness, dissolution of care.

He felt, suddenly, a surge of pleasure; as though Laurie was next to him and sharing the joy. But, of course, she wouldn't have shared the joy since the joy came hard on the heels of her departure. It was his joy, and it could only have come when she had gone. Truthfully he couldn't imagine wanting to be seated next to her on the plane. It wouldn't have worked. It wouldn't have been the same. Or rather, it *would* have been the same; they would not have been happy, not together.

He was aware that he ought to have been in tears, standing in the concourse. But sorrow seemed like a flippant, careless emotion. Love seemed more apt. Love flew away to any one of a hundred destinations, anywhere. Nowhere, and was lost anyhow in any direction. He waited and watched the departure screen.

Her flight was boarding. It was boarding for a long time and then she was gone.

She was out of his mind.

Maybe, he speculated, she was out of *her* mind, and always had been.

He looked around the concourse and saw that everyone was out of their mind, crazy and intent. You couldn't understand how anything, anyone, hung together.

He wasn't scared of his unhappiness. He had it covered.

He drove back to the office, late for his last appointment of the week.

"What's wrong?" Alice demanded.

"Nothing," he said.

His patient, attractive, even sexy, complained that his fingers were cold.

"Cold fingers, warm heart," he informed her, smiling, and ran his hands under the hot water faucet. Either her skin, or his fingers, were numb. He felt nothing. It wasn't that all women were the same; it was, suddenly, that all women had the same effect on him. He hoped that she didn't notice.

Abe poked his head around the door before leaving, and asked him if he wanted some dinner, and wasn't dismayed when Paul begged off.

"Are you stayin' late?" Alice enquired.

"Yes, I think I will."

"We have cleaners, you know, Doctor Matthiessen."

"I know. I'll see you all out."

"They went through the usual rigmarole of parading outside the office door. Nurses and staff dispersed to their cars, wishing each other a good weekend. He went back inside and locked the outer door, then washed his hands in the examination room. He saw that his office was in order, and that Monday's appointments offered no great surprise.

Neither would there be anything out of the ordinary at 1717, home. There wouldn't yet be any message from Laurie on the answering machine. Later on, the machine might go beeping its heart out along the empty hallway, its plaintive appeals asphyxiated by the thick carpet and overstuffed sitting-room chairs. 1717 made the grade in uncomforting comfort.

Paul lifted Alice's television up onto the reception desk, and found CNN. He turned one of the waiting-room chairs round to face the news; and settled, his legs resting on the pile of magazines which kept the low coffee table looking busy. He yawned agreeably, and within five minutes he was asleep.

He slept for an hour and a half. He stirred once, thinking that he had heard the sound of an answering machine, but this was only the small and unpleasant ending to a forgettable dream; he lifted his head further up the back of the chair and reclaimed his place amongst the luxury of sleep.

Coming back to consciousness reluctantly, he was stiff and dopey and not inclined to consider doing anything at all. CNN intruded, and persisted, and went on being intrusive, slithering its world from the reception desk. Paul killed it. It crossed his mind that he should go home to bed; but this was surely part of some pleasant memory, a resurrection of his late childhood days when there were no televisions in bedrooms, when the split between television and darkness was absolute; when, for Christ's sakes, you switched off the television and went *up stairs* to bed.

Standing by the reception desk, he remembered living at home – when his parents were out, and he was watching television alone, late; with a game of softball in the morning . . . and the junk car that never seemed to die. That was a great car. Over snow, rain, anything.

The Mercedes was a piece of elaborate technology which travelled at an average speed of twenty-five miles an hour, and for which he could never find the right music.

. . . and a patio . . . Los Angeles.

And seven-fifteen. He had arranged to meet Bill forty-five minutes ago.

Paul yawned and didn't want to care about anything. He didn't want to care about an expensive car. An expensive house was enough. He called for a cab. He had clothes and a clean shirt in his office but he didn't feel like changing. 1717 would be clean enough, a baptism of undisturbed cleanliness. When the cab arrived he had locked the front office doors and left everything to the night cleaners.

Sunday: 3.42a.m.

"No . . . "

FOURTEEN

Sunday: 3.43a.m.

Laurie put the gun down. She placed it on the arm of the desk chair, with the nose of the gun pointing towards the back of the chair, and the handle of the gun bulging stubbornly against the desk. She didn't say anything.

The movements of her arms and her fingers had been incredibly precise, minute and manicured signals of a dextrous performance. He couldn't tell, either from her face or from her T-shirted torso, that she felt anything. But her muscles showed rigid against the skin on her bare legs.

He could not tell what she was thinking, nor what she did, or did not, know.

He didn't know what had happened. One minute, or perhaps for some part of two hours on a March evening, he had been half soporific with Bill and a couple of Bill's friends, mixed company; and the next minute, sometime, he was half drunk, without Bill, in a bar where people came and went with disturbing irregularity. Bill had gone; Paul remembered hands slapping shoulders, buddy and laughter. Paul couldn't quite understand why Bill wanted to go and eat; but because of his trip to LAX they hadn't done the Friday lunch; so.

He wasn't hungry. Food would demand an effort and he was effortlessly slewing from doze to daze. The music in the bar wasn't too loud, the people were intelligent; there was no onus on any brittle zigzag of networking, no dutiful comparison of families. The men weren't dressed too stylishly, the women looked great and vital, the conversation flew lazily, of its own accord. It was good. Good people, warm and honest and humorous, having a good time: Paul didn't understand how it was that they all, nearly all, moved on. Why move on?

" . . . always moving! Why are we as a people, Americans, always moving?" He begged, off the one girl who had stayed. "I'll tell you, I'm not moving." She smiled, a broad soundless beam of teeth – one of Bill's? He considered patting her elbow, but thought not. "But I *am* just going to get washed up. For a moment." It was better not to touch her arm, it was better just to wheel casually and walk to the bathroom. She'd stay. She was one of the good people.

The bathroom had been silent. Clean and white. He was inclined to be a little drunk. He felt good, but he felt messy. He should have changed his shirt. He washed his hands. He felt dirty. He should eat some dinner.

However, he couldn't imagine anything worse than sitting at dinner somewhere with the girl, dressed like he was, making conversation. Hell, no. Why? Telling her what he did, listening to what she did, and not wanting to think what to do next. He didn't want it. He didn't need it.

Outside, on the sidewalk, he felt a little guilty. He wondered if he should go back inside. Maybe she was a friend of Bill's. He ought to go back inside and talk politely.

Hey, what was it with this guilt?! Guilt? That was one of his neighbor's normal tricks. Time enough for that at home, at 1717. All the guilt in the world.

But when he went back into the vestibule and looked through the glass door, the place was full of couples. There was no sign of the girl. She'd gone.

She'd left. She had already moved on. He felt a little cheated. He went back outside.

She'd left. So? Wasn't that what he wanted? All women had the same effect on him. She'd left, and Laurie had left, and that was great. He was on his own, he was all right with himself. There was no-one he had to answer to, no-one he had to talk to about himself, he was complete and intact. There was no goddamn neighbor to keep an eye on; it was *him*, unhappiness happy. Like a private dick. He smiled. Like a private eye. And he was now off the case. And he wanted to sit in a bar, on a stool, and eat a sandwich, and watch a game. It shouldn't be that difficult, not in LA.

He walked quickly. He tried three places before he found what he might be looking for: a pair of doors with portholed glass, a comfortably uncomfortable bar with a back room that infrequently spewed out agitating beat when the sealed doors were opened; a polished wooden bartop with a hung TV screening taped basketball.

Paul ordered a sandwich and sat, hunched over the bar, on his second beer before the sandwich came. The bar wasn't busy, the main action was in the back room, the traffic passed behind Paul's back, ignoring him. There was, briefly, an argument at the other end of the bar, which Paul ignored. He watched the game as it swept from end to end of the court, ten feet in front of his left shoulder, stuck in mid-air. It was a high-scoring game, remarkable only for rare lapses of skill; the big guys didn't make many mistakes, they were all finely tuned, incredibly organised, and in great shape.

Paul had been a good solo cross-country skier. He had never been one for participating in high-grade team sports, he didn't react to hyped group motivation; but he enjoyed watching the finished product, he appreciated the beauty of understanding between the players. Left to their own devices, these guys might be huge dinosaurs, tearing their surroundings and each other apart. Trained as they were, they created patterns and cohesions which were magnificent to watch. It hardly mattered whether or not the ball dropped into the basket. The scoreline only became important in the last thirty seconds, when there was an almost arbitrary decision as to the winning team. Many times, he had tried explaining this to Laurie, who inevitably assumed that the most part of the game was a pointless exercise.

The bartender seemed to feel the same way. He ejected the cassette.

"Hey . . . " Paul complained.

"Lakers win, one o nine to one o seven," the bartender said. "It's an old game."

"It's a great game. Have you got any others?"

"Man . . . " The bartender looked at the clock, which showed ten of eleven. "Time doesn't wait."

"Time waits for no man," said Paul. "That's the quotation, as the saying goes." He looked up at a tall black guy who had appeared next to him, and who was smiling with a slight twist of irony. "Time waits for no man, isn't that it?"

"May be. I would say that when time isn't flying, then maybe it's waiting for no man. You like basketball?"

"Sure. The game just finished."

"I know that. I was watching. David, put on another game, man."

"That's okay," Paul said quickly. "If anyone else wants to watch anything else."

"Then they wouldn't be in here watching it. I like to watch a little basketball. It's early. It's not serious."

"Any game in particular, Mel?" The bartender asked, a little sarcastically, Paul thought.

"Sure. You're going to have to show some discrimination."

"Oh sure."

"Angel, when will you learn to attract your clientele?"

They jived each other in a way which Paul would not have dared, with segregated repartee, until eventually the television again screened basketball and Paul had ordered drinks and Mel had smiled easily, including Paul in the irony of the charade. The bartender retreated to the busier end.

Mel sat back and lazily watched the game. His tongue clicked occasionally against the roof of his mouth, he looked away, down at his drink. The game wasn't as good as the first game. Paul presumed that he was irritated by the looseness of the play. The man was not much shorter than most of the players and even when relaxed he looked athletic. Strong, he looked strong alright. Quietly and comfortably dressed in slacks and a thin black sweater, like an off-duty athlete. And very expensive black Italian shoes. His tongue clicked again, and he bent his head to one side as though easing free the muscles in his neck.

"Do you play?" Paul asked. Mel cast an inquisitive, good-humored glance. "Basketball?" Paul wondered.

"Maybe I wasn't black enough."

"Oh . . . I apologise."

"Don't do that. I was looking for something else."

"Okay. I know the feeling. Right now, I want to move back to Colorado."

"You have someone there?"

"Yes and no. You ever been there?"

"No." Mel looked at him and Paul was struck by the consideration.

"Why not?"

"I never had a reason to go to Colorado, as the saying goes."

"It's a great place."

"Cold and white."

"Just in winter."

"This is the winter, isn't it? You know that my name is Mel."

"Paul Mathiessen."

"How's it going, Paul?"

"Pretty good."

Paul looked away, and down into his scotch. Maybe it was the scotch, maybe tiredness; maybe it was the sudden thick presence of his depression, loitering under the man's expectant stare; Paul looked up at Mel and sensed a concern which tugged his melancholy to the surface. "The next thing", he muttered bitterly, "is what do you do?"

Mel laughed and laid a hand on his shoulder. "The next thing, man, is what does your wife do?" He laughed again. "Shit . . . oh, man . . . "

Paul found himself laughing, he didn't know why. "Why?" He asked.

"You're in the wrong place."

"No I'm not."

He watched dumbly as Mel considered him. "On a Friday night?" Mel suggested.

"She's out of town."

"I'll bet she is."

"She's having a baby."

"That so? Paul, you're in the wrong place, man." Once again, the eyes looked at him generously. Paul felt cords loosen, a tightness detach itself and begin to rise.

"No I'm not," he repeated, and he stipulated it. "That's what *she* says."

The man considered him.

"Uh-huh." His reply was noncommittal.

Paul bit his lip and looked at the game.

"You want to stay up here at the bar?"

"Yes."

They watched the game through to the half, silently. Mel wanted to pay for the next drink but Paul wouldn't let him. Paul looked across the bar, and looked at the sealed door as it opened and closed. He didn't understand where he was or why he was there; but he didn't understand why he should be at 1717.

"I don't understand," he told Mel. "I just don't understand. I don't know what it is."

"Sure, that's okay, Paul."

The next scotch came with a lot of coffee, for which he was grateful, to Mel, who waited for him to talk. Paul couldn't meet his eyes, he couldn't bring himself up to Mel, not yet. The basketball had gone. Men worked out with weights in a gymnasium. Mel stood up.

" . . .'re you moving on?" Paul asked.

"Yes I am. You be okay now?"

"I want some more coffee. I *need* some more coffee."

"That's fine by me. But I don't want to have to watch this macho shit."

"That's because you didn't make it as a basketball player."

"Baby, you are right up there!"

He span away, his body poised, his attitude flared into contempt.

"Mel, I need another coffee."

"Sure you do!"

Paul followed him out to the street. He had a car, an old VW convertible.

"Where are we going?"

"You don't care. You want coffee, right?"

When he sat in the car, Paul nearly fell asleep. He sat with his head bowed forward, his hands loosely in his lap; every now and then he clenched his thighs together in a determined wakefulness. Mel drove with one hand, the other hanging over the side of the car, holding a cigarette. He said to Paul: "You must be crazy."

Paul said: "Yes. I don't think so."

"*I* am going home."

" 's okay." He cleared his throat. "I'll get a cab. Thank you."

"Oh sure you will."

When they got to where they were going, somewhere south and east of Larchmont Village, off Third, Paul sat in the car while Mel walked across a piece of faded grass and went into the side door of a white-boarded house, which had, Paul squinted through the soupy orange street light, a porch.

He had no idea where he was. He knew that it was late, although two cars had sped past with no regard for the hour. He was thirsty. He got out of the car and went round to the side of the house.

"Mel?" The door was left open. The first room, on the left, was the kitchen.

"Say who?"

Paul pushed open another door. Long burgundy velvet drapes covered the street wall, lighting fell from the spots which were set into the ceiling, rays which dissolved at the glare from the television. There was some style to the furniture, expensive wicker, Laurie would have known the designer. Mel was spread across the rug, his arm on a chair, watching the television. He gesticulated idly at the white lines which crossed a square platform of thick safety glass.

"Do you have any water?"

"Anything you want." He sniffed, and swallowed. His tongue clicked. "We have. You know how it is."

When Paul came back from the kitchen, Mel was still watching the television, which was given over to a news program. The sound was turned down, the pictures floated from a government building to an expensive suburban house to a number of photographs. Mel pushed the glass across to Paul and watched the report. Paul applied himself to the small glass tube.

Lead sprayed through his veins. His heart beat in tides. His head banked, his gaze swept in towards the TV, as though his mind might be programed to attack the screen, swirling in out of a burning light and always, always his mind overshooting its target. He didn't want to watch, but it mattered. His attention rolled and corkscrewed towards the horizon, and fell back upon the screen without disturbing him or his breath, which fanned shallowly across either side of his throat to spread and disappear. It was the most wonderful feeling, that every part of him was separate without being lost. This was easy to contemplate and yet simultaneously too urgent to restrain.

"Same, man."

"Yes," Paul observed.

"Liebermann." And the name was there beneath the photograph on the screen. "Dear man."

Mel stood up. He was so tall, and his eyes took corkscrews and dissolved them. He smiled quickly at Paul, his tongue clicked just once. "Seven. And why seven? Two into seven does not go. It just does not make it. The manifesto is going to have to say something more. Soon, baby. And you don't understand what it is. I don't believe you do." Standing there, he ran his hands through Paul's hair, and squeezed the back of his neck twice. He was strong; Paul shivered, gladly. "You figure it out . . . " he murmured.

Left alone, Paul stared blankly at the television. He sat in a chair, but couldn't make himself comfortable. He got up, with enormous effort, and sat on the floor, but he couldn't make himself at ease. He wondered how he kept his life together, how, time and time again, he put patients at their ease, and examined them, and made the right decision. How did he do this? How *could* he do this? His hands sweated now. How did he know that his hands would stop sweating? Every pattern, every surety was so fragile. It could all dissolve. It could fall apart. He was nothing but a small piece of fear, which flapped helplessly, like a crippled bird in the middle of a highway. Or in the middle of 1717, that polished wooden cage, made from the best, chainsawed trees.

He was top-heavy, ready to break apart and fall. He felt that he contained an untappable reservoir of tears. Knowing this was irrelevant. The knowledge was unhappy, and formed a crust, like a scab. Like death.

He was dying, was he? No, of course not. He was simply falling apart. He was defenseless. There was death on the television, without sound, for Liebermann, for others, for Doctor Suro Ky, there was death.

Paul concentrated. Didn't he know someone called Liebermann? Didn't that name have something to do with the land sale around Jerome? Wasn't there a pattern? Paul didn't know the man's face, but surely he knew the name. Surely he had seen the name somewhere, at the bottom of a piece of paper on his desk. Not headlining an office letter, not that big. But in normal print at the bottom of a piece of paper. Liebermann.

There was no remote control that Paul could see. The sound was of heavy rain, water splashing on plastic, hissing from a shower in the next room and beating against the thin wall partition. It was like being in a car wash. Water strafed the wall, the pipes pummelled the baseboards. Other names: Suro Ky, Hubris, Doctor Luke Rabik, Bonner, Kiesco, Mill. Deaths linked by thought. Thin lines of water hitting the wall, a sporadic slash of water dropping to the floor. The blood pummelling through his veins. A line of thought. The tension rising through the crust. Liebermann. Just a line of thought, all victims linked by thought and not touching unhappiness.

There was a metallic clunk, and the noise of the water stopped.

Where was Liebermann? At the bottom of what sheet of paper? And out of how many dozens of sheets of paper?

It didn't matter. All the lines were linked somehow. It really didn't matter. He would go back to 1717, and would wait. The horizon would settle. He had taken a night out and 1717 would be quiet, someone had killed Liebermann, someone had taken a night out, someone with the same rhythm but with a different ending for a different victim.

"Mel?"

"Prego?"

Mel didn't appear, so Paul got up and walked to the next room. The door was ajar. "Can I use your phone?"

"Sure."

Paul pushed the door open. Mel lay on the bed, his long legs half hidden by a bathrobe, an ashtray near his groin, his hand holding the cigarette away from his hip. On the table at the end of the bed a large TV screen showed a white man's naked body from the hip to the bottom of the thighs, side-on, with his large, clean penis held in a black hand, swollen and tense. The hand closed on the penis and squeezed. There was no sound, there was the tense hiss of static as the sound equipment strained for sound. The penis flushed and lifted as the hand relaxed, and then Paul heard a close groan. The white man moved sideways. He must have put his arm up around the black man's neck, because the nearest side of his body lifted slightly and his penis stood horizontal, and somehow neglected, before the camera. A white hand appeared, leading the black hand back towards his penis. Again the black hand squeezed, and relaxed, and then slowly masturbated the penis until it was swollen and heavily protuberant.

Paul felt his own blood descend, and his penis begin to tingle. He was utterly aroused. He had seen skin flicks before, when the laughter of his male companions was nervous, and the action was rawly bestial. The women – he felt both guilty for and annoyed with the women – they showed no care for the penis, the movie was about fucking and they were taking part in a time and motion study as to the erection of an implement. As though all that men wanted to do was to get lost in fucking. He had never before seen such attention, such adoration for the penis. Nor had he seen such beauty, such choreography, such respectful devotion to sensuality.

"You like that?" Mel murmured.

Paul's mouth was dry.

"Sure you do. You'd be crazy if you didn't."

The white penis reared lonely and inept. Again the black hand came in, the long index finger stroking against the ridge of darker skin underneath the crown of the erection, gently, conjuringly. The static hissed.

"Can I sit down?"

"*May* I sit down. You may. You want to take a shower?"

Yes, he wanted to take a shower. More than anything to get out of the room, away from the agony. Mel froze the tape; the black hand clasping the scarlet, safely. He slipped away down the bed, Paul caught a glimpse of his penis, long and smooth, soft clean skin like the silk of his robe. He gave Paul a towel. Paul wanted a shower, more than anything. He felt dirty, he wanted to be clean, to have his blood settle.

"Do you know Liebermann, Mel?"

"Who is that?"

"The man who was killed. On the television. The news report."

"No." Mel's eyes floated sadness across the bed. "I knew Timothy A. Hubris, man. Vice President Hung. The man had some sense of humor. Timbone Hubris. You want another line."

"Sure." Why not? It must be nearly dawn.

It got him to the glory of the shower, the safe, stinging warmth, the end of the dirt, the blood heavy, Mel's bedroom looking like a locker-room. He delayed in the shower. He thought that Mel might come into the shower. He thought this with a kind of fear, but nothing happened, there was no looming terror against the frosted glass door. Mel was not a bad man. He himself was ridiculously pathetic, plain morbid.

When he came out of the shower, there was a glass of scotch. They settled to watch the video: two kinds of sadness, Paul thought at first, two examples of unhappy loneliness. Until the beauty of the sex began, the slow tremulous gentility that introduced a panic of need in Paul.

"They come in twos, right, the murders?"

"Oh it takes two, babe. Each time it takes two."

All the lines of thought converged into the single tension. A pouch was gently removed. The black penis was slim and silky. A soft fatalism superseded terror. Paul glanced across at Mel and saw that Mel would take care of him, through the tension, towards death, in whatever way. He was of no mind to resist. The eyes were kind and generous. He turned his back on Mel and watched the screen, he watched the gentle stroking of the fingers, the firm insistence, the teasing cajolery, that rising pressure of need. And when he felt Mel hard against him, he reached behind to take his penis, and he squeezed, somehow so inept, but Mel would take care of him. Mel's hand closed on his penis and they masturbated each other, at first in imitation of what was happening on the screen, but then in disdain, in vigorous competition until Paul felt happily the sperm dance up his back and soon his own full lunges of discharge; . . . three, four, five, six; and the downy-feathered swansong of ecstasy.

As soon as he awoke, he had wanted to get out. Mel said something as he dressed, and Paul said something back. He felt dreadful, but was glad to feel dreadful in place of having to think. He thanked Mel politely and made a joke. As he walked out of the house he wondered if he had thanked Mel enough, if there was any claim on him that he hadn't settled. He didn't want to have to think. He wanted to get away, before a better daylight came, he had to get away.

He walked quickly to an intersection. There weren't any cabs. There came a bus and he got on it, paying for his ticket and sitting down, staring away from the dawnlight at the floor; and it dismayed him that the bus stopped, endlessly.

He had no idea where the bus was going. He glanced up and saw that the bus was half full of poor people with tired and spongey faces, a cargo of hopeless people going to work. They were somewhere downtown, endlessly downtown. He thought that Alice might get on the bus, the thought filled him with terror. When he saw a cab pulled in at the side of the road he persuaded the bus driver to stop, and he ran to the cab, which was empty.

He ran up the side of the road, startling people. His shirt collar scraped against his neck. At the next intersection he saw another cab, and called it over, and sat tired in the back while the cab took him to his office, where he picked up the car and drove back to 1717, nauseous with the fear that he might get stopped.

When he got to 1717, he walked violently through the house, treating the doors brutally, ensuring to his satisfaction that Laurie wasn't there.

The house knew nothing.

He was savagely grateful that the house knew nothing but was dumbly attentive. It was his house.

He stripped off his suit and threw it on the hall floor. He ripped his shirt into pieces and threw his tie into the trash, then his shorts. Shaking and naked, he pulled a beer out of the refrigerator and drank back half of it, tipping some of it down his chest and groin. Wilfully he lay on the kitchen couch. He felt suddenly and dirtily aroused, and masturbated.

He got up and fetched a pair of Laurie's underwear out of the bedroom and went back to the kitchen and masturbated over them, soiling the slack, black, cotton gusset and the floral cushion on which the panties lay, with some sharp memory of a penis being caressed, and at the very last a dim vagina waiting.

He awoke again at nine, chilled and shivering. He thought that he had gone mad.

1717 was quiet. Jerome was silent. The hillside was quiet. He had a headache.

Paul took two Tylenol and went into the bedroom. He showered and washed his hair, and shaved. On the bed was a note from Laurie which read: "Don't worry. I love you."

It had been a Saturday. It had been a normal day. He had dressed, and put on his loafers, and had gone to the club.

FIFTEEN

Sunday: 3.44a.m. to 3.46a.m.

What had happened?

He reached out for Laurie's shoulder, steadying her, as he thought; but to his consternation he found that he was in fact steadying his own balance. She was immoveable, the surface of her skin was cold, it was like touching a doll's cold plastic.

"Don't . . . " She said. "Don't touch me! There's a pain from the baby. I'm going to lie down."

"Yes," he said. "Jesus – "

"I mustn't get worked up."

"I'll come with you."

"No."

"You can make it on your own?"

"I think so."

"Okay then."

She turned and began to walk slowly up the stairs, so slowly that he went after her, thinking that she might fall.

"No, Paul. It's all right. I can do it on my own."

"It's a long way."

"It's all right. I'll make it." She looked back downstairs. "Paul, that's my room."

"This is? Yes, it is, Laurie." He looked at her, confused as to her state of mind as much as about anything else.

"Uh-huh," she said. "I'm going to lie down. I want to keep this baby."

"You will. Go and lie down. I'll clear this up. I promise."

He climbed to the top of the stairs and watched her walk, arms clasped in front of her hips, cautiously along the hallway. When she reached their bedroom, she went inside and shut the door behind her. He went back downstairs.

There was blood on the wall, and the body lay, still, across the easy chair, its head bent upwards against the window glass. Paul stood, horrified, unbelieving. This had happened. How?

What had happened, those five weeks ago?

Nothing. Absolutely nothing. It had been a Saturday, a perfect Saturday. He had dressed, and put on his loafers. On his way to the club, he dropped his suit and a cushion cover off at the dry-cleaners. He was a little later than usual, arriving at the club. He had taken his orange juice and had watched the swimmers lap the pool – jarring the surface of flat, early sunlight – making him feel dizzy and vulnerable. He went to the locker-room and fixed the thermostat inside the steamroom.

Someone passed him, on their way out to the pool, and said: "It's a beautiful morning."

"It sure is." He excused his own appearance, "After the night before. Are you heading for the pool?"

"You know, I think I'm going to see how it feels. These things are sent to try us." The man – late middle-aged and with tangles of white hair on his chest and belly – grinned affably.

Paul laughed. "That's right, they are. Good luck."

"Thank you. You too. Your family okay?"

"Great, thank you, sir. And yours?"

"Just fine. Take it easy now."

"I will."

The man shouldered his towel and went out.

That had been okay. That was a good conversation for the locker room, grade A.

Paul stared into the mirror over one of the basins. His tiredness didn't look so bad, it could have come from work; but his eyes were red and glassy and not suggestive of any ongoing status.

He would have to be careful. What had he said? What had the conversation been? "After the night before": that was bad, but it was a joky admission; he looked hungover but it was better to laugh this off as a freak occurrence, as if he were embarrassed. It would be worse to confine witnesses to a suspicion, which they would feel that they had to test out with somebody else. The locker-room members sharpened understatement to a fine edge. Any hesitant observation about alcoholic misuse might become a rumor which could cut Paul off from a lot of business.

"After the night before" was just about okay with the older men. It would pass, with the tone of dismissal offering a righteous perspective.

But how had his laugh been? He had laughed when the older man had said "These things are sent to try us". His laugh had been hollow, too forced. The laugh had seemed weird then, and its echo sounded weirder now.

Paul didn't care to look into his own eyes. They would reflect that stupid, nervous laugh. Superficial, evasive. Dangerously unconfident.

Jeez, but he was tired, and wasted. He looked at himself. Anyone might come in.

"Your family okay?"

"Great. Thank you, sir. And yours?"

"Great. Thank you, sir. And yours?"

"Thank you, sir. Great."

Anyone might come in, and he couldn't let them see him like this, examining his own weakness.

He went to sit – hunched – in the steamroom.

He sweated, emerging from behind the glass door occasionally to drink cup after cup of cold water.

From inside the steamroom he heard the swing-doors swing, and the faucets on the basins stream smoothly and monotonously and momentarily, and he overheard the slight variations on the standard locker-room greeting: the day praised, the easy joke, the familial enquiry. There wasn't much difference. There was a reliable normality which he hadn't upset. Every laugh sounded hollow, but probably wasn't.

Paul regained his balance. Outside it was, he recalled, a beautiful day. Truly so. Noticeably so. He just hadn't noticed: it would be so good to notice, when he chose to step out of the hot steam, and when the toxins were purged from his body.

He breathed deeply and regularly, pulling the steam into his lungs, the sweat dribbling down from all over his body, cleaner and purer, the poison washing out and away. In the locker-room, against the left wall of the steamroom, the showers beat sporadically. To Paul, sealed away in the hot mist, the experiences of the night before all seemed like too much of a dream, without any substance, drawn away with his sweat.

He was safe. Life distilled, purely. Nothing had happened.

He had been, if anything, seduced. And a man called Liebermann had died. The murders were in twos. He had escaped. He had wanted to die. The black, Mel, had something to do with it, but *he*, Paul, had escaped.

Nothing had happened. He had got away with it. Just one night, and he had got clean away with it. He had brushed with being a victim, but he had survived. Nothing had happened. Nothing at all. He wondered if Laurie would like the films, if she would react to them.

He wanted Laurie, not death.

He had got away with it.

Outside it was a beautiful day, warm, and the sky was an unusually clear light blue. He had shaved at the club, and secured his locker, and walked across the parking lot to sit in his

Mercedes. It wasn't until he had driven back home, and was sitting in the car while the garage doors slid down behind him, that he realised that he hadn't got his wallet.

His wallet wasn't on him. It wasn't in the car, and Paul knew that he hadn't taken it into the club. It wasn't in the kitchen. It wasn't in the bedroom. And the dry-cleaning company checked his suit and didn't find his wallet.

It was a beautiful day, for which there had to be a payment somewhere. Paul called up the credit card company and the card insurers, to cancel and re-issue. The black guy Mel had surely taken his cards. If he had time to use them, there wouldn't be much damage. It would be a simple matter of theft.

In a way, Paul was glad. It settled all accounts. Now, for sure, nobody owed anybody anything. Everything was clean.

He left the patio doors open and went through the kitchen to his study. He didn't find what he was looking for. He went downstairs to Laurie's room and looked through the files in her desk drawer, until he found the one relating to the purchase of 1717. Sure enough, amongst the list of law firm partners, was the name Leberger.

Paul C. Leberger.

It was nothing to do with James Liebermann.

He laughed. It was nothing, a mad brainstorm. He had been crazy. It was nothing. The black man Mel hadn't murdered Leberger. Almost certainly he hadn't killed Liebermann, or anyone. There had just been that moment of hyper-intensity, in that house, in that bedroom, when Paul had thought that Mel was the killer.

He had wanted to believe that. Everything had worked up to that certainty, when Paul had believed that he was going to die, that he deserved and wanted to die.

And what had happened?

Nothing.

There came a message from Laurie on the answering machine. It was Laurie. She had had a good flight, she guessed that he was at the club.

Light-hearted and bewildered by himself, Paul went upstairs to watch the Saturday football game.

Late in the afternoon, he called her. Her mother picked up the phone and handed him on quickly. To his enquiry, Laurie said that yes, she had had a good flight. "How is it?" she said. "How are things with you?"

"Good. It's quiet. I got back from the club."

"What are you doing?"

"Just hanging around. I haven't taken out the garbage."

"Don't leave it too long, Paul."

"I won't."

"You sound down."

"Well . . . I'm having a lazy day. I'm not down."

"Did you see Bill?"

"Last evening, yes. We had a few drinks."

"What did you talk about?"

"The usual crap. Nothing serious."

"Guys' stuff."

"Not really." He was already impatient with the call, and tired. They weren't getting along. She was appealing for his gloom, which he knew that he didn't feel. "We talked porches, manifestos, that kind of thing."

"You know that there's been another one. Did you know?"

"Uh-huh. Yes."

"You take care."

"Laurie, it's got nothing to do with me. You know how everybody in the east thinks that everybody on the west coast is going to die of craziness. You know? Who needs it? It's got nothing to do with me."

"I told you that."

"I'm telling you that. I know that. Okay?" He paused. She didn't fill in. "I'm fine."

"Good. Me too."

"That's good. Both of you."

"Yes."

"That's good. You take care."

"I am. Everyone's falling over themselves to take care of me."

"That's great."

"Don't leave it too long. Paul?"

"I won't. I'll call you soon. Okay?"

They said their goodbyes and hung up.

He was tired of being depressed and tired of the way she now relied on him to confess. If it was his fault, he wanted to change himself. He was glad to hang up, and to have the time to change. He slept like a drain. On the Sunday he worked on the garden for a while and sat in the sun, feeling that he had both shed and gained a skin.

They talked a couple more times on the phone. He made her parents laugh, and once or twice he knew that he had Laurie smirking. Their relationship began to lift, slowly and without any explanation or promise. Sometimes he missed her, to the point of getting pissed at her, privately. He could admit this to himself, and knew that he would tell her when he saw her, and that he could explain the delay. When she called one evening – it must have been very late at night on the east coast – he sat in his study and let the call come through on the answering machine. He listened to the sounds of a storm through the speaker. At the back of his mind, and very buried, lay the docile memory of that Friday night, another storm, burned out, having no significance and having caused no damage. Something that hadn't hardly happened. He sat in the study and listened to the sound of the weather on the east coast. He lit a candle and the flame didn't waver, not even slightly, unless he himself made a movement. He didn't think of Laurie. He thought of the baby secure inside

Laurie. He didn't pray, but with all his heart he wished it well. He didn't feel that he needed to pray.

When he saw Laurie at the airport, he was delighted, utterly and calmly happy. There hovered, about their relationship, a blessing. In the car, he couldn't put his finger on this blessing, he didn't know what it was, it made him slightly nervous about his happiness. And back at 1717 they half-made love so quickly, so ridiculously, and again in a blur before he went to work. It was all a blur, afterwards, of happiness and surety, with Laurie, as she moved, somehow a little detached, around their world. He had hardly known how to count his blessings, and the one time when he had tried to do so, to Diana Caviatti, the calculation had all gone haywire. For what could he have said? That he was just cluelessly contented and very, very safe? That Laurie and he had their own world.

The candle flame burned unwaveringly unless he made a move. He had no misgivings.

Sunday: 3.48a.m. to 3.50a.m.

And now. What had happened?

What could he have done?

"Babe . . ."

He might have gotten the gun off Laurie; that had been his plan, to get the gun and to threaten Mel, to keep him silent. Mel had stepped out of line, well out of line.

He had tried to blackmail Paul. Hadn't he?

Paul remembered. He didn't want Mel's understanding. Mel hadn't understood.

Mel was, now, silent. Niggers didn't go uphill.

Paul remembered.

"Oh Lord, please keep us safe, Lord God. Bless us and keep my child safe, don't let my child worry. Take this man's soul. Take him away with You, into Your perfect peace, which passes all understanding. Oh God, keep my family safe . . ."

Sunday: 3.50a.m. to 5.05a.m.

Where was the gun?

He stood up.

He couldn't believe that the gun was no longer on the arm of the chair. Where was the gun?

When would Mel move? If Mel was alive and had crawled over to get the gun, when would he make his move? Maybe Mel had the gun. He would move suddenly.

Paul stood by the chair, ready to use the chair, somehow as protection. One of Mel's arms was hidden, down beneath his side. Paul stood, and watched, and listened. Mel didn't move. For too long, he didn't move.

Paul went closer. "Mel?" He whispered. "Mel, it's me."

The man was dead. There was no movement, not even in the eyes. He was dead. He would say nothing. The other arm held nothing, the hand was empty.

Paul walked quickly upstairs and along the hallway. He knocked on the door of their bedroom, and when he heard no sound he opened the door.

Laurie sat in the middle of the bed and pointed the gun at him.

She stared at him, in some kind of a trance. Her breathing was deep and deliberately regular, as if she was in the middle of an exercise, while simultaneously, incongruously, her arms were stretched out, holding the gun, in another exercise, which she would not relax. She kept the gun pointing at him.

"It's me. It's okay, Laurie. He's dead. He's dead, downstairs. I checked. I came to see where the gun was."

She stared at him. It was an effort for her to speak. Her eyes were narrowed. "Are there any others?" she asked.

"He's alone."

"How do we know that? Paul? How do you know that?"

Objectively, how *could* he know that?

He said, "I don't know that. But there's no sign of any others."

"There might be, though. Think! Don't you ever think about us?!"

"Yes I do! I don't hear anything, Laurie. I haven't seen anything. I want you to get some rest."

He seemed to have made his point. She let her arms fall to her sides.

"I'll check," he said. "I'll take the gun. I'll check this part of the house first. I'll switch the alarm on again. Keep the gun for a moment. It'll be fine. I'm certain that it's just the one man. I'll check. I'll be back."

"Paul, don't go!"

"Okay. Okay. It'll be fine. I won't go."

He sat on the bed and whispered to her soothingly, how it would all be okay, how it was all over, words which he kept coming back to, about love and how things would be. He sat on the bed holding her arm in one hand and the gun in his other hand, thinking good thoughts and wishing goodness on them both, for them and for the baby. It would be okay. He knew that it would be okay.

She closed her eyes, and seemed to sink back into herself. He thought that she was sleeping. He ran out of things to say.

It pleased him that he wasn't at all emotional. He didn't feel any emotion about what had happened.

He thought: if he had have taken the gun off Laurie and stopped her killing Mel, then there would have been a lot more trouble.

He didn't know whether or not he would have been capable of dealing with Mel. Mel might have come back again, even if he had agreed to leave. Even if Paul had forced him to leave, Mel might have waited for the opportunity to show up again.

They had done the best thing. It was best this way.

They would have to redecorate the downstairs room. They would never tell the baby, or the child. They would pretend that nothing had happened. They would go on as if nothing had happened.

He should set the house alarm.

He let go of Laurie's arm, and moved cautiously off the bed, not wanting to disturb her.

She said, "Paul, what do we do now?"

He said, "It's okay, hon; I'm going to set the alarm in case there's anyone outside."

"Okay."

She didn't move.

He went along the hallway and set the alarm. Then he went downstairs and looked into the basement room. The body was as he had left it, the blood was drying on the walls. He stayed by the door and decided to turn off the light; and there, for the first time, he was struck by what it would be like to say goodnight to a child, his child, and to turn off the light, and close the door, the stuffed animals smiling from the bed.

He closed the door. He felt weak. He filled with a terrible emotion, an anguish which overflowed from his eyes as he leaned his forehead against the doorpost. His jaw hung open, tears dribbled down the frame.

He pushed himself upright, blind with tears and hot about the lips; and the weakness dropped into his legs.

God knows how long he sat on the stairs. Until the sobs slowed and his breath juddered spasmodically in and out of his lungs, and he was flat with fatigue. During the walk down the hallway he tried, and almost managed, to pull himself together, to the point whereby he paused to look at the sconces on the hall lights and realised that he liked them, as if he had never really looked at them before. But when he went in to Laurie he was so drained that he looked at her wonderingly and asked her, shaking his head: "What do we do now?"

She opened her eyes and faced him, worried for him. She reached for his hand. "It's all right," she said. "I called the police.

We have to wait. The police are all tied up with the riot. They told us to wait. Hush now. They'll come. We just have to wait."

He waited for as long as he could.

Suddenly, before dawn, he froze; in a burst of fear and disgust. Mel was in the house. If he slept near Laurie she would know that he had had sex with Mel. He had had sex with Mel. The knowledge would be contagious. She would feel the knowledge seeping, from him, into her. He didn't want her to know. He was carrying Mel. He didn't want Mel anywhere near him or Laurie.

He crawled away from Laurie, out of bed, drawing all the dirt with him. The bathroom was already steamy. He showered, not caring about the noise which was only one more chaos, like an acute time lag. He washed himself thoroughly, painstakingly.

When he went back into the bedroom he detected that she was awake in the darkness.

"Are you awake?" he whispered.

"Half. I took a shower. It will be all right, darling. Try and sleep. We just have to wait for the police to come."

He lay, for a while, next to her. She mumbled and turned onto her side, away from him.

Christ, she was strong. She was so strong, he thought. What would he have done if she hadn't have come downstairs with the gun? She had killed Mel, shot him calmly and deliberately. As she would have shot any intruder.

Mel was an intruder. They had every right to shoot him. And with the riots, especially in the context of the riots, people were jumpy. She had every right to be jumpy, and to defend the house and herself from any intruder. It was right. It was understandable. It was clear. She had every right to shoot at him. They had every right, under the law. It was clear, and would be clear to the police, when they arrived.

Why *had* Laurie killed him?

He fell down the echo. "Why *had* Laurie killed him . . . "

SIXTEEN

Sunday: 4.30a.m. to 5.00a.m.

It's okay. Laurie persisted. The baby will be okay. Just relax, and the baby will be okay. Slow the breathing, and the heartbeat; let the body act regularly; and comfort the child, feel the child. Think good thoughts. It will be okay. I will not lose the baby. It's strong. We are strong. Think good thoughts.

Her muscles contracted, suddenly, in a struggle. Laurie gasped. The foetus moved feebly, and she ran her hands over her belly, letting go of her breath, breathing regularly and staring at the ceiling. She closed her eyes.

She tried not to pray; she didn't want to plead, nor to admit despair. She thought for the baby, of seas and warm beaches and laughter, of all the wonderful times they would have together, mother and child. There was a feeling of Paul's presence, but this was in the child, this was in the baby's sense of wonder. Laurie herself felt no constraint whatsoever from Paul and no disturbance of her responsibility.

She soothed the baby, which lay calm inside her. She closed her eyes and her breathing was slow; beginning, and ceasing, and then again a slow break, like ripples from across a placid sea, one after another.

She didn't sleep. Tiredness floated through her, ebbing into her body, trickling past her mind, blurring her mind. She let her body absorb the tiredness, and her body rested. Her body was almost inanimate, succouring the baby. It was as if she had placed the baby in a cot of seashore, and the baby slept, and occasionally patted at the air, and curled its hand securely around the finger of love which she held out. The baby slept, and she watched, and she became absent-minded, just as securely.

She didn't sleep. Into her absent-mindedness came sadness, as monotonous and peaceful as the waves. Gentle and with no crescendo the tide came in, weeping sadness like a mist, not disturbing her or the baby. She knew that their bodies were shielded, comfortable and warm.

Here is Laurie, turned away, with Paul Mathiessen lying at her side. They are waiting for the police to come. She knows that they will wait for a long time but this does not disturb her, because she wants to wait; and the house is quiet. Seventeen Seventeen Jerome will quietly take away the tremors which are running through her body and her mind. Seventeen Seventeen will minister to her, Seventeen Seventeen is unmoved.

Blood dries. They are waiting for the police to come and they will wait for a long time, until she is ready. Until the baby has settled and Laurie has remembered what has happened. Until she is ready to remember what has happened, without it happening over and over again in her mind, which is what does happen. The body, of course, dies.

Laurie is here. Already she knows why she is sad with sadness like a mist, and this is because there is a decision which she understands that she has not yet made, but which is there waiting for her to take. She only has to reach. Yet she will wait. Already in waiting the decision is made but Laurie is proud, she regrets that she had not made the decision before, she should have known that she would leave Paul Mathiessen.

Perhaps she has known, has perhaps kept the knowledge to herself, making herself invulnerable to the decision. Laurie doesn't sleep. When she does sleep it is with her eyes half open, but now she stares absent-mindedly at the ceiling, her mind as settled as a wide expanse of beach at dawn, the baby keeping her warm, she keeping the baby warm, in her imagination her finger is clutched by a tiny hand, the sadness fanning across them both and disappearing into Seventeen Seventeen, leaving, as daylight's suggestion makes clear, a detritus of stark incident which she is able to consider.

She waits until she is ready to remember. As Laurie, she thinks back. But gently. Gently. Don't wake the baby.

She remembered herself walking down the hallway. She had shot and killed someone. She had climbed the stairs and was walking down the hallway. It was a horrible walk. She had her hands clasped in front of her, her left hand holding her belly, holding her baby, feeling for the warm life of her baby while her right hand held the cold slick metal of the gun. The smell was bitter, she had to try not to collapse into this smell, not to let the baby be smothered by this smell nor to feel the metal of the gun so near. The gun was in her right hand and she wondered all the while she was walking why she couldn't move the gun from her right hand to her left hand, so that the baby would have her stronger hand. But she couldn't change hands. She couldn't for one moment let go of the baby inside her, and she couldn't let go of the gun. She could not have dropped the gun, or she herself might have followed it to the floor. Nothing could be allowed to drop. She must carry both the oily metal and her own chilling flesh. They mustn't meet, ever. She felt as though she was carrying a terrible secret, one footstep after another, down the length of the hallway, the hall, even into her bedroom. There was no end to the responsibility; and during that walk there was, seemingly, no end to the shock, one jolt after another against her feet and up through her legs.

And the despair, which weakened her: for it didn't seem as if she was walking away from anything, it seemed as though she was bringing it all with her, as if the noise and the shock and the knowing about Paul was all attached to her by elastic: she was bringing it all down the hallway with her, one foot in front of another, dragging the despair towards her bedroom where it would devour her.

She should collapse – she had thought this, she remembered this – she should fall gently to the ground and not go on at all, she should settle for holding the baby and holding the gun, and whatever was following her would find her this way. She shouldn't walk any further, not into the bedroom. Whatever should happen, would happen. Why go on walking?

She remembered the walk.

But it was the noise, the terrifying and astounding noise, which she had been bringing with her. The noise which couldn't find any place to settle in the house.

What happened to the noise? What happened to noise? The noise had just withered as she reached the bed, withering her with it, until she had remembered her breathing. Until she had succeeded in shutting the noise out, first from her body and then from her mind; and then with her breathing to start talking to the baby, to explain to the baby and to herself that it was nothing.

Sometimes, she explained, when *she* was a baby, a child, planes from the airforce base suddenly had come in low over her head; like interesting monsters, until the terrible noise had chased them away from behind and scared her so much, so much; but it was nothing – just a loud noise – a loud noise which went away. It's nothing. You just have to run to your mom and hide away the noise. It's nothing. It's just a loud noise which goes away. It's all right, darling. It's gone away. There won't be any more noise. Hush now. There. You see? You're all right now. Hush now. Everything's fine. She remembered.

Here was Laurie. And she was driving the terror away, shepherding it away, every feeling of terror from herself. She had tried not to be scared, because the baby would pick up her fear, and she might lose the baby if she was scared of losing the baby. Hush now. The gun on the comforter, both her hands on her belly, wondering what her body would do, fearful that she had killed her baby, fearful that she would be filled only with fear. Hush now. Keep it a secret. Hush now. Take your mind off nasty things. There is no noise. There is no walk, one foot after the other. It's all over. It's all gone away. Sleep now. Sleep. Curl up, and try to go to sleep.

Hush now. Your pa will clear up.

Paul will clear up. She remembered thinking this. She remembered being sure of this. She was still certain of this.

Here is Laurie. She knows what has happened. She has shot at a man who has come into the house. Three or four shots – she can't remember. Like slaps. Jars to her elbow and shoulder. Her wrists were strong. But that wasn't it. She knew what was happening.

She knew what had happened. The man looked at her. He smirked. He had an utterly assured disdain for her, an intimate disdain. He had known that she would never use the gun, that she would be incapable of protecting herself and Paul. Confidently he had smirked at her. He came forward on a surge of contempt. It was so incomprehensible that, for a split second, it threw her. She looked to Paul, for his support; he had already asked for the gun. He did nothing. There was something to figure out. There was something she didn't understand. The man came towards her. She shot him in the leg, to stop him coming towards her. She wanted time. What was there to figure out? She wanted time, or she wanted Paul to say something. Because the man was going away now. She told Paul to say something. But he didn't. He looked at the man. There was such intimacy between them; between the three of them.

And when Paul turned to look at her she knew that he couldn't say anything. She knew that he would never tell her the truth. She knew instantly what was happening. The man was destroying her room, destroying everything.

She shot him to protect herself. She shot him to protect everything she knew, everything that was hers. And when she had killed him she had, just for a moment, and unaffected by the noise, everything back where it belonged.

She remembers. Everything had been back where it belonged.

The worst part of the walk along the hallway hadn't been the noise. It wasn't the blood, or the noise, which she had been dragging after her. It was Paul's betrayal of her; that was what would devour her, that helpless moment of intimacy before she had fired again. He had another lover. Everything else was a sham. He had a male lover.

She can't fight this. She doesn't want to fight. She wants to be sick. She couldn't hold it any longer. She went to the bathroom and was violently, sorrowfully, sick.

Then Paul had come into the bedroom. She remembers. She needed time. She didn't want to see him. She didn't want him to talk to her. She didn't want him to say anything. She didn't want his interference. She didn't want any more turmoil.

He had knocked on the door. It could have been anyone. *He* might have been anyone. She pointed the gun at him, the taste of vomit rising from her stomach. She didn't want him to know that she had been sick, she didn't want him to start talking about anything. Her stomach churned. She felt as though bits and pieces of herself and her baby might spew out of her mouth.

If there was one thing which had kept her intact, it was anger, a slowly churning anger. She might have shot Paul; but the anger would not travel out of her. It would not go down her arm and would not make the transition from her finger onto the trigger of the gun.

She saw that he was terrified of the gun as she held it out at arm's length and pointed it at him, and kept it steady. She couldn't tell which part of him she might hit if she fired. There was no room in her for any judgement, nor for any calculation as to what shooting Paul might do, what good or what resolution might ensue. She felt expressionless, that her face was expressionless. There was only the gun, pointing at Paul, at the end of her arms.

It seemed to her that Paul wasn't worth it. He wasn't worth her anger. She remembered.

If he had have started to talk, if he had tried to be confidential, she would not have put up with it. She would have shot him. She remembered. The trigger would have gotten pressed of its own accord. Her finger, even the pad of her finger, would have dismissed him. She didn't want the sound of his voice. She didn't want him to say anything.

She wanted time. She wanted to know what was happening to herself, to be certain what she was.

This was the only time in her life that she had wished that someone would tell her a story about herself. She wanted someone to decide for her what she was. She was tired of figuring it out for herself. Paul had never done that for her; he had never come close to being convincing.

It's me, he had said.

She kept the gun pointing at him.

He had said that the man downstairs was dead, and that he had come to see where the gun was.

The gun had been there, pointing at him. The gun was there, and she had stared past the gun, at Paul. He said nothing else.

Anger and despair remained. They didn't mingle. Her mind had started to work. She stared at Paul, scrutinising him. She had seen that he was being clever. He had decided to carry it through. He wasn't going to say anything, he wasn't going to try to explain, nor to plead. He was going to pretend that nothing existed, that everything was as it was meant to seem.

She needed time. She hadn't been prepared. She knew as much as he did, but this time he was the one who would conceal the knowledge. Her mind started to work. Let him hide. She needed time.

The gun had become distant. She should explain the gun, why she had the gun pointed. She had asked, are there any others? And how could he know that there weren't any others? He couldn't know. He couldn't explain.

She had watched him flounder.

"Think! Don't you ever think about us?!"

It had been too soon. Her anger had gotten the better of her. Those words had been a cheap and needless victory.

She didn't want him to think, not too much. *She* needed time to think. She wanted to shut herself away with her feelings until she had thought what to do. "Paul, don't go!"

And he hadn't gone. She had lain with her eyes closed, ignoring his ministrations, letting his thoughts be taken up with her.

Laurie remembers what happened next. Her mind is, and had been, working well. It had been part of her legal training. She had to consider every word, closely. And she does remember.

Paul had left her, and had gone to switch on the alarm. She had not felt sick any longer. As his weight had left the bed, so her thoughts had fallen into place. She had heard him set the alarm, and had heard him go away down the hallway.

She had moved her legs across and had sat up. She had reached for the phone and dialled 911.

"Los Angeles County Emergency Services. Which service do you require?"

"Police."

"I have your number as 643–7011 – "

"Yes, but we're – "

"That is the number registered to Mathiessen, 1717 Jerome."

"It is."

"That has been passed on to the police. Your call is being

recorded. Please stay on the phone. Are you in fear of immediate injury?"

"No. We have had an intruder."

"Yes, ma'am. Do I understand that you and your family are no longer in any immediate danger?"

"There is no immediate danger."

"I am going to re-route you. This call has been recorded and logged. Please hold the line."

It fell into place. She had time. She began to understand.

She had waited. She had thought quickly. The call went through.

"Mrs Sathison how am I help you?"

"We've had an intruder. Who am I talking to?"

"Mrs Sathison, this is the 911 service. My name is Consuela and I am a volunteer county worker for emergency service. We understand that you and your property are in no danger."

"That is correct."

"You will understand that in a civil disturbances the emergency must prioritise the call. In a present situation the police must respond only to maximum danger incident, where there is an . . . immediate . . . threat to life or property."

"I understand that. You mean that the system is overloaded."

"Mrs Sathison, we are doing what we do as back-up. The 911 service can only respond to the call dealing with serious – "

"Consuela, I understand that."

"Thank you, Mrs Sathison. You are having a prowler?"

"Yes, we have."

"If you are, or you feel to be, in danger, I can re-route you back through the priority 911 switchboard."

"No, we are not in danger. And I guess that this call is logged with the priority service and with you."

"We have no logging at this level. Your call have be logged at the 911 intercept."

"So I should call in again to the police direct, when things have quietened down."

"You report all these incident to the police. Yes, I guess when things are quieten. Are you alone, Mrs Sathison?"

"No, my husband is here."

"Okay, that is good. I will ask you if you like to call a neighbor."

"I think that we'll manage. Can you tell me what our rights are, with regard to an intruder?"

"But I can find. Will you hold this line?"

"Please. Yes I will."

Consuela returned.

"Mrs Sathison, if you are reasonably in fear of death or injury, you have the right to use reasonable force."

As she knew.

"I see."

"Can I assist you with something other?"

"No. Thank you for all your help."

"I have to advise you that there is a curfew in operation."

"We won't be going anywhere."

"Thank you."

"Thank you. Good night."

So this was how it was. She remembered. She had time to decide what to do, what Laurie should do.

And Laurie had put down the phone. As she had told Paul, there was nothing to do but to wait.

SEVENTEEN

Sunday: 5.00a.m. to 8.00a.m.

She hadn't expected Paul to sleep. She had never imagined that he would fold, subserviently, away from her.

When he had begged her – "What do we do now?" – and she had told him that they must wait, she was not prepared for his acquiescence.

She heard the sounds of automatic gunfire which rose from the city, muffled by the wailing of sirens and the shredded resonance of helicopter blades. Closer to home she heard the refrigerator kick in, the grinding of the ice-maker and the sharp taps as the ice-cubes fell into the plastic tray.

Her husband had plummeted into sleep. His mouth was half-open and the air grated across the back of his throat in the usual, reassuring, way.

It occurred to Laurie that she might leave. That she might slip out of bed, pull on a pair of sweatpants, and take the car. In the morning she might find herself miles away, without Paul, without a house, responsible only to her child. Mrs Laurie Sathison.

How bizarre it was that the volunteer staffer had mistaken her name. She remembered the staffer's name, Consuela. Why should Consuela have screwed up on her name? What was Mrs Sathison to Consuela? Surely an older woman, fearful about the riots, probably watching them on TV and terrified about every little noise around the house; someone who should call up a neighbor and go over there for safety and peace of mind. But Mrs Sathison had a husband, and that was all right, she had company.

Perhaps that was how it would be in fifteen or twenty years. She would live with Paul for company. Or she could leave, now, while he was asleep. All that she had to do was to get dressed and take the car.

No. She wouldn't go. She could find somewhere to go, no doubt; but why should she go? It would be pointless. It would be absolutely pointless. It would be making clear to herself that she cared, and she didn't want to care, not about Paul who would only set out to find her and dog her with pathetic misery.

He had betrayed her. He had humiliated her. There wasn't anything she could do about it. She wasn't sad, she was angry. She didn't want to understand it. She didn't want to understand him. There were actions, and there were people. Paul had betrayed her by his actions: the affair itself was a betrayal which she had suspected and known, inside herself. She had forgotten and so, apparently, had forgiven; as she understood. But the homosexuality was Paul. She couldn't forget Paul. She couldn't forget Paul while continuing to live with him. Forgiveness wasn't in the equation, all understanding was irrelevant. There was nothing which she could fight for. It would be stupid to pretend that she could ever forget, and an insult to pretend that she could continue to live with him. She would not live with this insult. She could not imagine pretending.

There was another, slow, contraction inside her. She wondered what would happen to her body. She tried to explain it to herself. Her world was contracting; it was nothing to be scared about.

She told the baby: if you stay with me, and you *will* stay with me, I promise you that there will be nothing to be scared about. There is no pretending between you and me. Nothing will happen to either of us. Our world is just contracting a tiny bit but this isn't going to affect either of us. We will just accept it for what it is, and it will pass.

Rest.

She didn't know what would happen. It came to seem that nothing was going to happen. Her body settled. She thought that the baby was perhaps scared of helicopters, and she tried to picture how they might be beautiful in flight, grunting like great-uncles, chattering like aunts. She invented for the baby a whole mechanical family from Los Angeles, whooping children, snarky brothers shouting across a playground. The little human bugs hid, like woodlice. Stinkbugs broadcast stink into the air. She felt the baby as a hummingbird, hovering in humid warmth, thirsty for the flower inside her.

Nothing was going to happen. She was above it all. She was tired, her body was tired; waiting. She wouldn't sleep.

She wanted to tell herself a story. What story should she tell?

She had killed a man, an intruder. It was the end of the story.

Why?

The sadness again washed through her, heavily, swabbing away her anger, swilling from head to toe, making her numb. She had shot the intruder in self-defence. She shot him for Paul, for both of them, for their family, to protect them, to keep their family together, to protect him. She had killed for Paul.

So that nothing would ever be known. So that it would be forgotten.

He was Paul's lover. His lover. That man and Paul had made love. How dare he! How could Paul do that? How could he be so deceitful, so cruel?

What was wrong with her? She wasn't ugly. Was she? He desired her. Didn't he? What had she done? What part had she played in this, in his choice, in repelling him?

She went through her conversation with the 911 services. She had done exactly right. She hadn't lied. They were in no danger. She was in no immediate danger and that was the truth of the matter. She had been truthful. It was the correct story. She knew what her legal position was. She had done everything right and she had to wait. Until she knew what her body was going to do and what she was going to do, she had to wait.

Why couldn't Paul have known about himself? He must have known this. He must have felt it – every time he made love to her – that he was gay. Paul and she had made love. Hadn't they? Hadn't they been in love all this time?

How could she not have seen through him before? Was she so much of a failure that she hadn't noticed it? Was that what *his* sadness was all about? How could she not have noticed? How could she not have seen?

That it was her fault.

But how? What should she have said? If only he had said something? Was it her fault because she was domineering?

How could she not have seen it? If only she had thought about it.

Or maybe she had known about it. Maybe she had known about it all along and had ignored it, and that was her fault; she had never noticed how he was with men.

There was nothing. She couldn't remember anything. She couldn't remember not admitting anything to herself.

God, how naïve she had been, how dumb . . .

She wasn't dumb! She was supremely capable of treading carefully through a 911 call, and things were no less chaotic inside her then than they were now. She wasn't dumb.

Had he ever really wanted her?

Had anybody ever really wanted her? Was she that much of a failure? Was she that much of a waste?

If only . . .

If only what?

She couldn't forget. She would never forget what a waste it all was. That was *her* fault, the betrayal was her fault. It made her angry; she filled then with anger.

Sadness, then anger; then sadness.

She had to wait. She had to withdraw. She told herself that she had to wait, that she needed time. Nothing could survive such chaos.

Had anybody ever really wanted her?

This baby wanted her.

There were no contractions. There was no sign that anything was wrong.

She didn't feel that anything was wrong with her body.

She felt fine. Tired, yes. Surely. But fine. With no pains and no repetitive contractions.

Paul slept.

She went into the bathroom. She felt fine, and took a shower Still no pains. Nothing was amiss.

She had killed an intruder. The man was innocent. So was she, and so was her child. She *had* been just another innocent. Innocence gets pissed on.

He had smirked at her. She had also, at times, been victorious.

It wasn't a time for innocence, not now.

She wound a towel over her hair and went back to bed, to lie down in darkness. She liked darkness.

She had always liked it, even when she was a child; and the dark had enabled her, ever since, to recall and retain her childishness, peopled by careless imaginings and flimsy fears and vapid ghouls which she could entertain and with whom she could play until she got bored. She liked darkness.

She lay down.

When the light was turned out, a moment which a child could never control, she had established her supremacy over the darkness.

She had had her own room, and her own real friends: bears and lions and soft dolls who took turns in finding favour with her, or in being discarded. She used to lie in the darkness, confident of their loyalty, and she would summon her sister, her mother, or the boys and girls whom she knew, to appear before them. Together they would figure out who deserved what. She herself was never quite sure who deserved what, but she relied upon suggestions which were supported by her friends, and upon mitigations which were again, hesitantly, supported by her friends, until she was sure that everybody had got what they deserved. Her tribunals always took place in darkness. Sometimes she awoke later, in darkness, and stumbled across the rug and opened the bedroom door, into light which was painful to her eyes. She would close her eyes and feel her way downstairs and find a babysitter or a maid or her parents sitting calmly in light, and she would come to tell them, frightened, that she hadn't meant to get it wrong. She asked a question and never got a very long answer but got, instead, carried back upstairs and put back in bed, and her friends were chided and put on the rug for disturbing her, with which she agreed and didn't bother the darkness again.

Childish, but everything was where it belonged.

And everything, now, was incongruous. She lay, with a baby inside her, next to a man whom she couldn't love, with his lover in the downstairs room. She lay in darkness with a life which she knew, unthinking, that she wanted.

She summoned Anger, and Despair, and wondered which deserved what, referring her suggestions to the sleeping baby, which lay inside her and agreed with her as they swung to and fro.

She didn't want to be disturbed.

When Paul got up, or slunk up, into the darkness, she didn't want to recognise him. He was entirely foreign.

Her sister or her mother or her father had sometimes come into her room after dark, to arrange her bedclothes or to kiss her or to look for something, and they were foreign. She didn't want to recognise them. She didn't want to recognise Paul, not sadly as he slunk away, nor, as he made such a noise in the bathroom, angrily. It sapped her strength, and her interest, to have to tell him to go to sleep, when he returned to disturb her tribunal.

Just before dawn, when she had decided who deserved what, everything was in place. The outside no longer mattered.

Two hours later the room was still in darkness but the darkness was old and flat and stale. The drapes were trimmed with daylight. She walked round the bottom of the bed to the bedroom door. Her stomach felt slightly nauseous, with anticipation, which was guiding her. She opened the bedroom door and the rest of the house was bright with morning, against which she closed her eyes. She felt her way. The house was unfamiliar, there were no stairs and no carpet. It was a cold house, full of responsibilities. She didn't want to open her eyes. She was cold. She just wanted to go back to bed alone, to have someone else take everything and everybody away. The doorbell rang again.

The doorbell rang and she immediately lost the feeling of nausea. With her eyes half-closed she went to the door and unbolted it, and opened it. The bright sunlight hit her eyes. And that sunlight reeled past as the house alarm went off.

She knew what was happening, she turned quickly and switched off the alarm. She was naked, but for underwear. She looked down at herself. She was pregnant. People were whispering on the other side of the door, out in the sunlight.

"I'm not ready," she said. "I'll get a bathrobe."

"Don't worry," said a woman's voice, "dear. We just came to see how you were and if you were all right."

She found a polo shirt by the washer, and a pair of sweatpants, and these she put on, and took a gulp of water, and smoothed her hair. How many stories were there?

Just one.

She went back to the doorway. There weren't any police, not

that she could see. There was an elderly man and an elderly woman, whom she had seen before, but she didn't know where.

"Laurie?" The woman said. She smiled timidly, with the self-effacing warmth of a grandmother. "I'm sorry that we disturbed you, dear. Zeke and I just came over to see if you were all right. Things have been so difficult for all of us, but thank the Lord we're just fine and safe and we dropped by to see if you and your husband were pulling through the same as we are."

Laurie said, "Yes, we are."

"It's been a bad business," Zeke said.

"It's such a terrible shame. We all feel that way. So many people killed and such . . . so much destruction. In the downtown areas. And it spread so far, you know? We – "

"Still going on, they say."

"But they say they've contained it."

"They have the National Guard moved into place. They're going to cap it right off."

"Oh, I'm glad," Laurie said. "Thank goodness. It's such a relief."

"We all are, Laurie dear. It's been a tragedy. And such a terrible shame for everybody. And for you carrying your baby, we didn't want anything to happen to you. We *worried* about you, you sweet girl; we love you both so much, and these things are so terrible. You shouldn't have to think about these things, you shouldn't even have to think about them. Zeke and I are *so* ashamed; I can't tell you how mortified we are."

They were sincere, good people. They touched her, straight through her sleep. She said: "It's not your fault. It's not anybody's fault."

"Well, it seems to me – " her husband began.

"Oh we don't want to think about whose fault it is," his wife said, "now do we? Not here and not now. We're mighty glad that nobody we know got hurt or injured, and that it didn't come here. There is enough to be thankful for. That it hasn't touched any of us, and that is a blessing. We are all safe, we have a lucky star."

"We sure do."

"We do," Laurie said.

"Is your husband with you?"

"Yes. He is."

"I am so relieved for you both. We were both so worried about you."

"Thank you so much. Thank you. I would ask you in for a coffee but Paul's asleep, he's exhausted."

"And you must be too. We wouldn't dream of disturbing you both. We just wanted to know that you were safe and well. It's a little selfish of us, I know, but we love you."

"I'll tell him."

"Now you'll embarrass him."

"It won't."

"Then you both get some rest and we won't count on seeing you at Sunday service."

Her husband shook his head. "You rest up now, Mrs Mathiessen. We're happy to see you both safe."

"Thank you." She tried to think, but it didn't need thinking through. She said, "We'll come to church. I hope so. We'll try to be there."

Into the woman's eyes darted a swell of pride and relief. "That would be so fine," she said. Her husband nodded and put his arm around her waist.

Laurie watched them walk to their car. They were somehow so sturdy, and so vulnerable. They had got into their car and had driven out to check on people, he in an ironed too-tight shirt and pressed pants, she in a skirt and cardigan and sensible shoes. Both sincere. Both anxious, and yet putting their anxiety into a concern for other people, caring for other people and all their safeties. They must know how rotten and decayed everything, and everyone, was. Did they know, that generation? Or did they choose not to know? Or did they choose to carry on regardless, sure of the belief in themselves.

She shuddered. Paul was behind her; and then beside her.

She remembered their names. She called out: "Oh, Mr and Mrs Hindsley?" And as they turned: "Thank you so much for coming by."

They waved, and got into their car.

"Wave!" she said to Paul.

He did so. "Who are they?" he asked.

"We see them at church."

Here is Laurie. She shuts the door. She leans back against it. Paul stands before her, in his bathrobe, unshaven, his face swollen, pale and ugly. Hands behind her back Laurie stares at him, defying tears. She asks him, "Why is the world such a bad place?"

When Paul mumbles, "I don't know," she walks past him and goes into the bedroom. He calls out, after her, "Shall I put the alarm back on?"

"Yes," she says, "put on the fucking alarm."

She has made up her mind and now she will make up her face.

EIGHTEEN

Sunday: 8.15a.m. to 9.30a.m.

Here is Paul. Paul – Paul – has made up his mind. He goes into the bedroom with a cup of tea for Laurie.

She lay in bed, turned away to face the opposite wall. "Are you all right?" he asked. "Laurie?"

"Hm?"

"Are you all right?"

"I think so."

"What about the baby?"

"It feels . . . okay."

"Do you want to sleep?"

"Maybe. I want to, but I can't."

"No . . . "

"Did you sleep?"

"Some."

She rolled over, onto her back, to look at him. "I can't think about it. It's just suddenly there. I'm half asleep, and then it's happening all over again, right in front of me. I can't stop it happening. I don't want it to happen, it scares me so much, but it keeps happening – "

"Okay, it's okay."

"I don't understand why the police haven't come! I just don't want them to come. Paul? I don't want to go through with all that. I can't, I don't know if the baby will make it."

"Are you all right? Is there any pain?"

"Not now. When you were asleep. I should have called an ambulance. But I didn't think that it would come, otherwise I would have woken you."

"We should call one."

"I don't think so, not now. I think that everything's okay. Everything is still in the right place."

"How do you know?"

"I'd know if it wasn't. You'll have to trust me. As long as I stay quiet and rest."

"Okay. I made some tea. Do you want it?"

"Not right now. Maybe later. Thank you."

"You're kidding. I love you."

"We love you too." She smiled wanly and turned away.

He was far too awake, and was wired up, and was unable to leave her without making a decision. "I don't understand why they haven't come. They're going to come, you know."

"Uh-huh, I know."

"Laurie, it would be best if I was the one who had used the gun. I've thought it through. It would be better for you."

"It doesn't make any difference, does it?"

"Yes, it will do."

"It doesn't make any difference which of us did it. I did it for both of us. I did it to protect both of us . . . "

She was crying. He reached out to hold her shoulder.

"I know you did."

"You would have done the same, so it doesn't matter."

"But I'm not pregnant, I'm not carrying the baby. So it's better that the police talk with me. It's better that you rest. It's better that you came downstairs when it was over." Laurie didn't say anything. He felt that he knew exactly what he was talking about: how he had walked downstairs – how he had heard something and had gone downstairs with the gun and had fired at an intruder. In self-defence. Defending his family. His wife who was pregnant upstairs. His responsibility. "Do you see that, hon? You've got to see that you have to take it easy."

"I'm not going to lose this baby."

"*We're* not going to lose this baby. We're not going to risk it. You should take things real easy. I can do this. Laurie, it isn't that much different to the truth. I would have killed him."

"I was so scared that we would drop the gun . . . "

"It's all right. You did fine. You did the right thing. But we should say that I did it. It doesn't make any difference. I should have done it. And it won't make any difference except that you won't have to make a lot of statements to the police, and you shouldn't have to do that. I don't want you to have to do that."

"I don't know."

"I know. There's more than just you. It's not just you."

"I'll think about it."

"You woke up and came downstairs when it was all over. Then you went back to bed because you were scared of losing the baby. That's the truth, Laurie. And you called 911, and we were told that we should wait. Yes?"

"Yes."

"It's better that we waited. It's better this way. Okay?"

"Yes."

"That's good." He smiled at her. He stroked the hair back from her forehead.

"I don't want to think about it," she said. "Why don't they come? I don't want to go back downstairs, ever."

That hit him. Maybe she would never go back downstairs, nor ever look at the stuffed animals, friends, again. "It will go away," he said, "I promise you. It will all go away."

She snuffled. "It had better!" She managed a smile. Jesus Christ, she was strong. "I'm going to stay in here until it does."

"Yes," he said, "that's what you should do. You want some tea?"

"That darned tea." He thought that she was coming round,

bravely; but she stared at him in all kinds of crazed fear. He had never seen her like this, her eyes were wide open and there was no sign of her behind them, her mind was way out and frantic somewhere.

"Laurie?"

And when she narrowed her eyes, the whole movement was muscular and impersonal, the pose was artificial and crazed; it seemed like she was fading, there was so little life behind her.

"Do you promise me, that man will go away, it will all go away!"

"I promise you. I promise you."

"Then it's all right. I guess it's all right."

"It is." And, to his relief, she seemed to return.

Her skin was cold and she didn't seem to want him to look at her. She seemed to be paralysed, not wanting anything. He wanted to believe that she was acting, but he was too scared to believe anything at all. He too felt cold. He went to the bedroom door and switched on the heating. "I'll come back," he said. "Try to rest and keep warm. I'll come back. That tea is cold." He went into the kitchen.

My God? What was happening? Please?

He vomited into the kitchen sink, dry, but he was wet around the eyes from his coughing.

Her voice called from the bedroom, "Paul, are you okay? Paul?"

"Yes."

"Paul?" She had come into the kitchen.

"I'm okay."

"We have to keep calm, both of us."

"I know."

"We have to talk."

"Right. Yes. I'm cold; aren't you cold?"

"A little."

"I'll turn the thermostat up."

"Do you want some breakfast?"

She had her bathrobe tied around the waist. She had brushed her hair. Had she gone crazy?

"Do you want some breakfast?" Politely she asked him.

"No."

"We have to talk. You should eat something. Some toast." She opened the freezer door. "Muffins? I'm not hungry either, but it doesn't matter. Muffins and hot chocolate, right?"

"I guess so. What are you doing?" He asked her.

"I'm just making sure that I don't let you down. We have to know exactly what you're going to say."

For a half hour they had been watching TV coverage of the riots. He had been picking at his food. Laurie had a paper towel between her cup and her saucer. She was unnervingly precise. He didn't see how she could be so precise. The wind direction had changed, and smoke from the city brushed against the top of the house, the kitchen held some of the smell.

"We can't leave," Laurie said.

No, they couldn't leave.

She wiped the edge of the table.

He couldn't interfere with her. She seemed very much in control of herself, very aware of herself, and he didn't want to interfere with her. He didn't understand her, but he didn't want to upset any understanding which she had with herself. He didn't want to lose her to that craziness into which she had fled, in the bedroom.

"Paul," she scrutinised him, "tell me what happened."

"There was a noise downstairs."

"Before that."

"Before what? How long before?"

On the television a line of National Guardsmen walked down a street. People leaned against the walls of buildings and watched them; the streets were littered with debris, supermarket trolleys, burned-out automobiles. Traffic signals were dull black and lifeless, steel girders bent free of collapsed roofs. The streets were wet, smoke and steam rose wistfully from gutted stores.

"The police are going to come. They're going to want to know what happened and why. Paul!" She shouted, and then lowered her voice, and placed her hands out on the table, palms facing, as though she was measuring something. "I came downstairs, and ran back to get the gun. I came back and shot a man who was in our house, who was dangerous and a threat to us. We were in reasonable fear of our lives. I don't have any doubt about that, Paul."

"No."

"So that's what you did. You went down – "

"He refused to leave."

"Did he? Why would he do that, if you had the gun?"

"I don't know, Laurie."

"Was he armed?"

"No."

"You don't know that. You didn't know that."

"No."

"You see, I had a right to shoot him; you maybe didn't."

"I had no way of knowing that he wasn't armed."

"He came towards me, I asked him not to. He didn't refuse to leave. He came towards me, so I had to shoot him. There was nothing else to do. You didn't do anything. You might as well have been asleep upstairs. But you weren't. You were me. He threatened you. He did threaten you."

"Yes."

"You didn't have time to talk. You had come downstairs with the gun. We had dinner with friends, we had gone to bed. You were woken by a noise. You had the gun ready because of the riots. You took the gun and went downstairs. looking for the noise. It sounded like someone talking to himself. You opened the door to the basement room and saw him. He didn't refuse to go; why should he? Why should he think about staying? What right did he have to stay?"

On the screen, twenty-five maybe thirty black and hispanic people, men and women with their hands tied, lay face down in an empty parking lot, guarded by police.

"You know why I'm asking you this, don't you? Last night I killed someone."

"You were right."

"No, Paul. I was asleep. *You* were right. Remember? He threatened you. He came towards you. You were in reasonable fear of injury, or maybe being killed. So you shot him. He had no reason at all for being here, or for staying here."

"He had no right."

"None. Do you understand that? I *know* that."

"I know it too."

"What is it then? Hon?"

"It's . . . " He looked up at the ceiling. "I feel sorry for him."

She whispered, absently, "I do too. I feel sorry for everything; us, this, everything."

"And that's reasonable, is it?"

"Look at it." She looked at the television. "What else is there to feel? I just want everything to go away."

She got up from the table. She crossed her arms and went into the bedroom.

There was talk of federal aid. Paul pushed back his chair. Laurie was in the bathroom. He took the gun from the bedside table and wiped the handle with a kitchen towel. The heating furnace started up, in the basement. He stood in the hallway, holding the gun in his right hand, listening to the noise.

He went along the hallway, holding the gun in front of him, glancing into the study, into the dining room and the sitting room. He followed the noise, down the stairs. The door to the basement room had been ajar. Now it was closed, but it had been ajar. So he would have kept the gun in both hands. Mel would have been quite close to him, coming towards him. He would have heard Paul coming down the stairs. And he didn't leave, when he had the chance. He was close when the door swung open. The light was on. He came closer. And Paul shot once. And then there was violence and panic, and he had shot twice more.

There was some blood on the carpet by the bathroom door, from the first shot. The body was over by the windows, trying to get away. And the blood was all over the walls. He had been trying to get away. There was no reason for shooting him again. There was panic. There was reasonable fear of injury. An intruder might have been going to get a gun. And Paul had put the gun on the arm of the chair and had gone to check for this other gun. And knew that the man was dead. Then Laurie had come down and had touched the gun, and Paul had taken her back to bed. From where she dialled 911.

He went back upstairs.

He put the gun down by the side of their bed, where it had been before.

"What did you say during the 911 call?"

"That we had a suspected intruder."

"Nothing else?"

"Then they went through their questions, and the bottom line was that we weren't in any immediate danger. So they said that they had logged the call and they told us to wait."

"So you didn't say anything really."

"That was their bottom line. The system was at breaking point and we weren't in any immediate danger. We weren't, Paul. It was all over."

"No, that's okay, that's right. Take it easy. And what about the people who came round, this morning?"

"I didn't say anything to them."

"Nothing?"

"They asked if we were all right, and I said yes. That's what they wanted to know. They didn't want to know anything else. We were waiting for the police. They wouldn't have wanted to hear about it."

"You deliberately told them nothing?"

"Yes, I deliberately told them nothing. Or not deliberately; I told them nothing. Why should I? You were asleep. What should I tell them? I'm not as clear-headed about this as you are. I hadn't even talked to you about it. Those two old people are good people, they don't deserve it. What would they do? We were waiting for the police."

He couldn't figure this through, what it meant. He couldn't imagine how strange this must be, for her to exchange chat on the front step when she – he – had killed someone downstairs. What would these people think later? That Laurie had lied, that she was mad? That she, or her husband, had killed an intruder in the house and were just lazy about getting out of bed!?

"They said that it was terrible – "

"*It*?"

"The riots. They were scared. And they worried about us. I didn't want to upset them. We haven't done anything. We're innocent. What have I done wrong?"

She was going again. He watched in horror as her eyes stretched open and her voice tightened into a shrill. He was appalled. He was powerless. And, grotesquely, he feared that the neighbors might hear, that people like the Hindsleys might hear and clamor to see what he had done to his wife.

"Nothing. Laurie, you haven't done anything wrong. There isn't anything wrong."

She stared at him, kneeling on the bed. He wondered how long she had been naked. She shouldn't be naked, not naked and frenzied.

He repeated: "There isn't anything wrong." He didn't believe it. He believed that everything was wrong. He knew that everything was wrong from way, way back, and that there was no way of putting it right. There was only waiting, and that was horribly wrong.

"You don't believe it," she murmured. "I look at you, and I know that I don't believe it."

"Hon, you must believe it. You have to believe."

She looked down at the bed, at her belly. She said, calmly, "I know."

He said, "Because I'm the one who's going to have to lie."

She looked over her shoulder and reached for her robe. She said, "Oh Paul, we're both going to have to lie. Don't you know that? It won't be wrong, it'll be for each other, as a family. Go away, and don't think about it too much, and let me get dressed."

He went back to the kitchen. Down in the city the smoke had flattened, a dull breeze scraping it out towards the ocean. He collected the dishes and ran them under the faucet before putting them into the dishwasher. There was a body downstairs, the body of a man who had been trying to get out, finally. The body was leaning against the windows. The man was unarmed. The windows were not broken, they were closed. Nothing, apart from a few bits of furniture, was broken. He wasn't an intruder. There was nothing to say that he was an intruder. But he was black.

How long should he wait? How long would they have to wait?

"Paul, it's nearly nine-thirty," Laurie's voice complained from the doorway.

He turned from the sink to look at her, not understanding her complaint. He didn't know what to say. She had on a dark blue flowered dress, pantyhose and court shoes. Her make-up was immaculate, her hair brushed into shape, some of it gathered back by a white bow. He stared.

"Do I look all right?"

The question was so normal; and he answered normally, "Sure you do."

"Well, you've only got a few minutes."

"Yes." He didn't know what to do with her. How should he interfere, how should he bring her back?

"The morning service starts at ten. It's Sunday, remember? So we go to church. Sweetheart?"

NINETEEN

Sunday: 9.30a.m. to 10.00a.m.

He ran the basin half-full of hot water and added a burst of cold. The bathroom was silent. Laurie, he knew, was sitting in the kitchen, waiting for him to appear.

What should he do about Laurie? What could he do?

He shrank from every movement; and when he moved he felt that he was nothing more than the small ball of sickness and fear which hurtled around inside his corpse.

They would come, sometime, the police would come. He couldn't think now of anything to say to them. The body was downstairs, shot and cold. There was no story. There was only his mind, which skipped through words that were as insubstantial and haphazard as television images. He couldn't imagine that his voice would be capable of making any sense, it would not be able to arrange or interpret or make convincing the words which flitted through his mind. Nothing would remain still long enough to hold together.

Oh God; he wished that Mel was still alive. He wished that Mel would rise up, and knock at the windows and ask him and Laurie if he could come in for safety, for care. They were kind, he and Laurie; they were not terrified, they wouldn't refuse Mel. He might have been anyone. Paul might have met him in a bar, he might have asked Paul for medical advice. He might have explained that he had to get away from the riots. They might have taken him at his word. Nothing wrong might have happened, in daylight.

He was kidding himself. He was being naïve. Laurie would not have been so naïve.

How would Laurie be? The thought scared him, it pulled him up. Laurie wasn't thinking. It scared him that she was no longer thinking, that she was beside herself with shock and worry, that he couldn't arrange her or seem to convince her of anything.

Whatever he said to the police, would depend on what she would say. All she had to do was to tell the truth, her truth: they had had an intruder and she had shot him. It *was* the truth. She had done the right thing. She was right. As long as he played no part in it, she was right. She had done nothing wrong.

His fear dissolved. There was nothing wrong. All that he was going to do was to substitute himself for her, because she was pregnant. He had done nothing wrong. Even if the story came apart at the seams, they would see that he was simply shielding her and protecting her, in all innocence; he was acting for her, saving her.

With his right hand he stirred the water in the washbasin. He looked at himself in the mirror. This would work, it would work. It was right. And of course Laurie knew that it was right.

He would redeem himself.

With his right hand he took the shaving-brush, and wet it, and worked it over the soap in the shaving-bowl. He took a brushful of lather and rubbed it into his stubble, as he had done for more than a dozen years. He had always wetshaved, ever since his father had given him his first shaving-brush and a boxed and cellophaned bar of Roger & Gallet soap. Even when he had been poor he had ordered this same soap, even when he had been mocked for its scent and his own ritual of lathering and scraping, by Laurie amongst others. There was no better sensation than this smooth, wet, perfumed, soapy, shave; the removal of hair and dead skin, the cleanliness and the smell which returned reliably, time after time along the years.

He remembered the shower at Mel's, that small bathroom. There was a cheap electric razor. It was a cheap place.

He wanted the police to come now. The whole thing should be over and done with. The police should come; now. It was over. It was grotesque: they were here on a hillside with a burnt-out city beneath them and a body in the basement, and the police did nothing about it. What were he and Laurie supposed to do! Yes, they should get dressed up; yes, they should start to live again. They were innocent, they had done nothing wrong.

He dressed quickly, in a light suit and tie.

When he went into the kitchen, he felt suddenly annoyed with her. She was watching the television, watching a politician in Washington talk about the riots. He didn't understand why she was watching this, staring vacantly at the screen, shrouded by indecision.

"I guess the telephone lines are down," he said.

She asked, "Why?"

"There hasn't been one single incoming call, not from anybody."

"Not from Bill?"

"What?"

"Not from Bill, to thank us for dinner."

He despaired. "Not from anyone, Laurie. Not from your parents, or from my parents, or from anybody. They don't know if we're all right. We have to call them. You'd think they would have called."

"I took the phone off the hook."

"Why? Why did you do that!"

"Don't shout at me."

He restrained himself. "Why did you do that?"

"I didn't want to talk to anybody."

"It's not right, Laurie," he said gently. "What if the police called?"

"*I* didn't want to talk to anybody, *I* didn't want to tell them. I don't want to hurt them, I don't want our parents to worry. You know what they'd do? They'd come here. I don't want my father to come here. I don't know what to say to anybody. You promised me, you *promised* me."

She shook her head from side to side, "You never remember, do you?"

"Laurie . . . " He couldn't think of how to get a hold on her.

She stood up and smoothed her dress.

"We're going to be late."

In the hallway, he heard the whine of the abandoned telephone, from his study. He went in and replaced the handset, and expected it to ring. It didn't. When he came back to the hallway, Laurie was standing, holding her purse, rooted to the spot as though she was waiting for an elevator. He understood immediately that she wouldn't or couldn't go down the hallway towards the garage door, to the stairs.

"I'll bring the car around," he said. He didn't look at her.

His shoes made a loud noise on the floorboards. He tried to think of this noise as purposeful, then as casually normal. He knew what was downstairs, but he didn't think about it. He thought that the stair carpet needed vacuuming, and then he opened the door to the garage, and closed it behind him.

Standing on the concrete, he thought that Laurie looked impeccable. She was impersonal, beyond understanding; the lower half of her body sheathed in Lycra, the top contained within loose cotton, her hair falling to a straight line, just above the collar. It was all so strange, as strange as himself standing in his suit and laced shoes amongst the faint garage smell of oil. Without thinking he pressed the button to open the garage door and the outside world crawled in, higher and higher until the sunlight straightened up and he blinked at its barefaced gall.

Half-blinded he walked past the car and stared outside and heard crickets and bugs and insects, a whole aggravated vibrancy coming from the glare, down by his feet, around his feet somewhere but flooding across from the distance; there was nothing at his feet but concrete, the life was a noise which reached in from the hillside.

He relaxed instantly. He was astonished at how he relaxed, how much he shed, how eccentric he felt in front of all this busy serenity.

There came the unwieldy thought that he ought to look around, that on the other side of the house there were riots, there was a life of riots, also in sunlight, also vibrant; and that he was in the middle, in this 1717, this cold house with a dead body underneath and a beautiful woman standing waiting with a live foetus sheltered within her.

There couldn't be much more to life. He ought to stop, and look. He ought to stop, right now, with his feet on bare concrete and look at all these things without taking a count of them. All these components *were*. And they were incredible, they were simply unbelievable. He shouldn't move, he shouldn't dislodge them. He shouldn't make any pathetic attempt to explain them. It was like a painting, or a photograph, with the focal point missing.

He had gone missing. For a moment he could imagine that he had gone missing. The sunlight was so warm, so absorbent. You could imagine that nothing would ever happen to you; that all life would carry on according to fine principles. That you could go missing. That you, your rotten scummy self, could go missing.

He looked around. It was stupid to feel secure. He walked back into the garage and opened the door to the Mercedes.

The interior of the car was cold, like inside the house. The seats were soft and unmarked; a creamy, pliant leather. If he had to come up with one single reason for buying the car, it was because of its smell, that powdery smell of the leather. He didn't like the seats themselves, and the smooth movements of the car always made him feel clammy and uncomfortable. Several times he had stalled the car. It wasn't a car that reacted well to anger, it needed the smallest of requests to purr, it ignored any human emotion.

The engine ticked quietly into life, and the car glided out of the garage with no pressure on the accelerator pedal. The only sounds were the hush of the power-steering and the sandpapery scratch of the tires on particles of concrete. He reached for the remote and the garage door shut itself, sealing the house away. He shifted the gear select, which clicked happily into place. He spun the steering wheel again and the car pulled gently forward. Outside the front door he dabbed at the brake, and the car stopped dead, brusquely rebuking his clumsiness. He pushed the select into P, for Park, detesting the wretched sensitivity of the machine and its defiance.

Laurie came out onto the doorstep and shut the door behind her, carrying her purse. He got out of the car.

"Did you set the alarm?"

"Yes, it's all set." She smiled. She looked beautiful, but he didn't want to tell her.

"Do you want to drive?"

"No," she said, "you drive."

He opened the passenger door for her. He didn't usually do this. She never liked him to do this. Long ago she had told him that it made her feel like an invalid, that she was quite capable of getting into a car by herself. He didn't know why he was doing it now, except that he was pathetically angry at her composure; and this made him feel weak, and childish. She sat down and swung her legs in after her, and tucked her dress in at the side of the seat. "Thank you," she said, demurely.

He closed the door and walked around the back of the car. She was already fiddling with the air-conditioning and the window-switches, closing the window which he had opened to air out the Mercedes from its garage sepulchre.

"Okay," he said, pulling his door shut, "are we going to do this thing?"

"Are we going to go to service? – Yes. Do you want the window down?"

"Not necessarily, if you're hot."

"Being pregnant makes me feel hot all the time, and wearing pantyhose isn't comfortable."

"Why don't you take them off?"

"Because I want to look nice."

"You do look nice."

"Thank you. So do you."

"How do you feel?"

"Fantastic."

"Laurie . . . "

"You feel fantastic, at this stage. Later on it gets to be really uncomfortable and a nuisance, but at this stage you just feel great and there's nothing that can stop you feeling that way. Nothing. Except for being hot. I guess it's one of those really selfish things, darling. You just have to go with it."

He hesitated. "O-kay." He nodded.

They drove down Jerome. There was no other traffic. Most of the houses were shut up as though, if there were any occupants, they were asleep. Where Jerome hit Francis, at the intersection, a group of people stood and talked. Paul knew them by sight, as neighbors, but he didn't wave and they stood stiffly, close together, and watched the car go by like nothing so foreign should impinge upon the roadside.

"People are uptight," Laurie murmured, as though they came from another planet.

"They're scared."

"They shouldn't be. Nothing could happen to them that hasn't already happened to us. They're hiding it."

"Aren't you scared?" He felt that maybe they could begin to talk rationally, that maybe the horizon might solidify.

"No. I don't have any room to feel scared."

He took a left, and they started climbing up towards the pass. It might have been any beautiful Sunday. They came to a viewing point and he pulled in against the white concrete kerb. Laurie continued to look ahead. He put the shift into Park. She looked at him, maybe sad, maybe charitable, even maybe coy. "Do you want me to drive?"

"No, it's not that."

"What is it then?"

"I want to kiss you."

She said, "Sure."

Their lips met. Firmly, and he went on, tasting her tongue, meeting no refusal. He put his hand on her thigh. Breaking the kiss he looked past her, out of the car window at the smouldering basement of the city. "I love you."

"I know."

"Do you know?" Her body was pliant, and accepting.

"Yes, I know that you love me. I don't know that you love me now. I know that you're nervous and you're feeling insecure, and that's understandable."

He withdrew his hand. When he leaned back he saw that she was looking, bemused, at him. His hand moved naturally to the shift. "Right," he said, "okay. As long as you know that I love you."

"It doesn't hurt to say it."

They both started to smooth the ruffle in her dress, but she let him complete the move; her hand pushed her hair away from the nape of her neck, she complaining again that it was hot, and she leaned forward away from the back of the car seat. He felt quite alone, but this time it didn't bother him. The days of losing himself in her were long over. She wouldn't harbor him; he accepted that. He loved her anyway. And he loved her for giving him something to live up to. He didn't have to be scared of her.

There was a safety of responsibility, which was his. He shifted the Merc into Drive, and they went up into the pass.

Range Rovers, Suburbans, BMWs, Lexus, and the older, classier Jaguars and Lincolns. Pick-ups and station wagons, Japanese and the occasional American. There was nowhere to park. He left Laurie in the one piece of shade outside the church and drove back to the first unoccupied space.

He locked the car and walked through the heat. There was still the smell of smoke, he wondered if there would ever be an end to that smell. Pinpoints of black ash settled on the arms of his suit. There was another man in front of him, and two men some way behind, but there was no talking and an almost deliberate attempt not to walk together. It was like going to a funeral, the church building seeming to exert a magnetic pull towards death by sunlight. He saw Laurie, looking fresh and pretty under the tree, waiting for him, and his heart filled with pride. He was so glad of her, the confident way she stood waiting for him as if he would in some way add to her. There would be no kind of life without her. Jesus Christ but she was pretty. She needn't have said that she felt fantastic: she looked it, every bit of a beautiful girl, or woman. His. It was hardly believable. He could almost envy himself. If she had not been his, he could have stood still and envied the man who took her arm and walked with her. It would have been a lucky man, and almost certainly someone who didn't deserve her, whom she didn't get along with. Maybe someone who didn't appreciate her, and who cheated on her. Someone who must be a blind fool.

Thank God he had got away with it. How could he ever have been so stupid? Thank God it was all over without destroying them.

"Are you all right?" she asked.

"Yes I am. I am. I had to park the car miles away."

She smiled at the two men who were passing, who both

looked at her as if they couldn't decide what expression to wear. "What's with those guys?" she whispered.

"Laurie, you look beautiful. Out of this world."

"Let me take your arm."

"You don't feel good?"

"Just let me take your arm. It's no big deal. I'm your wife. I want everybody to know that. Don't you?"

TWENTY

Sunday: 10.00a.m. to 11.20a.m.

Together, they walked into the church.

She didn't look at Paul, she held to his arm while he guided her to a pew at the back of the church, on the left side of the left aisle, this being one of the last unoccupied spaces. They usually sat nearer the front, but the church was much fuller than usual and they had left the house much later than usual. She was glad that they were not nearer the front. There was a palpable tension amongst the congregation, she felt, not arising from the congregation; because their mood was flat, and depressed. They waited patiently in defeat.

She knelt and prayed insistently, walling herself in from the despair which threatened to rise through her, separating herself from Paul. She adjusted herself to the quiet sadness which eddied through the church. She asked for forgiveness, but felt only its impotence. She prayed for her mother and father and child, for the grace of God, for peace and an end to evil, for goodness to survive, for her doubts to disappear.

When she rose up off her knees and sat, she felt no godliness in the people, no confidence. She was glad that she was not sitting near to the front, hemmed into the center of the other people who were so tense with surrender. She felt the mass of this simple reaction, not as a weight but as a headless, disparate abnegation. Simple, trusting people were fine in ones or twos – she saw Mr and Mrs Hindsley on the other side of the church – but as a mass they were implausible: perhaps senseless, perhaps morose. She wondered just how many hypocrites there were, here. How many cruel people, how many liars. The church was inevitably well furnished with usurers – how else would most of the congregation keep their Christian dreams alive, or be able to afford to pass them on to their children?

I must not despise myself, she thought. And why do I despise Paul? Is it so important? Are my feelings so important?

They would both have to be tested for Aids.

Wouldn't that be enough? She had no doubt but that they would both test negative, Paul wasn't an utter imbecile. Wouldn't that humiliation be sufficient?

She looked down at her dress, the new, favorite dress. Flowered crepe. Drop. Nice gathers down the front. She had been saving it. She would have saved it longer, and not for a time when she needed it. It might just last through the end of the pregnancy.

Maybe she felt so out-of-place amongst all these people because she was the only person who was angry, who was so darned angry that she despised them all.

She couldn't see Paul for detesting him. She couldn't see past him. She couldn't imagine ever seeing past him.

She said a quick prayer for her father. She wondered if she should tell him. Maybe she should fly back east and tell him everything. It would be a way out. But would it? It wouldn't be a way out for her, and she didn't want a way out, not that way. It wouldn't stop or change how she felt, it would only change her surroundings. She didn't like those surroundings and she wouldn't find anything there. Arriving on the doorstep with her suitcase full of unwashed feelings would be like bringing home trophies and trying to find a place for them on the sideboard, which was exactly what her sister always tried to do. Poor Debbie, she always met with exactly the same lack of success. Maybe Paul should have married her, she had plenty of feelings to spare. Debbie was never as hard as she was, maybe Paul wouldn't have cheated on her, or been driven to cheat on her. Debbie was not as hard. As she was.

The choir sang their way in. Two lines drew up behind the altar, she watched them form. They had a certain authority, a staunch civic pride in the city of God which they advertised by their spotless, creaseless surplices. She liked the choir. They were two shelves of stuffed animals, with all the acceptable varieties, American-Afro-Caribbean, American-Chinese, American-Italian, American-Greek, American-Hispanic, American-shaken-and-stirred. Some of the singing she liked, although sometimes she didn't care for the mix of twelve male and twelve female voices, lost in unison. She had once mentionned this to Paul and had asked him what he thought, and he had replied that he hadn't paid much attention because he had been trying to think up two dozen menus. That had been months ago.

Months ago. Before anything had happened. Or *maybe* before he had been unfaithful – she had to believe that. She couldn't have been that easily fooled for so long, could she? She couldn't have been that easily brought to laughter, so easily disarmed by his two dozen menus. No way.

She looked down. Someone in front of her, two or three rows in front of her, was crying. She refused to believe that it could have anything to do with personal sadness.

When she looked up again, the church was silent. The minister, John Pearson, stood in front of the altar. He opened his arms to the congregation, and then dropped them. She saw that he had lost it. His head bent forward. There was a huge tension between wanting to bury yourself, and wanting to cry out something vast, almost as brutally as at a football game. Someone coughed. The minister looked up, as if he sought whatever strength was in the noise, and he opened his arms, holding them out, stricken with self-consciousness and uneasy at this, his, theatricality.

"Friends. My friends." He lowered his hands and clasped them in front of him.

He spoke without looking at anybody, and it seemed that nobody wanted their eyes to meet, although they wanted to look at him. Laurie wanted to look at him. She didn't want to know that Paul was next to her.

"Welcome to you all. This is the last Sunday before Pentecost. This is the first Sunday after a terrible tragedy, which has not avoided any of us. Not any single one of us. There isn't a heart in this . . . place . . . which hasn't been crushed and anguished by what has happened to our community. *Our* community, which is of every race and color and creed.

"There is no-one here who doesn't recognise the full extent of this . . . great . . . unhappiness. We do not know what to feel. We do not know how to feel. We cannot say what we feel because there are no words to express how we feel. But it is right that after so much destruction and despair, we express ourselves together.

"Our Father – "

They joined, with him, as one. "Who art in Heaven. Hallowed be Thy name. Thy kingdom come. Thy will be done. As in Heaven, so on Earth. Give us this day . . . "

"Amen."

"Amen."

"Let us pray."

For guidance. For peace. For the sick and the old. For all those people who had suffered the pain of loss. For all those people who worked in danger to restore calm. For understanding.

They remained on their knees, led in their prayers by John Pearson, until he fell silent, having called upon them for a period of private reflection, which he himself described as a privilege that, in the Lord's name, should not be misused. Laurie saw that

Paul was bent forward, as though shielding himself, with his hands clasped over the back of his head.

She didn't wish for any private reflection, not now. Her mind had focused when she had first entered the church, and she could not now pick through the bits and pieces which were flung up by her emotions. Her mind was a blank.

She drifted away on a daydream, the memory of a shoreline and a long expanse of unmarked sand over which she walked, the sea fallen back on her right, a line of debris thrown up, away to her left. There was no wind, not even the lightest of breezes, and so there was no smell; and her hair never touched her face. She had no sense of the air. But she was exalted. Inside her was a paean of joy, a triumphant confusion which she waited passively to deliver. Sadness? No. Perhaps behind her, but she had no eyes in the back of her head and she wasn't supposed to turn around. She was supposed to lift her head, to see, to hear . . .

She opened her eyes. One of the choir, a black woman, was singing. A beautiful song, moving powerfully from her chest to the rich pride of her eyes, issuing strength, demanding strength:

"Lord lift us up where we belong . . .
Where the eagles cry, on a mountain high . . .
Lord lift us up where we belong . . .
Far from the world we know, where the clear wind blows . . ."

No, Laurie thought, no; this is, who is this? This is from a movie. This is Joe Cocker, isn't it? And a woman. No, Luther Vandross. This is a song from a movie?! This must be LA.

But this *was* LA. And the song was powerful and was beautiful, and was spiritually uplifting. She herself was kneeling, others were kneeling, some were sitting. This was their cry to God, for His grace, for their salvation. And the woman's solo voice was fantastic, reaching to them all and for them all. Stricken and mute as they were, she pleaded and wept and sang out for all of them, each and every heart. Sitting, kneeling, some standing, their voices joined her for the final chorus.

She couldn't help but wonder what the minister, John Pearson, had been doing over the last twenty-four hours, where he had been, what he had seen, and how he had planned and prepared this service.

Drained and frail as he looked, his words were always careful. Not for one moment did he give way to anger or sorrow, although these emotions were never far from the surface and were quite clear to his congregation. The hymns which he had chosen were not melancholy, nor were they evasive. The Lord could not rely upon being praised, the congregation could not rely upon being succored. The still, small voice of calm would have to be well matched.

He didn't walk to the lectern. Laurie wondered for a moment if he had the energy or the need to give a sermon. The congregation sat down, and this, surely, was the time for reflection, to reconcile the inner soul with the turbulence that had been vividly and publicly expressed, and united. People needed to be blessed. They waited to be blessed. Their minister stood with his hands clasped in front of him.

"*Nobody* is going to throw me out of my neighborhood." He stopped.

Laurie, as everyone else, watched him.

"Nobody is going to do that. This is our city. This is *our* problem.

"How many of you feel frightened here, in this church, on this Sunday, now? And how many of you feel terrified, *here*, inside, deep down?

"Every single one of us feels that way.

"Nobody is going to throw *me* out of my neighborhood.

"I thank you for coming here, to this place, for taking part in our service of thanksgiving and worship. It wouldn't be right to stay at home and count your blessings, nor to count your losses. It is our duty, as human beings, to help make things better, to be together. I thank you all for having the courage to come here, for having the courage to show your courage.

"It hasn't been a fun weekend, has it? Eight hundred and fifty families homeless, one hundred killed, nineteen thousand arrested, five thousand arson attacks. I don't know if these figures are correct. I don't know how we can count our losses. I do know that we have been declared a disaster area. *We* have been declared a disaster area.

"No. No! This is *our* city. This is *our* problem. Money is needed to restore the buildings. Much, much more will be needed to restore the heart of this city. Much more still will be needed to rebuild the hearts and souls and minds of our citizens.

"The system says that we are a disaster area. But we are *not* a disaster area.

"How can you believe in the system?! How can you believe in something you see doesn't work?!

"How can you believe in God's presence, His mercy, His grace? But you do. You believe. And by believing and by helping out and by coming together, you show that *you* believe that things in the future will be better.

"Nobody is going to throw me out of my faith.

"We feel not scared, but inadequate.

"We breathe smog. The rivers wash mud into our houses. We fight brush fires with small garden hoses. We grasp for our lives to an earth which has always tried to throw us off.

"Nobody is going to throw me out of my neighborhood. Says who? Says God? But the words were spoken to me by an African American who stared at the looted, battle-scarred, half-burned store beneath her apartment. This morning I offered her sympathy as I do, as one does. I commiserated. And she said to me: nobody is going to throw me out of my neighborhood.

"Neither she, nor thousands like her, of whatever sex, color or race, are a disaster area. They are frightened, they are displaced, they are desperate. They have been trashed. And they tell their children: this is our neighborhood, this is our city, this is our problem – you take those useless things which you have looted, you put them right back in that store.

"I ask you, I beg you: be adequate. Donations, yes. Of money, and food, and clothing. To here or to the First AME Church in the midtown, with whom we must work. But, more important, *show* that you are adequate. Show that this is your city. Show the world, by all means; but show yourselves. That you have belief in this city. That you refuse to accept its racial boundaries and its inequalities.

"How can you not believe in something you see work?

"There are bulletin boards in my office here. There are bulletin boards in the entrance to the church. If we can get down there and in there and help out, if we can share the disaster and the cleaning up, if we respond together, then we can get together in our lives. This city is our neighborhood! Show that we care. Show that we are together, and that nobody is going to throw us out of our neighborhood!

"May God bless us, and keep us, all of us together."

As soon as John Pearson's voice ceased, the organist began his introduction. The choir lifted their hymn books. The final hymn was habitually meditative, the members of the congregation tending to sing out in relief at the end of the sermon while considering whom they might greet and buttonhole outside the church, and to whom they should pay their respects.

This was not the mood. What would they talk about? Everybody knew that everybody had a story about the riots, and that no story could match the minister's valediction. He had not comforted them, nor urged them to seek comfort. He had not offered them any confidential sympathy, nor absolved their fears. He had, concisely, offered them the challenge to prove to themselves that they were not inept and vulnerable bystanders. The choir sang out:

"Lift up your heart, lift up your voice,
Rejoice, again I say Rejoice!"

It was agreed.

It was strange, Laurie saw, how men and women agreed differently. The men clustered around the bulletin board, rejoicing in the activity of organisation, while the women assembled a database of contacts who might have access to what might be needed, and how it could be obtained through their husbands or their own working lives. Many of them wanted to make useful what they had at home. They wanted something to come from their homes. It wasn't a source to which the men referred, as far as Laurie could overhear. Their authority would be contrived elsewhere.

She was being unfair. There were couples who talked quietly to each other near the bulletin board, and younger people in groups undifferentiated according to sex. And there was Mr Hindsley and another older man in her group, talking about brooms and blankets and what they could do; guided by Mrs Hindsley who had obviously survived several instances of deprivation, and most obviously The Depression.

Where was Paul? Where was he? She looked around for him, not wanting this to be noticed. Her condition had, by unstated general consent, precluded her involvement in any organisation or action, which both touched and annoyed her. Where was Paul?

Suddenly she saw Paul coming out of the church. He put on his sunglasses and walked past the crowd. Then, as if it had occurred to him that he had neglected his duties, he returned and stood on the edge of the people around the bulletin board. He leaned forward to look at the notices. He took off his sunglasses. Laurie saw that he was pretending to read, he looked shocked and abstracted. A girl came up and tried to talk to him, he stepped back to avoid her, smiling in a ghostly way, nodding as he replied to her, replacing his sunglasses. They both agreed with something that was on the board. Paul nodded affirmatively. His hand came up and he pointed one way, then another, as if confirming a street direction; and then they disengaged, the girl went back to her group.

Paul walked away, towards the road. He lifted his glasses and rubbed his hand over his forehead and through his hair. He shook his head, as if there was a wasp around him, but Laurie saw that he was nervous and bewildered.

"Has your husband forgotten about you, Laurie, dear?" Mrs Hindsley said. "My husband does exactly the same. Sometime ago he drove down to K-Mart to look for me and I was in the kitchen. It's not that he doesn't know where I am, for goshsakes, he just doesn't know where *he* is."

"I think that's it," Laurie agreed. She watched Paul. She watched for any sign of what he was thinking, of what he was going to do.

"Doctor Mathiessen?!" Mrs Hindsley called.

He walked abruptly towards them.

"I think that we should go," Laurie said.

"I think that you should, too. It is just enough for all of us to see you here like this, such a fine hope for the future."

"You'll keep me in touch, Mrs Hindsley?"

"I will, sweetheart. Have Paul take you home and make sure you get your rest."

"Oh, I will," Paul said.

"I know you will. You are both such good people."

They said goodbye to the group. Other people were too involved to notice them leave.

"Do you want me to get the car?" Paul asked.

"No, I want to walk."

"It's quite a-ways."

"It doesn't matter. It isn't going to rain. I want to walk with you, out here, like this."

She put on her sunglasses. She took his arm. He was tense. She relaxed. They walked through an avenue of automobiles.

She said, "Nobody else is going home."

He said nothing.

She said, "I guess that it was a fine sermon. John always finds some way through to us. He has a way of lifting people's hearts, and minds." She waited. "Don't you think?"

"What!?" He snapped, and then retreated. "Yes. He gets the best out of people."

"And that's all you can do: whatever happens."

"Yes."

"What's wrong? You don't like this new dress?"

"Yes. Yes, I do."

"Do you want to go back there and join in with everybody? – you don't have to take me home. Just because I'm pregnant it doesn't mean that I can't drive the car. Darling? Tell me what's wrong. I'm worried about you. Paul?"

"The police didn't log our call." He let go of her arm. "The goddamn police didn't log our call! Jesus Christ . . . !" She waited for his anger to swirl, and turn. " . . . useless fucking police."

"So? We can call again." She took his hand, which was wet with sweat. "When we get back to the house we can call again."

"I *have* called again! Laurie, there is no record. I have called again and there's nothing!"

"Well," she said timidly, "we can just call them, can't we? Why can't we do that? They'll come. They will. Remember: 'this is our neighborhood'? No-one's going to make us leave. Don't be scared, Paul. It makes me scared. We'll call them, and they'll come!"

He looked at her. She saw him trying to feel how she was, trying to calculate. "It's all right," he said gently. "Everything will be all right. Stay here and I'll get the car." He put his arm round her and squeezed her.

She shuddered, involuntarily. "Let's walk," she said. "It's a beautiful day. I have a new dress on and I want to feel beautiful."

TWENTY-ONE

Sunday: 11.20a.m. to 1.15p.m.

They walked.

He couldn't believe it. He couldn't believe in anything, not the sunshine, not the sound of his feet on the road surface, not the greasy feel of the sunglasses on the bridge of his nose.

He had to hold onto her and keep her stable, he had to keep her on some sort of level, he had to maintain some sanity. For it was as though she was constantly on the point of losing herself. He had no idea whether she would collapse downwards or disappear upwards. He had to keep her. He had to protect her. She trusted him to protect her.

At times, during the church service, it had been as though there were moods, or visions, or emotions crawling up through her body, devastating her. He had thought that she would never get up off her knees from praying, and yet, when she stood up, she blazed up through the dampness of tears, terrifyingly naked in expression. And he couldn't tell whether this had anything to do with the past or whether this had anything to do with the future. There was no restraint. There was just this slipstream of a blue flowered dress which held off from wherever her mind was. And not merely her mind, but her self. He prayed only that the service would be over.

And when it was over, he thought, he knew, that he had to speak to the minister.

He had left her with the Hindsleys, talking about sleep, his own apparent ability to sleep perplexing Mrs Hindsley. He accepted the rebuke, which Laurie had laughed off. He left Laurie with them and went back through the church, into the minister's room.

There was no-one there. A female member of the choir had come in. Paul apologised for being in the room and asked if Mr Pearson was out front. As a matter of fact, the minister was exhausted. The minister would be down at the First AME Church in the afternoon, everybody would be basing themselves in that district. Paul would be very welcome. There were many details on the bulletin board over the desk. Any help, any help at all . . .

She had hugged him. She had asked him what his own situation was, whether he was in trouble. He had smiled, and had said something encouraging, and she had gone, telling him that of course he could use the phone.

He had begun to dial, but he cancelled the call. He dialled 1717 instead, and listened to the answering machine. Then he dialled again with the message withdrawal code, and there were messages from his parents and Laurie's parents, and from one of his brothers; maybe a half-dozen messages and none of them from the police department.

He couldn't understand how this could be so. Or why it should be so! Why should this happen? The riots were calmed down. There were a hundred deaths. Nobody knew the figures. One of them was in his house. How could they not care? How could they not be interested? How could this happen! What else then was happening that stopped this death being confirmed?

He looked at the bulletin board above a trestle-table. There was a large map of the county, with arrows and tags: Blankets, Food, E Welfare Checks, Prescriptions, Hot Meals, Red Cross. Everything to do with the logistics of support, everything to do with emergency, and dozens of numbers for information. There was a Clean-up Rally on the intersection between Olympic

Boulevard and Normandie Avenue, its schedule and its aims in widening circles. And there, to the northwest, was Jerome, some distance away, unmarked, uninvolved, private. Nothing touched Jerome. Nothing would approach Jerome. Nothing had happened at Jerome. Just an incident, becoming ever more isolated.

He had then dialled the police department, and had said that he didn't know whether it was an emergency or not. Yes, he was at the First Episcopal Church. They were missing some members of their congregation and he was enquiring if there had been any reports of an accident or . . . or any trouble on their street. Jerome.

There was nothing logged.

Nothing?

He should understand that they could give out no further information to any member of the public. Maybe the people had gone away. A lot of people had left. There was a call-in number for missing people.

Nothing had been reported?

Nothing. There was nothing on the log.

Thank you.

Thank you, sir.

He replaced the phone. The minister's room was silent. His desk was leather-topped, polished and expensive. The opposite wall was lined with bookcases which were filled with books; theological, reference, and literary. It was very quiet and civilised, a retreat for the purposes of study, somewhere where sermons would be researched, written, and considered. The trestle-table was a recent addition, Paul remembered seeing two easy chairs removed to the hallway.

Again he had scrutinised the map above the table and had seen Jerome, and his eyes fell upon the slight bend in the road off which ran the driveway to 1717. He put his hands in his pockets and clasped his coat around him. He was so angry. It didn't matter what happened at 1717. They didn't matter. Jesus Christ, the blacks could trash their own trashy part of town, and everyone came running. He and Laurie were alone and nobody came. There was just the two of them and nobody cared.

He left the minister's room and walked through the empty church, his footsteps echoing noisily on the parquet floor, ringing with anger amongst the empty chairs. There was a crowd of people at the church doors, a hive of enthusiastic and serious helpers. Intimidated, he slowed his step. He was so angry. He stared uncomprehendingly at the lists of volunteers and plans and appeals, and someone talked to him and got him enrolled to do he didn't know what; and then he was free, walking away with his anger, which beat up as the sun beat down; and he had wanted his anger to triumph, to hold out, with each footstep. He didn't want to think. He wanted to be angry. If he could just hold on to this anger, this crowding anger, against the sun and the people. He didn't want to have to think.

But the thinking had come. He felt himself weakening. In his house, at home, they had the body of an unarmed man. Who had been dead for twelve hours. Which had not been reported. And during that time, the alarm system had been on and off and on, all recorded, and people had called, and they themselves had gone out. And there was no sign of intrusion. The french windows were shut, the alarm system was faithful unto itself. Inside his house was an unexplained and unexplainable body. The man had been shot. The walls were covered in blood. There was no riot, no reason, no . . .

It was homicide.

She had a new dress. She took his arm. He couldn't tell her. He didn't want her to be scared. She wanted to trust him.

They came to the car. She looked at it awry, then squeezed his arm and laughed. "Such a horrible car," she said. "But no worse than any of the others." She leaned against the side of the car and turned her face to the sun. "We could get into the car and go anywhere, and yet we usually get into the car and drive home, and have lunch, and stay home. We maybe do some gardening and watch television and you get ready to go to work on Monday. I like all of that. And it's what we have to do." She took off her sunglasses and leaned back again, closing her eyes against the glare. "There are times out, like this, when it's really great to be with you. We have some wonderful times together. Truly. I never, ever, regret being married to you."

He coughed nervously.

"Don't worry, Paul. Everything's fine." She stood up and put on her sunglasses. "I might duck out on the gardening."

"Please, Laurie, take it easy. You can't do . . . nobody would expect you . . . I don't want you to get involved with anything. We have to figure out – " He heard his voice running wild again, and made himself stop. "We just have to wait. And you have to rest up."

"You're right. I don't want to walk anymore."

"We have to get into the car and go home."

"Yes." She waited. He unlocked the doors, and held her door open for her. She thanked him.

He walked round the front of the car. As he opened the driver's door he thought, I need a lawyer. He paused. He looked along the roof of the car, out at the hillside. He said to himself, I need a lawyer. I'm going to need a criminal lawyer. We're going to need something other than ourselves to protect us.

His anger was still there, but it was righteous. He felt happier. He sat in the car next to Laurie and started the engine. "I want to call by the office," he told her.

"Sure."

"I want to see if it's still there."

"It will be, won't it?"

"It should be."

Although, he thought, God knows what "should" meant

anymore. There was no value in "should". It was a pretty flimsy guideline.

"Paul, don't drive so fast."

"I am? Okay. Sorry."

They came over the top of the pass and looked down over the city, smouldering in sunlight. He thought, I have things to do. I have to do this. We need help. I don't need a way out, I need a way in. I need a way back in to the police.

He took the freeway towards the office. There was no traffic. It was Sunday. He was pleased. It was his freeway and it was the only empty space he had had for what seemed like a lifetime. Laurie sat expressionless beside him. The car moved perfectly over the ripples of concrete. It was easy. The freeway was empty. There was no traffic at all. He deserved this. It was a break. There was no other human being on the road.

And then he saw why. He took his foot off the accelerator. There was a highway patrol roadblock up ahead, black and white and shining in the sun. And, as he drew closer and slowed, there was a military convoy pulled up on the other side of the roadblock.

There was no way out. Two patrolmen flagged him into the slow lane and he stopped. A group of National Guardsmen cradled automatic weapons and stepped forward from the crash barrier. One of the patrolman lifted a bullhorn. "Turn off your engine, and get out of your car." He did so. "Stand away from the car."

He did so, and shouted: "My wife is pregnant!"

The patrolman put the bullhorn down on the freeway and came towards him, followed at a distance by his back-up. He stood staring at Paul, the normal tinted precaution.

"This lady's pregnant? The lady in the car?"

"Yes, sir."

"And you're taking her to the hospital."

"No, she's not that pregnant. We were going to my office. I'm a doctor. She's my wife."

"This is not an emergency?"

"No. I want to stop by at my office."

"I understand that. May I see inside the trunk of the car?"

"Yes. Sure. Certainly."

Paul opened the trunk. The patrolman looked, and scanned the interior of the car. He straightened up and signalled an all clear to his back-up.

"What are you doing on this freeway, sir?"

"Stopping by at the office. My office."

"How did you get here?" His colleague said.

"We came from church, the First Episcopal Church, in the valley. And we got on the freeway maybe a couple of ramps back."

"They missed the first roadblock."

"I guess we did. I didn't see anything."

"Did you know that the freeways are closed to civilian traffic?"

"No I didn't."

"You don't watch or listen to news broadcasts?"

"I haven't, no, not recently."

"Well, sir, the freeways are closed. There has been some unrest and violent incidents in the mid and downtown areas of Los Angeles, and these areas have been sealed off to prevent the incidents spreading and to prevent looters coming into these areas."

"I didn't know that."

"The freeways are shut down for the use of the emergency services and National Guard vehicles."

"Like those guys?" Paul looked past the roadblock to the convoy.

"No, sir. That is a military convoy waiting for clearance to pull out."

"Is it that bad? The military are pulling out?"

The patrolman stiffened. "Nobody's pulling out. You got that clear? If the shit inside those sealed trucks ever got loose, excuse me, ma'am, you might consider pulling out. You may have something to lose, they don't. They're going somewhere real safe."

"It's ironic, isn't it."

"Pardon me?"

"What are they? Pre-trial homicide?"

"Multiples."

Paul looked across at the convoy of sealed trucks, and the soldiers standing armed; half were facing the convoy, half were watching over the freeway. He looked at the sky above the freeway, at the barred windows high up the sides of the trucks. "Really!"

"May I see – "

John Paul Stanton.

"Your driver's license. Sir!"

He felt in his pockets for the temporary license. He realised, with a shock, that his old wallet was somewhere in 1717. Mel had given it to him, and he didn't know where it was.

"I only have a temporary driver's license with me. I lost my wallet. It might be at my office. I thought it must be. That's where we're going, to check."

"This lady's your wife, you say?"

"Yes, she is."

"Ma'am, do you have your driver's license?"

"Yes, I think so. It should be in my purse. It's right here somewhere. Here it is." Laurie handed it out of the car window.

"Mrs Mathiessen? 1717 Jerome?"

"Yes."

"And this is your husband – Doctor Mathiessen?"

"Doctor Paul Mathiessen. And I know where his driver's license is, too. I found his wallet, in his sweatpants, by the bed."

He didn't look at her, and Laurie didn't look at him. Mel had returned the wallet, and Laurie had found it. At some point she had been through it the same way Mel had. Maybe it had still been warm from Mel's hands, from his fingers on the leather. And his fingerprints. Where else would they be? What else was there? It was all impossible. He couldn't hide everything. How could he go on hiding? He should tell it all, here, on this empty freeway up high in the open; he couldn't keep a track of anything. He looked down at the right front tire, there was a piece of gravel stuck in the tread. One question – if they asked him one question, he would tell them everything. It would slip so sweetly out. He wanted to say: We've killed someone too!

"Your husband lives at that same address, 1717 Jerome?"

"Yes, he does."

"One moment please, Mrs Mathiessen."

The patrolman walked away and spoke into his radio, which crackled and silenced. They waited, isolate and high up on the freeway.

He said, "You found my wallet."

Laurie said, "It was just lucky. I don't know how many times I've washed those sweatpants without checking the pockets. It's something you have to learn to do when you have a child."

The radio crackled, and the patrolman said, "Affirmative." He came back to their car. "Doctor Mathiessen, we have to run a check on everyone we stop. Most all traffic intercepts are being logged."

"I understand that."

"Where is your office, sir?"

"It's a few blocks east."

"And this is an urgent visit?"

"It is."

"Well we have a priority clearance for medical personnel. You can't get through here, but if you follow some way behind the convoy to the last entry ramp, I can call through to the cars at the bottom of that ramp to let you through."

"They aren't turning into the city?"

"No, sir, you will at that time drop back from the convoy. And you shouldn't go any farther into the downtown without a police escort."

"I won't."

"Wc don't have the manpower to seal off all residential routes. This situation is not yet stabilised."

"I understand."

"You want to turn around here? They'll be moving off in a couple of minutes."

"Okay. Thank you."

"Take it slow."

Paul got back into the car and three-pointed it, and waited, air-conditioned once more.

"Do we have to go to the office?" Laurie said.

"That's what we've told them we'll do. And they're waiting to check at the ramp."

He thought, And they've logged us.

In the rear-view mirror he saw the soldiers run towards jeeps and the spurts of diesel fumes as the trucks started up. The outriders came past, and the trucks strained to pick up speed. He looked at the barred windows, one by one, as they went past. There were no faces. He didn't see John Paul Stanton, sealed in his container. Maybe he was writing, maybe he was thinking through the rationale for what he did. Secure. Being taken out of town. Picking his way through dualism, on the freeway.

"What are you trying to see?" Laurie asked.

"Nothing," he said, slipping the car into gear. "Nothing seems to have a lot to do with me."

"I know what you're thinking," she said, "but it's only skin-deep. Don't think about it. Thank you for not telling me."

They followed the convoy back along the freeway. She suddenly reached across a hand and gripped the loose material of his pants, at his thigh. She said, "We should have told them, shouldn't we? Paul?"

"What about?"

"About everything."

"Maybe. I don't know, hon. They're traffic policemen. I don't know if we should tell them."

"They're like the 911 people."

He glanced across at her and saw that she was biting her lip. She reached into her purse. She took a tissue and wiped her eyes, beneath the sunglasses.

"It's okay," he said.

"They just don't ask enough questions. You can't go any farther, can you? You can't just say everything. They want you to panic and be in danger. They don't want to know how things are, they don't care. They don't care if people are dead." She sobbed. "They don't want to know."

"No. But it's okay. I promise you. It'll be okay."

"I don't want to go home."

"We have to. You have to be strong, Laurie."

"Why can't we just stay at the office?" she moaned. "Abe will help us."

"Of course he will. I have to get a phone number. You have to let me do this. Be strong."

"I'm sorry."

"Me too. Really sorry. But we have to go back to the house. Laurie? Hon?"

"I don't know why they didn't burn the house down."

"It's okay. Things will be okay."

He too had thought about it, burning the house down; but it was too late. They were approaching the ramp and another police roadblock. The convoy went on towards the hills.

When they got to the office, he pulled Diana Caviatti's phone number off the files. He came out of his room to find Laurie solemnly feeding the fish, which swam to and fro, indifferently, in the clear, still water of the tank.

TWENTY-TWO

Sunday: 1.35p.m. to 2.25p.m.

Up the hill, to Jerome; and along the side of the hill. Laurie stared out of the car window. Most of the houses had short driveways. There was no-one in the street, the neighbors had gone to their homes. Twice she caught sight of a television screen, through windows, and a group of people sitting, watching, eating. It was what people did. They didn't sit outside, their children didn't play on the lawn outside.

She wouldn't have played outside; the grass was somehow too perfectly kept. To play outside would be lonely. She would feel lonely. Any child would feel lonely. The children would stay inside, with the television picture moving from one exterior shot to another. And that way, of course, they would stay out of the harmful sun and they would not, in later life, need a skin doctor to run his hands over the surfaces of face, and arms, and body.

She recoiled from the thought of Paul doing this to her. But she would have to be nice to Paul. He was in a difficult situation. He would have to find a way out. He would do so but she mustn't let her confidence show. She didn't want to get drawn into him, or to have him try to get close to her. She had to be on her guard to ensure that he didn't go to pieces and behave stupidly, and to make sure that she didn't fall for the old trick of making his decisions for him.

She looked out at Jerome. The lawns were perfect, but there were cracks in the concrete road, with weeds and grasses pushing their way through the cracks. The road couldn't have been more than ten years old, transitory and already breaking up. Temporary, as things were. As everything was. It stayed while it served a purpose. Then it just made you sad . . .

But not guilty. This wasn't *her* purpose. This wasn't her plan. This was Paul's affair, and it was his responsibility. She didn't want to be cynical, but she didn't want to interfere.

She considered the reasons why he had driven them to the office and what he had wanted from the office, but none of them fit or made sense. She would have to watch him. She stared out of the window. 1717 was the nicest house in the street.

He pulled up at the front of the house. She sat mute until he had opened her door. "It's okay," he said. She wondered how many more times she would have to hear him say that, and for how long she could make herself nod her head in dumb gratitude when she felt disgusted by him, when she wished that he, with all his miserableness, would disappear. "If you go in this way, I'll put the car in the garage, hon."

She replied: "I think that I'll go and lie down for a while."

She unlocked the house, switched off the alarm, and shut the door behind her. The house was silent; she liked it that way. She didn't want him to bustle in from the garage and clomp his announcement down the hallway towards her: how was your day?

How was my day?

She thought, I have had enough of my day, I have lost any sort of interest in my day, and my life with you. Other than this baby, I have lost any interest. I don't want lunch, I don't want to sit around, I don't want to go outside. I was quite happy walking along that road, knowing that I hardly needed you, almost forgetting about you. I will never go down those stairs again, and I won't stay in this house. I will never make love with you again, no matter what you do. And what you do is entirely up to you,

you and your little, mean self. Whatever you do, it will not be with me.

A part of her cried out, You'll be all right, I hope and pray that you will, I know that you will!

She stood there, intrigued as to whether she was praying for herself or for him. But when she heard Paul put the key into the garage door lock, she knew that the prayer wasn't for anyone, and that prayer on its own wasn't good enough anyway; so she went into the bedroom to get away from him and she shut the door.

He didn't intrude. She heard him go into the kitchen and then she heard the low sound of the television, which was like a baby listener, reassuring her that she would not need to be disturbed by him.

She felt tired, but she couldn't bring herself to lie on the bed. She sat on her chair. She reached behind her and threw the black slip towards the laundry basket in the bathroom, and closed her eyes.

She couldn't have slept for more than five minutes; waking, she needed the bathroom. She gathered the black slip on her way through, noticing that Paul hadn't cleaned his basin after shaving. Black bristles stuck to the bowl, oily with soap. She washed her hands in her basin and dried them on her towel, disliking the proximity and slovenliness of his mess. She couldn't be bothered to change her clothes.

It was a beautiful dress. She got rid of her pantyhose. She went into the bedroom and opened the top cupboards, and pulled out old clothes, his and hers, and threw them on the bed. From his chest of drawers she took all the clothes she disliked and added them to the pile.

Then she went into the kitchen. He was watching a live broadcast of the situation downtown, groups of looters darting across otherwise unpopulated streets, circling tranquil debris.

"I thought you were asleep," he said, standing ill at ease.

"Uh-huh," she replied. She yawned, trying to look drowsy, wanting to keep her distance. "Do we have any garbage sacks? You know, the large black ones?"

"There's a box in the garage."

"Oh."

"I'll get them."

She went back to the bedroom. When he came in, he saw the piles of clothes and he said, "What are you doing? Laurie?"

"I'm giving these clothes away to the church. They want them."

"But these are my clothes."

"And mine. Some of them are nice. People will like them. And I won't wear them again."

He held up a plaid shirt and a ski jacket. "But I like them. They're mine."

"But you don't need them."

"Laurie, why are you doing this?"

"People need them!" She felt her voice shrilling, and saw his reaction, and carried on. "We don't need them! People are stealing them, you can see it on television, people are breaking in and stealing them, that's why people are breaking in everywhere!"

"It's okay . . . " he said, with excruciating gentleness, " . . . It's okay."

"It isn't okay!" she screamed at him. "Don't you understand that it isn't okay! And look at your washbasin, it's filthy and dirty . . . and everything is messy!" The phone rang. She stopped, suddenly more surprised than he was. His fright wavered. He held out his hands, as if to stifle her, and he went out of the room.

She went to the door to listen. She knew exactly what she would say to her family, pretence spread calmingly over pretence. She listened to what Paul would say. She padded to the study door, ready to intercede. She didn't want him to give anything away.

"Diana?" She heard him say. "Hi, this is Paul Mathiessen. No, we are okay. Are you? That's great, it's a great relief for all of us . . ."

Diana? Who on the face of the earth was Diana? What skunkskirt was he going to hide in now?

She went into the study. "Paul!"

He covered the mouthpiece with his hand. "Just let me do this, Laurie."

"Do what?"

He spoke again. "Diana? Hi, yes. No. Not really. We're not entirely out of a situation. I don't think so, but what I wanted to ask you was if you had the number of a lawyer, a friend. A law firm. No, it's just something I have to talk over. Fairly urgently." Some moments later he wrote down a name and a number. "And he'll be at his home number. Right. You will? That's great. So I'll call him in a while. That's so great. Thank you. Well, thanks. No, we are." He reached for her hand. "We are. I will. And thanks, Diana. Bye now. Goodbye."

He put down the phone. "Are you all right?"

"Yes." She wondered what he was doing, and asked him.

"I'm getting a lawyer, hon."

She murmured, "Yes . . . but why . . . I don't understand." She looked at the telephone. "Why didn't you take it in the bedroom?" She shook off his hand, and turned away.

Back in the bedroom she started to put the clothes into a plastic sack, and went on doing this when he came to find her.

"Laurie, this waiting around is too much for us. We're going to need help. We're going to need a lawyer."

"I am a lawyer. Remember?"

"You're not a criminal lawyer."

"Is that what I should be? What else do you want me to be?"

She decided to give him one more chance. She didn't think that things would be any different if he took it. She didn't believe that he would take it. But he was owed one more opportunity to tell the truth, he owed it to himself, to at least square with her and tell her what she already knew. "Why should we need a criminal lawyer? Paul, what have we done? I don't understand what's wrong. Why don't you call the police? What do we have to hide?"

She would never forgive him, but she might understand him and have him understand her; and they might not be so stupid as to refuse each other that opportunity. They wouldn't have to part on a lie. "Who is Diana?"

"Diana Caviatti."

"And is she a criminal lawyer?"

"No, she isn't, Laurie."

She wondered how, and why, he was so condescending. She quelled her anger, and set herself to traipse painstakingly through the innocence of logic.

"Then why are you calling her? What is she? We don't know her, do we?"

"She is a patient of mine. She's well connected."

"To who?"

"To who?" he repeated, taken aback.

"Who is she connected to?"

"To a good lawyer."

"And to you."

"Why? What is this?" He was wary, she saw, and getting defensive.

"Diana Caviatti . . . "

"Yes. A patient."

"Is she attractive?" She saw that, yes, Diana Caviatti was attractive. And so she went on. "She is, isn't she?"

"I guess so." He looked sheepish. She would usually have laughed at him, at his harmlessness; he knew that, she knew.

She said, "I know that when I went away at Easter, you had an affair."

"I did?"

"Yes, you did." She waited for it to sink into him. "I didn't know who it was with. I didn't know that it was with this Diana Caviatti, whoever she is. I thought that it must have been with a patient. Just a short-term thing." She watched him, his head was bowed, emotion begining to show. She laughed. "I'd kind of forgotten about it really. It was somehow . . . meaningless."

"Oh God, I'm sorry!" His face was white when he lifted it. "I am so sorry."

"I don't blame you, Paul. I was being . . . me, and pregnant."

"I felt so guilty. So useless."

"Is it over?"

"Oh yes, believe me. Do you?"

"I do. And is it over for her? Diana? It was Diana, wasn't it?"

"Yes."

"*Mrs* Caviatti?"

"Yes, she's married. We meant nothing to each other."

"That's a shame."

"It was just, I guess, loneliness."

"I see. And is she, has she been, lonely often?"

"Just once. Honestly, just once. Only once, that was all."

She believed him. "Once with you."

He understood immediately. "I was protected, I promise you. I don't think she's, or that she has . . . "

"You were special."

"No, not really."

No, she thought, you aren't really special. You never will be. You're pitiful, but I haven't got any pity. You are so pleased to be able to lie to yourself and to me. You are so pleased to find a shelter, where you can lay down and lie. With your lover dead in the basement.

"Well," she said, "it doesn't matter. I wanted you to know that I knew, then you wouldn't have to worry so much. You wouldn't have to run around trying to hide little meaningless affairs, or contact little meaningless lawyers."

He glanced at her. He almost pleaded, but she smiled charitably at him. She saw that the strain of relief and panic was too much for him. He didn't know what to do with himself. She thought that he was going to pass out. He walked to the easy chair, and sat down very cautiously; once seated, the top half of his body slumped dismally.

"Mrs Caviatti's lawyer isn't a divorce lawyer; is he?" She trilled brightly, watching these ludicrous words pierce him like shrapnel. "Paul, I don't want that. I want us to go on. This affair is finished and it's nothing. It's so unlike you to fool around. Does it do you any good?"

"God, Laurie, no!"

"What does it matter . . . "

"Sorry?"

"I said: what does it matter? I shouldn't have brought it up, not now; but I can't go on watching you try to hide something. You're not there. You're not doing anything. Paul, we shouldn't wait any longer. We should call the police again, and tell them. I don't want to wait any longer. We don't, do we, Paul? We have to start over. We have to call them."

"I don't know. I don't know."

"Why not?"

"We need a lawyer."

"We don't know these people, why do we need them?"

"Because we've killed someone, who was unarmed."

"An intruder."

"Laurie, there aren't any signs of a break-in."

"But this man is in our house. We don't know this man, Paul. He's in our house. We didn't ask him to come here, we don't know him, do we?"

"No."

"Do you?"

"No."

"Then we're innocent. Aren't we innocent?"

"We haven't reported it, Laurie. It isn't logged."

"I am innocent!"

He was crying. She watched him sob and choke everything to the surface. She waited, and she watched it dissolve. Finally he said: "We're innocent."

"We are so innocent," she said. "I don't know what we're going to do together. It makes me sad. We have to sort it out. We have to go back to the beginning, as if nothing had ever happened. If you hide these things then you can forget them. I can. Maybe I shouldn't have said anything."

She left him. She thought, If he can lie through his teeth with such conviction, then maybe I can pretend to be crazy. He's had his last opportunity. And we'll see which of us ends up being better served by coming clean.

She folded the rest of the clothes neatly and bagged them. She dragged the bags to the bedroom door.

He remained in his study. She passed the open door on her way to the dining room, and she saw him, with his head in his hands, sitting in the same chair. "It's okay . . . " she murmured gently. "I forgive you. I want you to know that."

He looked up at her and thanked her.

She said, "I can't wait until this is over, I can't do nothing. I'm going to clear up."

"Wait."

"Why?" She looked round the door again. He didn't seem to need comforting, and she wasn't about to comfort him. She wanted him to do whatever he wanted to do, as long as it had nothing to do with her.

He tried to be plain-speaking and authoritative. "Laurie?"

"Yes?"

"Hon, to all intents and purposes we have murdered this man."

She furrowed her brow. "To whose intents and purposes?"

"It looks as though we murdered him."

"Why would we do that? I don't understand."

"That's the way it looks."

"It doesn't look that way to me."

"But it's why I can't call the police."

"But we can't pretend that nothing happened. I'm sure they'll clear it up." She shrugged. "We can't go on living with a dead man downstairs, can we? I mean, not the three of us living together. Or four. Those old clothes are all set to go, when you're ready."

TWENTY-THREE

Sunday: 2.25p.m. to 4.00p.m.

Maybe.

He tried to clear his head.

He had gotten away with having an affair with Diana Caviatti.

Laurie would care. She would put it out of the way. That was Laurie. She would put it out of the way for a while, and then the seriousness would make itself felt.

But it was nothing. And he could convince her that it was nothing.

Or maybe he should convince her that it *was* something.

If only it had have been with Diana Caviatti. If only it had been with her.

He imagined it. He imagined making love to her. Lingerie and skin.

How could he imagine this, now, at this time! How could his mind do this? How was he sitting here with a hard-on, revelling in sexual delirium? It was the thought of freedom, so much freedom.

How could he sit here, snivelling for freedom?

The clatter of cutlery came through from the dining room. Drawers slid open and banged shut.

Feelings of despair and gratitude and relief and panic tumbled inconsequentially through his body. His mind could give them no coherence. He lost track of them and sat, numb with trepidation. He couldn't believe that she had let him get away with cheating on her, that he had confessed and had been forgiven. It was finished, and it was so simple, like weeping.

The simplest of thoughts came to him. The two things were separate. Now it was simple: he had had an affair, and they had shot an intruder. There were two separate things and there was no need to mix them or to confuse them. They would be sorted out separately.

He didn't think that he should go to Laurie.

He should probably change his clothes.

No, he would keep his suit on. He wanted to keep his suit on. He wanted to think. Laurie was one hundred percent behind him and would help him, but he shouldn't take her too much for granted. He still had to protect her.

Whatever happened, he would have to get rid of his wallet; because that came from the basement and led upstairs to the bedroom. The wallet had Mel's fingerprints on it and it would link Mel personally to them and to the house.

He unlaced his shoes.

Laurie had her back to him, returning place mats to the sideboard. He carried his shoes into the bedroom. His sweatpants were on the floor, the wallet stuck out of a pocket. He took it. He held it and wondered what to do with it. They didn't have a furnace, nobody had a furnace. There was no way of burning the wallet, nor of forcing it to rot. The waste disposal wasn't powerful enough to destroy it.

He took the wallet into the bathroom, withdrawing the cards and his drivers license. Reaching under the basin for a scouring pad, he scrubbed the surface of the wallet until the soft leather began to disintegrate, falling shredded into the basin.

Laurie's voice called: "Paul?"

"I'm in here cleaning the basin."

"I just wondered where you were." She stayed in the kitchen.

"I've got to start somewhere."

"Do these crystal glasses go in the dishwasher?"

"No. Leave them out."

He wanted there to be silence. She might then say something which would tell him how she felt, something which would indicate her approval. But he heard her start to load the dishwasher. And he began to use the scourer on the plastic cover of his driver's license.

He put the license in his pocket. He wrapped the wallet in a cleaning rag and put it in amongst the bagged clothes. Wearing a pair of rubber gloves, he scrubbed the basin and the credit cards, which he dried and cut in half and placed in the safe in the study.

He went back to use the bathroom. He saw that the toilet bowl needed cleaning, and there came to him the memory of the long-running dispute which he and Laurie had had about cleaning toilets. It was an absurd historical accuracy. His mind was clearer now and more balanced, which both surprised him and made him wary.

When the cleaner came, did she never use the bathroom? Didn't housecleaners do that? He guessed that she would discreetly use the bathroom downstairs, if she had to.

He remembered vividly: Mel had used the bathroom downstairs. If cleaners were impersonal, then why would intruders get so casually personal? It would be another link. Thank God they had waited, thank God the police hadn't come.

The phone rang. Laurie picked it up in the kitchen. He went to the door to listen. She was talking to her father. She was laughing. Her father was making her laugh. When he walked past the kitchen, she caught sight of him and smiled. She said into the phone: "Oh, Paul's fine. He's really pulled through on this one . . ."

He no longer knew what to think about her reactions. Clearly he had to clean out the basement bathroom, and he went down the hallway, and down the stairs.

There was so much blood in the room, and the arched, sprawled body with its head turned towards the window. But he had to do the bathroom. He turned away. He had to do the bowl with the scourer, and take the pubic hair from between the seat and the rim of the bowl, and clean in under the rim. He choked at the sourly stagnant smell, and retched a half-dozen times. When he stood up and looked at himself in the mirror he was crimson, his eyes protruded and his lips were suffused with blood. He turned and flushed the toilet. He didn't know if the police could tell when a toilet had last been flushed. Should he now go on to clean the top of the cistern, or the washbasin? Or the walls, against which maybe someone urinating would lean a hand to steady their balance. Or the mirror? Or the carpet for drops of male urine; should he clean the whole carpet? It would be impossible.

It was impossible. He looked around. All of it was impossible. It couldn't be done. Fuck you, he whispered; fuck you! He looked across at the dead body, "Fuck you."

How would, could, a lawyer clear this up? *No-one* could make this clean.

He crouched down. He went back over his reasoning. His own reasoning had been exactly right. It was too late to call the police. He was right. It was too late. They wouldn't believe anything. Would they believe that Laurie had called her father, calmly, after waiting around for twelve – fifteen! – hours?

They had run out of "intruder" hours ago! How could they possibly be innocent?

He picked up a stuffed dinosaur, his future child's friend, and he looked at the blank, black eyes in its green and white smiling face.

"We *are* innocent," he said.

He didn't know how to believe this. Rising to his feet he tossed the dinosaur away. It bounced off the dead body, and against the window glass, and fell out of sight. He couldn't let that happen, not to his child's friend. He went over to the body and leaned across it, and retrieved the little animal, which he took and placed on the daybed; he made it sit up. He noticed that he had a bloodstain on his pants.

Walking slowly up the stairs, practicing mindlessly "but we are innocent, we're innocent"; he tested it against the unyielding mass of impossibility. He heard Laurie's voice from the kitchen – she was telling her mother about the church service and clearing out all the old clothes, something good coming out of something bad.

It suddenly occurred to him, But yes, we *are* innocent; as far as anyone knows. As far as anyone from the church knows, or the police, or Laurie's parents.

He thought excitedly: No-one knows any different. Only *we* know. Only *I* know. No-one else knows anything. As far as they know, nothing has happened. Only Laurie and I know, and Laurie doesn't want to know. Not in her condition, she doesn't want to know. So, it might be that, outside of what I know, nothing has happened. There has been a one-night stand, an irrelevant affair with a married patient, and that's all that's happened. No-one knows any different. Did anyone need to know?

He had something to think about. Something to get clear: why should anyone have to know?

Laurie was off the phone. He went into the kitchen. "Don't make any more phone calls", he said. "Not for a while."

"No? Okay." She nodded vacantly at him, then smiled. "George says hi, and my mother says that we must be either crazy or something else not to dump the house and run. They're kind of proud of us. They must be telling their friends."

"That's good. Do you want to make anymore calls?"

"No."

"We'll let the answering machine take everything."

"Right." She smiled hesitantly at him. "Are you feeling better?"

"Yes, I am. I guess so."

"You had me worried."

"I couldn't go on. Deceiving you isn't my . . . I can't do anything without you. Except get lost." He hugged her. "Thank God you're you. Thank you."

"Careful," she murmured. "Not too tight."

"You're not angry?"

"What do *you* think, Paul? Sure I am. But being angry is better than being sad, and much better than watching you being stupid. Yes, I'm angry, but what good is that going to do us? We're in trouble, you're going to have to think what to do. Promise me? Promise me that you'll think it through. You say that we can't call the police now?"

"I don't see how they're going to believe us. I have thought it through."

"So we need a lawyer?"

"With or without a lawyer they're not going to believe us. This whole thing is unbelievable." He glanced at her and saw her eyes beginning to stretch wide. She blinked and walked away towards the closet in the hallway. "What are you doing?"

"I'm going to vacuum the dining room, then I'm going to lie down. If the police aren't going to come, there isn't any hurry. Why don't you call your parents?"

He followed her out of the kitchen. "Now?"

"You better had. Otherwise they'll worry. Give them my love."

"What shall I tell them?"

"Tell them the truth. Tell them everything's fine. I'm sure that they don't want to hear about Mrs Diana Caviatti."

He sat in his study. The vacuum cleaner started up, and Laurie began to vacuum the carpet noisily, banging the arm against the chairs. He looked out of the door and called, "I'm going to close this door!" She didn't hear him. He went up to her and touched her on the arm. She looked at him irritably. He switched off the vacuum cleaner with his foot. He said, "I'm going to close the study door, I can't hear anything."

"Close it then," she said, and switched the vacuum cleaner back on.

He went into the study and sat with the door closed. He wondered if she was crazy, and what difference it made. Did it matter if she was crazy? It didn't matter to anything at all. It only mattered to the house, which she wanted clean; even at the cost of vacuuming, which she hated. That was the only difference between this Sunday and a normal Sunday, in the upstairs of this house.

He picked up the remote and flicked the TV on. There was no local sport, there were riots. Or not riots, but an aftermath: the surveillance of sporadic incidents amongst an applied calm. There was talk of clearing up. There was a baseball game on one of the networks. ESPN replayed basketball. Which was a peculiarly vicious return to the start of his own recent circle. He went back to the downtown coverage and killed the sound.

The phone call to his parents passed off with his being more or less a caricature of his usual lackadaisical self. Once he had told them that everything was okay and the house was okay, they wanted him and Laurie to fly up for a rest, which he said they would do a little later. The airport wasn't open yet, and they would be busy: even now Laurie was cleaning house and he really had to go because there was a lot of dirt from the smoke in the atmosphere, and otherwise things were fine. They only had a lot of clearing up to do, but the whole community was pulling together and the neighborhood hadn't been in any serious trouble. His mother, relieved of anxiety, told him that she loved him and he said that Laurie and he loved both of them, and that they would talk soon.

There was a click, but Paul suspected that the line hadn't cut off. His mother asked if he was still there, and then she told him that his father had some trouble with his prostate.

"Is it serious?" he asked, worried and immediately hating the worry. His mother began to answer.

There was another click. His father must have picked up the phone again. He said, "No it isn't serious. Not in the middle of a civil war it isn't serious. You concern yourself with Laurie. We have some great doctors right here. I'll hand you back to your mother."

He waited, then said to his mother, "Is it serious, mom?"

She said, "You know how your father is. He's more worried about you. There isn't any crisis, but I hate waiting for results of tests."

He asked her to let him know. He knew that she wanted to talk with him and he promised to call back the next day, when his father was out of the house.

It touched him that they wanted his opinion. He was the only doctor in the family; although he had no in-depth knowledge about prostates, they wanted him involved. He must be intelligent, somewhere along the line. He turned the volume up on the TV.

He sat watching it long after the noise from the vacuum cleaner had ceased. Laurie didn't come in. So she had gone to lie down. He watched the lines of National Guard form up and move into the streets. It was patchy. It was some way away from the Jerome area, and further away from the central and eastern downtown, which is where there were the incidents. There were no riots. There were incidents, which would claim investigation.

Nobody knew about the incident at 1717, but it was not now a part of a riot. Nobody in their neighborhood was jumpy now. In their neighborhood, people were going to clear up. They were no more terrified than usual of intruders. There wouldn't be such a thing as an unarmed intruder. That climate had gone. The screen of smoke and violence and chaos had gone. People were going back to baseball games and prostate cancers and skin doctors, and motivated murders. If he dialled 911 now, he knew exactly what they would find at 1717 Jerome. It would be as clear as daylight, of which there were maybe four hours left.

And there on TV was the clean-up rally, on Normandie and Olympic, a crowd of people. Who, Paul heard, had been told to come back tomorrow, because it wasn't yet safe enough to begin. He himself had pledged that he would go down there.

It was so grotesque. It was as grotesque, as crazy, as Laurie vacuuming the carpet; when their own house had its feet sprayed with blood. It was crazy; when all they wanted to do, and all they had to do, was to clear up their own mess, to get rid of the body and the blood and the incident.

Nobody would help them. The police wouldn't do it for them. They would have to do it for themselves. He would have to do it for himself and Laurie.

Everyone else was clearing up. Everyone wanted things back to normal. Things could be gotten back, almost, to normal. He had to make that decision.

There was no other way the decision could go. There was no other way back, not parents, not system, not friends, and, really, not Laurie.

He had to do it himself.

How could he do it?

In his medical experience, bodies went to the hospital or to the morgue. The morgue was a no-go because they needed too many details; the body might as well be handed in to the police. The hospital was a possibility; they must be in chaos.

But he was a doctor, of sorts, and no doctor would deliver a body and pretend that he didn't know that it had been dead for over half a day. Where would he have found it, and why would he deliver it? It would arouse too many suspicions. The police would check back, and no amount of crazy vacuuming would sanitize the basement.

He might leave the body in the hospital parking lot, where it would be found. He could leave it in the chaos. If there were one hundred dead, this body would not be the strangest circumstance. It wasn't white. It could be the product of any lousy incident at all. Mel had lived alone. Who knew if he had a family in LA? Or a regular lover? Maybe his pattern was to take advantage of people who weren't gay, who didn't want to be known as gay. His identity might never be traced, and if it was traced to being gay, then the police would, maximum, look for someone who was in the gay world.

So it could be done. The body could be left. At the hospital.

He tried to think of flaws. The body could be left, that was fine.

So why at the hospital?

The body could be left anywhere. Why should it be at the hospital, where someone might recognise him, or the car? The body could be dumped anywhere. His seizing on the hospital was developed from a false precept that the body needed some medical tie-in. Whereas it was a dead body, it was no different from trash, it needed no medical tie-in. It could be found anywhere.

He thought further: did he have to do this? If it was just a question of dumping a body, did *he* have to do this? There must be people who would do it.

Fatuously, he thought of having this conversation with Bill over lunch. Bill would say: Well, I guess that you could look in the Yellow Pages. If you don't hit lucky with Disposal, you could try Restaurants.

He was crazy. He was going crazy.

But he started to think about Bill, seriously. He wondered what kind of a friend Bill was: with his Korean family, that tight family who defended their own people and their own property in an organised group with automatic weapons. He wondered if Bill would help him. They could maybe use a truck, at night. Three or four of them. They could pick up the body, through the garage, and take it away and drop it somewhere. They would know how to do that. They might do it for Bill or for one of Bill's friends who was in trouble with the same kind of people they were in trouble with. Out of friendship, or solidarity. He would go with them if he had to, or there could surely be some kind of deal, money or a trade-off.

How would he put this to Bill? He would tell them about the failure of the police to log it. He could tell them about the whole situation as it was. Laurie could maybe talk to Helen. They had gotten along well. They could talk after he had talked first to Bill, and had told him what the situation was, and had sounded him out. Then Bill could get his people moving, somehow.

He thought of what he would say. He dialled Bill's number. A woman answered.

"Helen?"

"No, she is not here."

"Is Bill there? Let me speak with Bill?" He waited, not sure whether she had understood, until Bill came on the line.

"Hello, who is this?"

"Bill? Hi, it's Paul. Paul!"

"Hiya, buddy."

"How are things with you? It seems like it's been a long time."

"It sure does. Jesus, you're not kidding. What a night!"

"So what's happening? Are you okay?"

"Uh-huh, everything's happening. So far we're okay. Helen's taken a beating in terms of business property, a bit like the goddamn Alamo. Her people are still out there. We're bunkered down with like two dozen hysterical domestic staff. Is Jerome okay?"

"Laurie's got to rest."

"Yeah, she should."

"So did your guys get involved with any of the violence?"

"I understand that there was some shooting, yeah. Over in that neighborhood it was pretty hairy. I don't think that anyone on our side got hurt too bad."

"Self-defence, right?"

"Sure, isn't it always? I don't know about the other side, they don't have too much left to defend, I guess. Jesus Christ, man, it's crazy talking like this. I must need some sleep."

"So how do you get rid of the bodies?"

"What do you mean?"

"Well, do your guys load them up and drive them out somewhere or what?"

There was a pause. "Yeah, by the dozen." Bill laughed. "Sorry, I was a little slow there. Things have been kind of serious around this part of the world. I lost my sense of humor after the third jug of coffee. It's lucky you called up. I was begining to think that civilisation was going to hell in a handbasket. If everyone's starting to make jokes about it, then we're getting back to normal. Okay. I've got you. How many Afros can you fit in a Daewoo delivery truck?"

"Seriously."

"I don't know: they have to load them in half at a time and the Kories don't ship anything in halves."

"But seriously, Bill, if you – "

"I know what you mean. It's too serious for any sick joke. We'll be tied up for months. I don't expect that we'll be shipping anything for a while. We'll have to search for a nice easy restaurant. Maybe Portuguese, buddy. I'm going to have to go. That was a great dinner, will you pass it on to Laurie?"

"Yes. Take care now."

"You too."

TWENTY-FOUR

Sunday: 4.00p.m. to 4.10p.m.

He must have been crazy, trying to get Bill involved.

It was lucky he hadn't blurted out anything real to Bill. That was lucky. But he was starting to make his own luck. He felt more confident.

Laurie was asleep. He was alone. Of course he was alone; and therefore he was gaining control. The choices were disappearing. He didn't have to think so fast, for there would be no more surprises and no more considerations and no more dependency. He felt confident that he knew, for the first time, what to do. And that he no longer had to refer to anybody, not even to Laurie. Whom he was protecting. Which they both understood.

He had advantages. He was a doctor and he could go anywhere in the present situation, and he could explain injuries authoritatively. These were his own strengths, and he could play to them and exploit them. He was the only person who knew what truth to construct. And if one truth broke under examination, then there was the fallback upon the truth that he was protecting Laurie. He was confident that one of these truths would stand up.

Sunday: 4.00p.m. to 4.10p.m.

Laurie lay awake. She had changed the bedsheet and the cover for the comforter, and she might even get used to lying in the bed again, alone.

It wasn't difficult to read Paul's thoughts. In fact it was easier now that she felt that he was no longer a part of her life. She knew him very well. She knew to what conclusion he would have to come, she knew what he would resolve to do; but she had to wonder whether he would do it.

He would, for her.

Her mind wandered cautiously over and around the shooting. He was right about the alarm system and the closed windows, and the implications of there being no logged call. Maybe he had been right in his decision to lie to her, for if he had told the truth there would have been far too many complications for him to think his way through, and she would not have been able to stop herself from behaving vindictively. As it was, they now had a lie which could be maintained by both of them, and which he would feel that he could go on maintaining. He would feel guilty, but he would feel secure. He would do anything for her. He would be able to think what to do.

He would have to get rid of the body of his lover.

And then, afterwards, she had to get rid of him.

There was just this one opportunity.

Paul wouldn't go of his own accord. He wouldn't be capable of ridding her of himself. It would be better for her if he was dead. She wanted him away from her, she wanted nothing to do with him, she wanted no contact with him; but he would drag on and on and on, lying to himself and to her.

She thought through the shooting: the intruder who had broken in downstairs, the alarm that hadn't been set and hadn't sounded. She had come downstairs and had shot.

She had a right to use reasonable force if there was a reasonable fear of death or injury. Did Paul have the capacity to get violent? She had never provoked him, she had chosen not, ever, to provoke him, once she had known that she would marry him. If she provoked him, savagely, then he might respond; right?

No, probably not. He habitually evaded any question of self-respect.

She wished that he was dead.

Sunday: 4.10p.m. to 4.50p.m.

He went and turned on the heating downstairs. If the temperature was higher, it might delay the full onset of rigor mortis in the body, making it easier to handle.

He went back up. He opened the garage door and began to drag the sacks of clothes along the hallway, to the garage, and into the trunk of the Mercedes. He unwrapped the wallet and put it into his coat pocket, and retrieved his cut-up credit cards from the study. He stuffed them into his pocket.

He left a note for Laurie. "Gone to take clothes to church. Back by" – he looked at his watch – "five. Leave everything. Love you."

He drove up to the pass. He dropped all but one of the bags off at the church and accepted the charitable deduction form from one of the helpers. On the way back he stopped by a dumpster on the deserted building project. This was clever. He carried the last bag of clothes across and dropped it inside. He put his hands in his coat pocket, clasping the cards. As if in afterthought, he reached into the dumpster and tucked the cards down amongst the rubble, straightening up with his old plaid shirt and a pair of blue jeans in his hand. He took them back to the car, and when he reached a bend in the road, he threw the wallet out of the open window.

Sunday: 4.20p.m. to 5.00p.m.

When she heard him go, and was sure that he had gone, Laurie got off the bed and checked that the house alarm was switched on. She went into his study, and through his filing cabinet, and found under "Appliances" the alarm instruction manual. She skipped through it, and read carefully the penultimate page.

There was an override switch, located in a small compartment under the main and individual room switches, which allowed the alarm to function even when the disarm code had been tapped in. She fetched a screwdriver from the garage and opened the compartment, and tested the switch. Then she replaced the cover, and put the screwdriver in the drawer by her side of the bed.

She checked the bolts on the front door, and the patio door, and the garage doors. She ignored the basement.

In Paul's study she found bullets for the handgun, which she reloaded. She took the gun and sat on the top step of the second flight of stairs, momentarily, while she recalled each moment of the shooting of the intruder; and then she walked back down the hallway to the bedroom, and placed the gun next to the screwdriver.

In the kitchen she ate a turkey and pickle sandwich and a bowl of ice cream, before returning to bed.

Sunday: 5.30p.m. to 6.00p.m.

As Paul approached the house, the light was already beginning to fade. He reached into the glove compartment for the remote, and as he pressed it, so the garage door started to rise. He parked the Mercedes. He got out and pressed the button to close the doors, ducking under it out into the driveway. Going round to the front door, he unlocked it, and disarmed the alarm.

Softly, he opened the bedroom door. Laurie was still asleep. He picked up the roll of garbage bags from off the carpet. Re-entering the garage from the house, he collected his shirt and blue jeans and took them back to the study, where he changed his clothes, folding his suit over the back of the desk chair and keeping an eye on the TV.

He thought for a moment, and then he dialled Alice's home number.

"Alice? It's Doctor Mathiessen." He asked her if she was all right, and he asked her how things were in her neighborhood, and when he heard that she was afraid, he said that he would come get her. She refused. He asked her what she needed. She must need something. He would see if he could get through. Doctors had a priority clearance. He would see what he could do.

She demurred. He wanted to know if she was safe. He heard voices and sirens outside, drowning her voice. He would see what he could do.

He put down the phone, and wrote her address on a piece of paper, which he put in the back pocket of his suit trousers. Looking out of the study door he saw the vacuum cleaner lying in the dining room. Laurie never put it away. That was one of his chores. He gathered it up and took it to the hallway closet. Then he took rags and sponges, rubber gloves and a bucket from the kitchen, and went downstairs.

Sunday: 5.00p.m. to 6.30p.m.

Once the body has gone, Laurie thought, there is just the blood. There will always be some blood, some of that blood, in that room. There is no way of either cleaning the room, or of being certain that the room is clean. I can never be certain of that. I should presume exactly the opposite – that the blood of that man will be discovered. I will never be rid of the traces and the influence of that man. He'll have been here, and left traces, and gone.

But there is nothing to say that this isn't what happened.

This is what would happen: my husband would have shot at him and wounded him, and he would have escaped. This is what happened, and it's what I reported. The man had escaped, and therefore I was not in any immediate danger.

But the man knows his way in. He knows the weak points of the house. So I am afraid that he will come back, in revenge, maybe with others. He doesn't know about the alarm system. However, he has got in once through those glass doors, and he knows that he will again. This is the easiest way to get in, when the house is locked. It is the only way to get in. He might try the other doors, but they are bolted. There's no other way to get in, and I know that he will have to come in through those downstairs doors.

My husband wouldn't think about coming in that way. I would never have expected him to consider that way of entry. Only an intruder would think about breaking in through the downstairs, because he knew that way in, and because he couldn't find any other way in. And I would hear it, and I would go downstairs with the gun, in reasonable fear of my life, and I would use the gun on that intruder, as my husband did before.

This is not unreasonable. I have good reason. I have every good reason.

She ran through them over and over again; until night fell, and it was time to come out from under the covers.

Sunday: 6.30p.m. to 7.30p.m.

The body was not bleeding any longer. There was a pool of blood on the chair and on the carpet underneath, where it had spilled. He absorbed what he could with the sponge, and frequently changed the water in the bucket. When he had taken up the volume of the blood, he attacked the stain which it had left. He remembered that once, when he had fallen and sliced open his leg and had gotten blood over the cushion in his mother's kitchen, the maid had tried all kinds of cleaning liquids and powders, and his mother had come in and had said that clean cold water was the best thing to use.

It was hot in the room, and he was glad of the coldness of the water. He sweated only at the back of his neck and from his forehead. But he could not get rid of the darker stain on the green carpet. They would have to change the carpet. They would have to cause a small fire, or maybe a chemical spillage. He could find out about that kind of thing. They would have to peel the carpet back and check the underlay, and dispose of the cushion; maybe run up to Colorado with the whole chair, where it could be burned or dumped.

He wondered if they could ever live through this, if they could ever forget it and carry on as though nothing had happened, whether they would be able to seal it shut as a horrible two days, or a horrible two months: starting with his affair and ending with the carpet company disrupting the house, everything happening at once. Maybe this was a good thing. Maybe it was so much – too much – that they would only be able to let it go. But there would always be the riots. People would ask them about their experiences during the riots, and what would they say? Maybe that the riots happened just before the baby was born. And the baby, or the child, would be in the room, or would come into the room, and they wouldn't talk about it anymore; life being so much larger and so much happier, and too precious to be linked with such a horrible time.

It was dark. He drew the curtains and switched on the overhead light. He collected the pieces of the shattered table lamp and put them into the wastepaper basket. He emptied his bucket down the toilet bowl, and refilled it from the handbasin, happier now that he was doing something and that the room was on its way to being clean. He started on the wall. The clotted surface of the blood came away on the sponge, but smeared clean areas of the paintwork. It would need some product, maybe a kitchen cleaner, and then he would have to re-paint the wall; but there would be time. There would be a warm afternoon, when the sun had come round and through the windows, and Laurie might be in the garden and he had fetched the CD player down from the kitchen. He didn't mind house painting. He enjoyed it. Sooner rather than later. He was owed time off from work. It didn't have to be a weekend.

The exertion of the sponging made his skin itchy. The room was hot. He thought longingly of the steam-room at the club, of being naked with the steam drawing every memory out of him. There would be a time, maybe for a week starting tomorrow, when he and Abe would have to work hard to make things reassuringly normal. And then he would take a vacation. He had some money saved to take a vacation with Laurie, to get away before the final months of the pregnancy. If they had've been getting along better, they would have gone before; he would have asked her, and surprised her. They might have been away this weekend. Would that sonofabitch still have broken in? Maybe; and maybe it would have been worse. He and Laurie couldn't go any further down, and they were still together. They would take a vacation. He would have gotten rid of the body. He would have taken care of the incident, and of her. He would have gone some way to redeeming himself in her eyes. He had protected her and had made sure that every bit of disaster was a long ways away from the house.

There was a tap on the door.

"Yes?" he said.

"Hi. What're you doing?"

"I'm getting it cleaned up, Laurie."

"Oh, you're cleaning up?"

"Yeah, it's the only thing to do. Trust me."

"Okay. I don't want to come in there."

"No. Don't."

"I brought you a sandwich, and a soda."

He put the sponge in the bucket and went to the door, which he opened a little way so that he could see her. She was dishevelled from sleep, she was puffy-eyed and warm-skinned and wearing a long sweatshirt, holding the sandwich on a plate with a Diet Pepsi in the other hand, damp with condensation. He filled with love for her.

"Thank you. That's great."

"Sure." She smiled timidly, then with a forced and tired pleasure. "What're you doing?"

He took the plate, and then the soda.

"I'm cleaning it up, all of it."

"Okay."

He watched her think and try to understand, and look at him trustingly.

He said, "I have to do it. No-one else is going to help us. But it's not going to be impossible, I promise you."

"Isn't it?"

"No. I'll come upstairs in a couple of minutes, and I'll tell you."

"I want to know."

"You don't need to; but sure you do. And I want to talk it through. A couple of minutes?"

"Okay." She nodded at him, wide-eyed.

"I'll be up there," he said, and began to close the door.

She said, "Paul, I'm so proud of you."

He bit his lip. He couldn't think of anything to say, so he smiled and said, "Me too. I guess."

Sunday: 7.30p.m. to 8.00p.m.

He brought the bucket and the sponge into the kitchen, and ran the sink full of hot soapy water. He asked her what she was watching on TV, and she really couldn't say; it was a Discovery Channel special about the types of sea creatures which lived near to the South African coasts, their intricacies of courtship, their patterns of reproduction. In lagoons. So was it South Africa, or had they switched to one of the groups of South Pacific islands? She wasn't sure. She liked the way the tiny creatures scuttled and floated like weightless astronauts, across the seabed, through the translucent and seemingly immobile water. She found it easy to drift along a continuum of wonder. She had never liked endlessly restless fish, such as those in the tank at Paul's office.

He asked her if they had stopped covering the stuff downtown. No, she said. She knew that he had the television coverage on in his study, and that he must have seen it on his way along the hallway. She wondered why he didn't get angry with her, why he hid behind his self-restraint. She thanked him for putting the vacuum cleaner away, just as she always did.

"Sure." He came and sat down beside her in order, she thought, to let her know that he was about to treat her gently. There was something repellently creepy about him. There had always been something creepy about him in the way he arrived with a statement of his attitude towards her, which was supposed to proclaim his neediness by making her feel that she could never quite match his expectations.

"Laurie, I'm going to take the body to the hospital."

"You are?"

"There isn't any other way, hon. Nobody is going to understand what happened."

"You look tired," she said. "Don't do anymore cleaning up, I'll do it. I can't go down there while . . . you know . . . "

"I'll take your car."

"Why?"

"It will be easier to clean the seats. You're not thinking."

"I am. What will you say if you get stopped?"

"I'll say that I'm going to Alice's apartment. I called her. Help me think."

"You won't take the gun. You can't, because it's the gun that killed him."

"Okay."

"Which hospital will you go to?"

"Cedars."

"Too upmarket."

"But I'd have a better chance of getting through."

"You think so?"

"It doesn't matter," his voice snapped angrily, and then his shoulders slumped in self-pity. She changed the TV channel to riot coverage.

"Check that you have your driver's license. Take a white T-shirt, and paint a red cross on it."

He agreed, absent-mindedly.

She stood up. She wouldn't touch him, but she urged him: "It's just one last thing to do, Paul, to get everything cleared up. And then we can start over. We start over with a blank sheet, everything back where it should be. What else can we do!?" she shouted; anguish to him, anger and exasperation to her. "You promised me!"

"I know. I know!" He pleaded with her. "It's about thinking it through, it's not – "

"It isn't about thinking it through. It's about doing it or not doing it. I *did* it. I am the one to blame, it's my fault! Is that better?! Tell me what to do and I'll do it myself!"

"No." He said. "No. I suppose that I wanted to know that we were in it together."

"Really?" she asked. "Really? That's something I've wanted to know for a long time. Which was stupid of me. In the end, I saw that it has to be taken for granted."

TWENTY-FIVE

Sunday: 8.15p.m. to 8.45p.m.

He had the body in two garbage sacks, drawn tight and tied around the waist.

The plastic was slippery. There were no arms for him to get a hold of. He went up to the garage, but couldn't find any rope; he searched the laundry room and the kitchen, until Laurie asked him what he was looking for and he told her that he didn't think that he could manage to drag or carry the body upstairs.

She tensed. He saw that he had made a mistake. She didn't want the body upstairs. He argued with her. He had to get the body into the car, he had to get it up to the garage in order to get it into the car. Was there any other way? *Any* other way?

She looked away from him, at the television screen.

"But if they come here, they'll find that he has been upstairs in the house. There'll be traces on the stair carpet. I don't want anyone to know that this person has been in my house. It isn't fair, Paul."

"What else can I do?"

"I just wish that you'd stop behaving as though he was dead."

He was amazed.

"But, Laurie, he *is* dead!"

She sat stonily, ignoring the rebuff.

She said, "Then why are you taking him to the hospital? I'd like to know, because they might call and ask me. I won't know what to tell them. You haven't thought about it. This is a man, it isn't garbage." Her voice broke. "This man had feelings and a family and maybe someone who is in love with him . . . "

"Maybe."

She restrained herself. "But it's not our business."

"No, it isn't, hon."

"I don't see how you can drive along with a human being in a plastic sack. It looks criminal."

He removed the plastic sacks, he killed the outside lights and opened the french windows.

Lifting the body under the armpits, he dragged it out of the basement room and round the side of the house to the waiting car. He hauled it up into the front passenger's seat, and shut the door. From the driver's seat he propped the body up against the door.

Then he took a rake and scuffed the gravel path. There might be some blood, but there wouldn't be the marks of the heels furrowing the earth and stone. He placed the rake against the patio wall, on one of the terraces.

If Mel was to be alive, then he was going to have to be recently wounded. There would have to be blood, as there had been in the basement.

He went back to the car and reached across to the body. With a pair of grips he picked at the wound above the knee, loosening the clot and the stiffened pants. Then he worked on the thigh, pushing and squeezing until the blood came down; with difficulty, because the blood was hardly warm and dribbled from the wound with the greatest reluctance. With his two hands he then braced himself against Mel's chest and pumped, and pumped, until his skin was sticky with gore and the last foul air had left the lungs. There was a smell of excrement from the car seat, and a smell of warm meat. He took the head and moved it from side to side, and blew hot breath into the mouth, and pinched and slapped the cheeks; and left the body with its head leaning forward and the two hands clasping the wounds in stomach and chest.

He washed his hands in the basement, and closed the french windows. He undressed and threw his clothes in the washer, starting it on cold wash, full load; then he put on his suit, checked that he had his driver's license and wallet and medical ID, a small clip of cash, Alice's address, house keys, car keys.

"I'm going," he called.

"Right now?" Laurie came out of the kitchen in an apron.

"Yes, I have to go right now."

"I was going to fix dinner. I was going to fix tofu and gingered pork. But it'll keep."

"I have to go now."

"You'll call me; you will, won't you, on the mobile?"

"Yes, I guess so. On the way home. I won't call you until then. I have to go, Laurie."

"I know. We'll just mess around here, like us chickens always do."

"Love you."

"Love you too."

Sunday: 8.50p.m. to 9.15p.m.

He went out of the front door. She heard the car drive off.

It might be the last time she ever heard his voice.

She didn't want him to say anything when he saw her again. She would come into the basement room with the gun, she would switch on the light and kill him.

If he said anything she wouldn't hear it.

The noise from the alarm would shut out every other sound, maybe even the sound from the gun.

Love you; love you too.

It was the last time she would hear his voice or admit to being part of that equation.

For some reason she was irritated that he had gone out of the front door instead of walking away down the hallway, when she might have imagined shooting him in the back like shooting so much insignificant asshole.

She slid the bolts on the front door. Walking along the hallway, she marvelled at how quiet her footsteps were; she eased past the Mercedes and slid the bolts on the garage doors, and returned to the hallway and bolted the entry to the garage. Then she went into the bedroom to fetch the screwdriver, and she set the override switch on the alarm. On all the TVs she channelled riot coverage; except on the bedroom TV, before which she would lie and watch something else – an old movie, maybe, or a jazz concert, or a soap – until she heard him intrude.

From the kitchen she dialled 911.

"Los Angeles County Emergency Services. Which service do you require?"

"Can you get me the police!"

"I have your number as 643–7011, 1717 Jerome. Please stay calm."

"I want the police, please, please get them here!"

"Your address is being passed on to the police, your call is being recorded. Are you in immediate danger?"

"Yes I am, really I am!"

"Please just keep talking, as calmly as you can, and say what is happening."

"You don't understand!"

"The police have been alerted, they will be with you as soon as they can. Please just keep talking. Describe your situation."

"I'm alone. We had an intruder last night, and I think that he may come back!"

"Is he in the house at this time?"

"No but I think he'll come back. I don't know what to do."

"If you stay on this line, then nothing is going to happen; if you stay calm and keep talking, and make it clear that you are in contact with the police. You must understand that. Is there anyone in the house?"

"Not at the moment. Oh, thank you!"

"We have this under control, Mrs Mathiessen. Now, do you hear anyone around the house?"

"No, I don't think so."

"Okay, so the house is secure. You are alone in the house."

"Yes I am, that's the trouble; my husband has gone out."

"I understand. And as far as you know, nobody has broken into the house."

"They did last night, and I'm sure they'll come back. He ran away. And my husband was here then."

"And you secured the house?"

"Yes."

"And the house is still secure?"

"Yes. But I'm afraid that he'll come back."

"Do you hear any suspicious noise outside the house?"

"No, not now."

"So the situation is that you are alone inside the house, and the house is secured, and there is no sign or noise that would lead you to believe that you are in any immediate danger."

"No, not at the moment, no."

She imagined the operator cancelling the police alert; she would now be on stand-by, awaiting any definite emergency.

"Well, we have this logged, Mrs Mathiessen, and I understand your concern."

"Do you have time? To talk with me?"

"Yes, ma'am, I do. We would like you to stay calm and to dial 911 again if you have any definite suspicion of any intruder on your property."

"You didn't have any time last night, when this man broke into my house."

"Ma'am, you will appreciate that we had any number of

priorities last night, and you say that the incident at your address did not place you in danger."

"But it did, and we defended ourselves, and he ran away. But I'm here on my own now and I'm pregnant and I'm scared!"

"Mrs Mathiessen, the situation has pretty much normalised outside of the eastern central area. If you have reasonable grounds for suspecting an intruder, we can have a police presence with you inside seven minutes. I can still make this call operational if you are convinced that you or your property are in immediate danger. Do you consider that to be the case?"

"No. Not right now! But he might come back!"

"Yes, ma'am. But he might not, and he probably won't."

"Thank you. That's what I needed to hear. I just can't tell you how frightened I get when my husband isn't here."

"Ma'am, Laurie?"

"Yes?"

"If the house is secured, Laurie, then you should be safe. You should feel that way. Those houses up on Jerome are a long way from any trouble. The security is well organised up there, isn't it? You have Southgate-McGrath patrolling that neighborhood, you might consider calling them up to run a regular check around the house while your husband is away. Mrs Mathiessen?"

"Thank you. I feel a little better. I get – well, I get jumpy."

"I think that we've all gotten that way. But if you're certain, or suspicious, that anything's wrong, then you come straight back to us on 911, okay?"

"I will, yes."

"You take care of that baby."

"Oh? Yes. Sure I will. Thank you. Thank you for everything you've done. I was going crazy after last night. It's so good to talk to someone."

"My pleasure. Okay now?"

"Thank you, yes. Goodbye."

And logged. She put down the phone.

Sunday: 9.00p.m. to 9.45p.m.

He came down Curson and turned left onto Hawthorn, crossing Hollywood two blocks above the West Hollywood hospital. Lighting from the street lamps slid across the wet blood which had spread over Mel's chest. He avoided the studios and continued southeast, zigzagging one block east, one block south, down the small streets, down the residential ladder from Hollywood through Hancock Park towards Koreatown.

He cut across Beverly and Third as fast as he dared, the white T-shirt flapping its red cross from the radio aerial. He lost the street lamps. There was no-one on the streets, the houses were darkened, his headlights picked out a sculpted detritus of mangled steel and smouldering wood. He came down Kenmore to Wilshire, and as he looked right he saw a large congregation of National Guard personnel carriers and armored vehicles, drawn up around a helicopter as if to protect it.

Overhead, invulnerably, other helicopters circled, their search-lights stabbing and slicing through the fabric of the pock-marked city. He started to see faces in doorways, groups of people hiding from the beams of sharp white light. There was a gun store on the corner of Eleventh and Gramercy, and he was shocked to see that it was both open and trading.

He couldn't go much further. The streets were scattered with debris, and he would soon come up against the Santa Monica Freeway, which he assumed would be heavily patrolled. He was way out of his depth. This was not his part of town, not a part that he would ever visit in the middle of a normal day. He would have been too scared. He should, now, be scared.

He started to sweat, on the palms of his hands, which slipped on the steering wheel as he spun it first one way and then the other, trying to negotiate the littered street, like swinging the Isuzu along a rock-strewn mountain track.

He thought quickly of Wyoming: how he would drive this

way in Wyoming, way up there, bucking the wilderness with a hunting rifle in the back of an old pick-up, heading for a lodge and a drink, telling someone that he had learned his driving skills in the Rockies, and more such in downtown Los Angeles.

He saw the supermarket basket but couldn't miss it; there was a tinny crash and one of his headlights went out, the basket skittered away into the darkness.

It came to him that he was being stupid, that he had been stupid: because he could have dropped the body out long ago in a quieter, empty area. And he was fighting his way through to God knows where – he was looking for what? He was looking for a right place which he would never find, feeling the panic rise, losing any power of decision. He was going to have to think laterally. And the car would soon break up like everything else. Like trash. Like the line of forlorn baskets which spread like dulled trenchwire across the road now, between him and the burned-out cars beside him.

He pulled over and stopped, and got quickly out of the car. He ran down the side, and then he felt his face rolling along the back window, his arms lifted behind his back, and his face slammed against the glass, his coat ripped and tangled with the rear wiper. And obscenities, and blows from something dull and heavy against both shoulders. The fresh smell from the car exhaust was overpowering, but the air was full of heavier toxic fumes from other fires.

"I'm a doctor!" he shouted. "I'm a doctor, fuck it!"

"What you doin'!" And threats, and proclamations, and pride. There were three men at least, and more in a doorway, waiting.

He was hit in the ribs. But not hard. Nothing was broken. He could breathe. He could breathe anger, and turn his head. His cheek was smashed against the glass. "Do nothin'!"

He shouted: "There's a man inside, one of your people! He's going to die unless I get him to a hospital! I don't have a gun!"

They frisked him.

"See what's inside!"

They dragged him round to the side of the car, and forced his head against the passenger's window, where he saw Mel's head, not two inches away, and his blood.

"He's dying, fuck you!" The grip relaxed. "Get off my ass, man, I have to get him to the hospital. I'm a fucking doctor, right?!"

They were all suddenly lit up, blinded, hit by light. He felt nothing. He was alone, pinned by light, against the car, senses stunned; but he was alone.

The chopper was way off, on a diagonal. He shut his eyes and held out his arms, and then made his hands move, one to give a thumbs up, one to give a clenched sign of gratitude.

The chopper circled, holding the searchlight on him. He felt his way around the car and stretched out the white T-shirt as though he was having a conversation with the chopper. He gave another thumbs up, and then he turned and shouted into the heavily shadowed doorways. "He's one of your people! He's been shot! If you want him, then you take him! Or let me get him to the hospital! You understand?" He waited for a split second. He got into the car, which was a balmy pool of brightness.

He let off the handbrake and nudged the car forward amongst the eerily brilliant baskets. Which was like intruding into an art gallery, with slumbering blackened hulks pressed back against the edges of the wall of light. He thought that it was over, that in the light he was safe. He was a doctor. He had found a body. He was being escorted to the hospital.

And then he was overtaken by black people. Three, four, a half-dozen ran past the car and began to clear the road. One of them held up a white flag in the light, one of them appeared suddenly at his window, knocking at it with his knuckle, an automatic rifle held against his hip by his other hand.

The chopper came right down over the roof of the car in

ceaselessly dementing blasts of sound. The black guy was shouting something through the window. He hung on to the roof of the car and rode the step beneath Paul's door.

The chopper pulled up and away, lighting the street, and Paul heard his passenger's voice.

"You drive, man! You got protection in this neighborhood!"

They cleared the wrecked cars. The lights of the Santa Monica Freeway showed up ahead. The chopper wheeled its searchlight across and away, leaving them back in darkness.

Sunday: 9.30p.m. to 9.40p.m.

Laurie shut down the houselights. She left the bedside lamp burning, above the drawer in the bedside table. She checked the gun. She left a light burning in the hallway outside her bedroom, and one at the top of the stairs. She lay on the bed, and waited.

Sunday: 9.45p.m. to 9.52p.m.

Once the light had left him, he didn't know what would happen. Things were not poised, and were no longer immutable.

He started to think. Nothing had changed. They would still find out that the body had been dead for all those hours. He had the rubber gloves in the map compartment, smeared with dated blood, the body smeared with traces of 1717. The police chopper would have recorded the license plate. He wouldn't get away with it. He couldn't get away with it, not with the man riding shotgun, making sure that he got to the hospital and filled in the forms, and did it right.

There were two blocks until the freeway.

He had to decide. He had to do it. There was a pile of broken glass spewing out from the sidewalk. Lose a tire.

The bang.

Lose control. Up on the sidewalk.

Accelerate.

He hit the blackened shop front. He was thrown forward

against the steering column, his foot pushed into the accelerator, the lights went dead.

He was winded.

He wasn't injured. He was up against the side of a wall and there was no-one next to him. The man with the gun had gone. There was a smell of gasoline.

He switched off the racing engine. He unlocked his seat belt.

He got the rubber gloves out of the map compartment and put them on, then he unlocked Mel's door and kicked the body out, and followed, scrambling across the front seats.

It was utterly silent, until the broken glass crunched under his feet. He dropped the gloves.

There was a lighter in the map compartment. He took it and climbed over grocery tins and brooms and found his escort lying against the wall at the shopfront. He went back in to the stench of gasoline, which was gushing over Mel's body. He backed off, lined up his way out, and took a dust mop which he lit and threw over Mel's body.

The explosion came just as he reached the sidewalk, and was bending down to drag the other man clear.

Sunday: 9.45p.m. to 9.52p.m.

To the baby she whispered, "Everything's going to be fine, I promise you it's going to be that way. You sleep now; you hush and go to sleep. There's going to be a loud noise but we know that the noise will go away and you won't remember what it was, you will be so warm and so loved. You will never see this house, pumpkin, there won't be anything to remember. Sleep tight, sleep safe, my angel."

She sat up, and took the gun out of the drawer – dull, lifeless and heavy. With its thin smell of oil that . . . reminded her of the electric train set. Which her father had bought for her and her sister one disappointing Christmas. And her sister pleading and wailing in panic, cowering on the rug in the playroom while she,

Laurie, proudly threw the locomotive at the wall, time and time again, the pieces falling off it until it smashed.

She thought, we didn't want a train set.

Her father had joked about it for weeks beforehand. She had told her father, that she didn't want a train set. Debbie didn't want a train set either, but Debbie always gave in and wanted whatever she was given, whatever was presented to her by their father. When it was broken Debbie wanted to cry and she wanted to collect the pieces; with fear, with love, with hypocrisy Debbie clung on to the pieces while their father laughed and comforted her and sent Laurie upstairs to her room, in recognition of her victory.

Lights arced across the ceiling of the bedroom. She heard the motor, of a pick-up or a four-wheel drive.

She took the remote and changed to the local live channel, where, from a helicopter, they were transmitting a searchlit tour of the gutted downtown, desolate and motionless, like picking across an underwater reef.

The car swung around the driveway, its lights disappearing from the bedroom. She took the gun and followed these patterns into the hallway. Her husband would try the garage doors first, and then he would try the front door, and then he would break in through the french windows in the basement. The pattern on the ceiling disappeared as the lights shut off. She heard nothing. She sat on the top stair with the gun held out in front of her, resting on her knees, and she waited.

Sunday: 10.33p.m. to 10.42p.m.

He picked himself up off the ground. His face was bloodied and he nearly fell, several splinters of glass protruding from his left leg. But his eyes were fine, unscathed, and he could see the freeway high up and two blocks ahead, the lights and the line of uniforms under them. He set off towards them with his story, away from the fire into the darkness, holding on to his story; line by line he would drag himself out of this city and take his wife and his child with him.

When he fell, he never knew whether it was his fault or someone else's fault, and he couldn't understand why the people around him didn't help him. At the last, maybe, warm blood clinging to him like steam, he accepted perfectly the sensation of being a victim.

Sunday: 10.33p.m. to 10.42p.m.

The security company vehicle had gone. The lights had gone. There was no sound. She was so very tired and cold; her eyelids drooped. Snake-eyes, her father had teased her gently; but then not even he had ever managed to sway her determination.

There was no sign of her husband. She remembered that he had promised to call, but then it was only one of his promises. She stood up stiffly and walked back down the hallway, the gun hanging from her right hand. As she passed the front door, she thought that he would almost certainly use the intercom to try to reach her, when he came home and found it bolted against him. He would wake her; she could count on her same determination, she would never lose it. As she passed his study she stared absent-mindedly at the television, the searchlight weaving amongst the streets and buildings, a small fire blurring the picture at the top left of the screen. The camera was jumpy. It seemed to have no power of decision, trying to reach the flames but falling back reliant on the light.

She wandered on, into the bedroom and around the bed, to replace the gun in the drawer. She lay down and reached for the remote. On the screen the searchlight came up to an intersection, edging forward. There was a man on the ground, being dragged by other men across a beach of broken glass, the blackness held back on either side. As the light stopped – and intensified – the men lashed out with sticks and with their feet. And then they ran off, leaving the body, into a sea of darkness.

She pressed the remote, surfing the channels until she found the cordiality she wanted.

TWENTY-SIX

Friday: Noon to 4p.m.

Another exactitude. Lunch with Andy Townsend. Californian-Balti cuisine. Andy goes for the choice of restaurant in a big way, Bill sees. This is good, because they haven't yet established any kind of a reliable index and Bill doesn't know what the priorities are in Andy's life. Vice-versa. And so they have to circle the conversation cautiously, adopt maybe a new sympathy, discover when to laugh. Thank God for the freshness of the coriander; praise comes consensually.

This is the third Friday that Bill has done lunch with Andy. It is a lullingly warm Friday, the sky is blue and Bill has driven from his offices. Along the way there are demolition crews and construction teams, it's hard to tell which is which, trucks are delivering, trucks are hauling away, the road was blocked, Bill was a little late.

They talk about Paul. Christ, it could have happened to any of us!

They both worry. Nevertheless they are hungry. Perhaps hungrier than usual because of the worry, but Andy only knows about Paul by hearsay, he shakes his head, and Bill feels that he has communicated one of his priorities, let loose a little of himself.

Their waitress does not happen upon them at the right moment. They have to wait, there is an awkward kind of a silence. When she does come Bill says, No this is my tab, let me get it, and he puts down his card feeling that he probably won't do lunch with Andy again, Andy somehow isn't a sensitive person. And this intuition is reinforced by the way that Andy shows some sign of wanting to continue the conversation, any conversation, outside on the sidewalk, which really isn't on Bill's agenda, and not a sensitive behavioral pattern.

But, there again, patterns weren't normal, or back to normal. There was a lot of tension around. You couldn't pinpoint it. There was no tense situation, but *people* were hyper; they were keeping the lid on themselves. You gave everyone a lot of room, you kept for yourself a larger private space; even on the sidewalk, you kept your eyes down, you stayed away from other people, you didn't connect. That was what was happening.

Initially there had been a rush of touching base, a rush to touch base, calling around, checking in. People had come in for dental work when it wasn't necessary, just to check that dental work still existed. People couldn't convince themselves that the sun still shone, they hadn't liked to say what a beautiful day it was; you couldn't really think how to start a conversation with anybody, or even how to come out with any kind of a commonplace greeting. You didn't take anything for granted, you didn't accept that the sun still shone; and the blueness in the sky, what was that?

That was weird, that time had been weird. And then came the lull. Like apathy. There were plenty of spare dental appointments, especially on the Fridays. When Bill and Andy might just as well have shot the breeze on the sidewalk. But you didn't do that, you didn't invest, you didn't expand. Most of the guys called it quits early Friday morning and took their families out of town, a mass of sombre refugees gathering at LAX with update bulletins in their heads for out-of-state acquaintances.

Bill and Helen stayed. This afternoon Bill got stuck in traffic. He took the car on the freeway north, without music. The sky was blue, bits of the city were blackened. Glints of sunshine rolled across glass surfaces like a dazzle from neon dice. He took a space in the slow drive to the hills, at long last crawling off the freeway, turning left and up across the side of the hill, into Jerome.

Things weren't normal. Coming up here, to Jerome, wasn't normal. Maybe things wouldn't go back to normal, so it wouldn't be out so strange for him to swing by! at 1717. Friday afternoon, nothing much to do. Bill was inquisitive, maybe just to see the house again.

There was a rental pick-up in the driveway, a ladder on its roof. Bill pushed a button by the front door and heard the chimes inside. A man came to the door in coveralls and a cap, paint stains on the coveralls. Nothing struck Bill so strange as that the man was middle-aged and white, house decorators of that . . . well, they would cost a hell of a lot of money, Bill figured!

It seemed like the man was from the east coast – Maine, New Hampshire, somewhere – from the way he spoke and the bleak resignation. Someplace where they had the habit of not expecting to pass their time answering questions.

"Is Laurie Mathiessen in?"

"Mrs Mathiessen? No."

The man stood by the partly opened door.

"Okay . . . Well . . . "

The man watched him in the same way as he might have watched his paint dry.

"So . . . would you tell her that Bill Matson called?"

"Yep."

"I called before, on the phone."

"I'll tell her that."

"Bill Matson?" It was her voice, coming closer. "Bill?"

For some reason he thought of calling her Mrs Mathiessen, but the man moved away and he found himself saying to her, "Laurie, hi there," and looking at her as she stood at the door in a pair of blue jeans and an oversized blue workshirt, her hair tied back.

"Hi," she said, "I didn't know who it was. And the house is a mess, and . . . I haven't really wanted to see anyone."

"Sure."

She looked down. "I don't know . . . how to see anyone."

"I can understand."

That was it. That was the end, he thought. He wanted to get away and couldn't think how to do it, but she said: "Sooner or later people will fight their way in, I guess."

"Hey," he smiled weakly and backed away, "Laurie, I didn't want to intrude. It was a Friday and, I don't know, I just drove up here."

Then she said, as if she hadn't heard him: "But it's a mess right now, the paint isn't dry and there are dropcloths everywhere. I'll bring some coffee outside. Or do you want a beer?"

"Coffee would be fine," he didn't mean to say.

"Wait there," she called. "Cream and no sugar?"

"Yes."

"I remembered."

He waited by the door. Then he couldn't wait by the door any longer, he stepped back from the house, and waited by his car, looking up at the house for a moment and then looking anywhere else. Until she came out, with a single cup of coffee, which she handed to him.

He never could remember what she talked about. He never forgot how she talked. It was like hearing a report in a newspaper, or a paragraph out of a biography, her biography. It was too unnerving. Once, months later, over lunch with someone, he recalled her telling him that the house was being redecorated – she had passed on this information – that the house would be sold; not then, of course, but when the real estate market stabilised.

Also available in Vintage

Eddie Little

ANOTHER DAY IN PARADISE

'A raw, gutsy debut'
Observer

'Imagine the aesthetic of Quentin Tarantino colluding with the amoral goofiness of Clark's *Kids*, and you have something of the novel's spirit...glides along with all the unnerving facility of an experienced mainliner cooking up his junk'
Independent

'Bobbie is a teenage petty thief with an addiction to speed who falls among bigtime thieves and develops a taste for heroin. Moving to Chicago to pull a bank job, he meets a number of caricature villains, including Mel, the brains of the operation with his comically wide vocabulary, and the Reverend Cook, who sermonises on the virtues of dum dum bullets...the comparisons American critics have made between this book and Jean Genet's fiction are probably not too wide of the mark'
Daily Telegraph

Also available in Vintage

Martin Amis

NIGHT TRAIN

'Tough, *noir*, Chandleresque...Amis is still the finest English fiction writer of his generation'
Sunday Independent

'I worked one hundred murders,' says Detective Mike Hoolihan, an American policewoman. 'In my time I have come in on the aftermath of maybe a thousand suspicious deaths, most of which turned out to be suicides, accidentals or plain unattendeds. So I've seen them all: Jumpers, stumpers, dumpers, dunkers, bleeders, floaters, poppers, bursters. But of all the bodies I have ever seen none has stayed with me, in my gut, like the body of Jennifer Rockwell'

'Exhilarating...hugely enjoyable to read...*Night Train*, like everything Martin Amis has written, shines with disciplined linguistic exuberance in every syllable...You would be mad not to read this book at the first opportunity'
Sebastian Faulks, *Harpers & Queen*

'*Night Train* is both delicate and bruising – a long drawn-out blue note. The book hangs around in the mind like smoke in a jazz club'
Allison Pearson, *Telegraph Magazine*

Martin Amis's ninth novel is a mystery story which lingers in the reader's mind long after Mike Hoolihan declares the case closed.

Also available in Vintage

John Burnside

THE DUMB HOUSE

'One of the most beautiful, disturbing debuts for a long time...brilliant'
Guardian

'An exceptionally sinister book...It is the story of Luke, whose experiments into the nature of human language are recounted with all the beguiling reasonableness of the highly intelligent madman...The horror is tempered and fine-tuned by the exceptional beauty of Burnside's writing...In Luke, Burnside has produced one of the most chilling voices in recent fiction'
Phil Baker, *Times Literary Supplement*

'A wonderfully disturbing book – chillingly focused and lyrically amoral with moments of remarkable stillness and beauty. A poetic novel in the best and most troubling sense'
A.L. Kennedy

'Burnside's prose is exquisite and he dissects his themes with delicacy to produce a novel resonant with poetic menace'
Sunday Times

'A haunting and fascinating tale'
Ra Page, *Literary Review*

Also available in Vintage

Mordecai Richler

BARNEY'S VERSION

'A wildly funny, satiric, virtuoso performance'
Daily Telegraph

'The funniest book of the year, and maybe the saddest...Mordecai Richler has never written with greater voice or more puckish verve. Barney Panofsky is his mouthpiece, truth, lies and lousy memory are his aces, every card in the deck is a picture, every rasp shoots an arc of grievance: bile with style...You will love it, laugh with it, and treasure it'
Tom Adair, *Scotland on Sunday*

'A delightfully curmudgeonly mock memoir, describing the life of one Barney Panofsky, a boozy Montreal Jew, from Paris *atelier*-bound aspirant writer circa 1950 to present... An enticing, intelligent and bloody funny non-PC read'
Wally Hammond, *Time Out*

'The narrator of Richler's new novel is as much a figure of satire as a satirist. He is a complex, endearing, at times plain frightening old reprobate and one of Richler's finest creations...Richler is magisterially in command of his material'
Guardian